KEITH

KEITH DOUGLAS

A Study

William Scammell

faber and faber
LONDON · BOSTON

First published in 1988 by
Faber and Faber Limited
3 Queen Square London WC1N 3AU

Photoset by Wilmaset, Birkenhead, Wirral
Printed in Great Britain by
Richard Clay Ltd, Bungay, Suffolk
All rights reserved

British Library Cataloguing in Publication Data

Scammell, William
Keith Douglas: *a study.*——
1. Douglas, Keith——Criticism and interpretation
I. Title
821'912   PR6007.0872Z/
ISBN 0–571–14500–9

In an age when critical theory promises, or threatens, to 'cross over' into literature and to become its own object of study, there is a powerful case for re-asserting the primacy of the literary text. These studies are intended in the first instance to provide substantial critical introductions to writers of major importance. Although each contributor inevitably writes from a considered critical position, it is not the aim of the series to impose a uniformity of theoretical approach. Each book will make use of biographical material and each will conclude with a select bibliography which will in all cases take note of the latest developments usefully relevant to the subject. Beyond that, however, contributors have been chosen for their critical abilities as well as for their familiarity with the subject of their choice.

Although the primary aim of the series is to focus attention on individual writers, there will be exceptions. And although the majority of writers or periods studied will be of the twentieth century, this is not intended to preclude other writers or periods. Above all, the series aims to return readers to a sharpened awareness of those texts without which there would be no criticism.

John Lucas

Kent thy birthdays, and Oxford held thy youth;
The heavens made haste, and stay'd nor years nor time;
The fruits of age grew ripe in thy first prime;
Thy will, thy words; thy words the seals of truth.

                   . . .

England doth hold thy limbs, that bred the same;
Flanders thy valour, where it last was tried;
The camp thy sorrow, where the body died;
Thy friends thy want; the world thy virtue's fame.

— Walter Ralegh, *Epitaph on Sir Philip Sidney*

She never undertook to know
What death with love should have to do . . .

— Richard Crashaw, *Hymn to Saint Teresa*

Angel and doll! Then there's at last a play.
Then there unites what we continually
part by our mere existence.

— Rilke, *Fourth Elegy*, trans. Leishman and Spender

Contents

Preface

The poets of the First World War made an immediate impact on the public, and on the next generation of writers. The poets of the Second have not been so fortunate. Their work was part of the poetry boom of the 1940s, which produced a great deal of mediocre verse, and was left stranded when the high tide of little magazines and poetry publishers receded. It did not lend itself easily to categorization like the 'committed' poetry of the thirties, the formulaic romanticism of the New Apocalypse in the forties, or the Beveridge Plan for poetry implicitly adopted by the Movement poets in the fifties. The 'war poet' label had to cover such diverse talents as Keith Douglas, Alun Lewis, Roy Fuller, Sidney Keyes, Drummond Allison, Henry Reed, Charles Causley, F. T. Prince, Bernard Gutteridge, Hamish Henderson, Alan Ross, and many more. Unlike Owen, Rosenberg and Sassoon, who all endured essentially the same experiences, the later poets each had a different war; and the civilians, who were now almost as heavily involved as the enlisted men, had different ones again. War was not so much a subject as something to be endured, like a protracted winter. 'The common mood ... was one of dour resolution, sceptical, lugubrious, resigned' (Vernon Scannell, *Not Without Glory*, p. 19). Once it was over the sensible thing to do was to forget it.

Critics have been deploring this neglect of forties' poets for a good many years but the literary histories, and public opinion, have been very slow to change. 'The

. . . now notorious forties has been thoroughly written off,' observed Ian Hamilton in 1964. Twelve years later Vernon Scannell wrote: 'The notion that from the First World War came a wealth of fine poetry and from the Second little of any merit is still extraordinarily widespread, even among educated people.' And yet the title of his own sympathetic study of the period, *Not Without Glory*, taken from the worst, concluding line of Henry Reed's famous poem 'Lessons of the War', seems to half-concede the justice of the popular view. That such a view is still commonplace is confirmed by Michael Stapleton's *Cambridge Guide to English Literature* (1983): 'It is generally agreed that World War II, unlike World War I, did not produce poets of the level of accomplishment of Wilfred Owen, Isaac Rosenberg, or Edward Thomas.'

This orthodoxy is perhaps breaking down a little now, and is certainly due for revision. Ted Hughes's edition of Douglas's *Selected Poems*, with its brilliant Introduction (1964), marked a watershed in Douglas's posthumous career. Since that time two further editions of the collected poems have appeared, Desmond Graham has written an excellent biography, and the admirers of Douglas, Lewis and other good poets of the period have grown in number and influence. In a recent poll in *Poetry Review* Douglas's successors voted his *Collected Poems* one of the best books to have been published since 1939. He absorbed the lessons of Eliot and Auden and carried modernism forward into our own age, combining honesty and passion in a deceptively casual idiom of great rigour and penetration. As Ted Hughes has said, the longer his poetry lives, the fresher it looks. I hope this study will help to increase our understanding of his achievement, and that it will bring him new readers.

All readers and students of Douglas are indebted to his first editors, John Waller, G. S. Fraser and J. C. Hall, and especially to his later editor and biographer Desmond Graham. My thanks to him both for his published labours, without which this study would have been much poorer, and for other friendly assistance, despite the fact that I have quite often disagreed with his editorial judgement. I should also like to thank other friends and correspondents who have helped me by supplying, books, magazines and reviews, including Geoffrey Holloway, David Scott, Christopher Pilling, Michael Meyer, David Wright, Louis and Miriam Simpson, J. C. Hall, Dr Brian Powell, Charles and Brenda Tomlinson, Norman Nicholson, Mike Bacon and Jonathan Barker of the Arts Council Poetry Library.

Note on Texts and Abbreviations

There are three editions of Douglas's poems: (i) *The Collected Poems of Keith Douglas*, ed. John Waller and G. S. Fraser (Editions Poetry London, Nicholson and Watson, 1951); (ii) *Keith Douglas Collected Poems*, edited by John Waller, G. S. Fraser and J. C. Hall, with an Introduction by Edmund Blunden (Faber and Faber, 1966); (iii) *The Complete Poems of Keith Douglas*, edited by Desmond Graham (Oxford University Press, 1978; paperback, 1979).These are abbreviated in this book as *CP(PL)*, *CP* and *TCP* respectively. *Selected Poems Keith Douglas*, edited with an Introduction by Ted Hughes (Faber and Faber, 1964) uses the *CP(PL)* text, and is abbreviated as *SP*.

TCP is the most recent and scholarly edition, and aims to be definitive. It omits some interesting juvenilia, however, so I have taken the opportunity of printing some examples at the end of chapter III. Desmond Graham's policy of using the 'latest known text' (*TCP* p. x) also leads him to print what seem to me to be inferior versions of some of Douglas's best poems – notably 'Aristocrats' ('Sportsmen' in *TCP*) and 'The Behaviour of Fish in an Egyptian Tea Garden'. I have therefore occasionally preferred to use the *CP* text, or an eclectic blend of *CP* and *TCP*. In all such cases I have indicated where and why I have departed from *TCP*, which is otherwise used throughout. My preferences are based purely on literary-critical considerations – which version makes for the best poem? – not on textual ones, or any quarrel with Graham's scholarship.

There are also three editions of Douglas's prose memoir *Alamein to Zem Zem*: (i) Editions Poetry London, Nicholson and Watson, 1946 (with poems and drawings); (ii) Faber and Faber, 1966 (with drawings), edited by John Waller, G. S. Fraser and J. C. Hall, with an Introduction by Lawrence Durrell; reprinted, with corrections, as a Penguin Modern Classic, 1969. (iii) Oxford University Press, 1979 (with drawings), edited with an Introduction by Desmond Graham. All quotations are from the OUP edition, abbreviated as *AZZ*. A *Prose Miscellany*, compiled and introduced by Desmond Graham (Carcanet 1985), is abbreviated as *PM*. *Keith Douglas 1920–1944*, a biography by Desmond Graham (Oxford University Press, 1974) is abbreviated as *KD*.

I

Life

Keith Castellain Douglas was born on 24 January 1920 at Tunbridge Wells in Kent. His father, also named Keith, had served with distinction in the First World War, winning the MC and rising to the rank of captain. His mother, Marie Josephine Castellain, worked as a secretary to an artist, and had artistic and intellectual leanings. Douglas Senior had difficulty finding work after the war and was away a good deal, so the young Keith (who remained an only child) was brought up by his mother and by his maternal grandparents, who had a small private income. From an early date, his mother later wrote, 'Keith shewed interest in art. First, shapes interested him. Then words. (He started to draw things at two years old.) Always very independent, he usually spurned advice till his own mistakes had proved him wrong. He had few "advantages" in the generally accepted sense of the word and as a baby had to spend long spells on his own. But he was never at a loss for amusement. He "talked" stories to his various toys till he learned to write and then he attempted to write them. He drew on every available scrap of paper; on doors and walls and any soft flat surface he could find in the garden which he could scrape with a stick. He pored over books he couldn't possibly read, comparing shapes of words he knew with shapes he didn't know and trying to guess their meaning' (*CP*, p. 13).

In 1923 Captain Douglas bought a house in Cranleigh, Surrey, with two and a half acres of land, and established a chicken farm. Keith now got to know his boisterous father, and was soon dressing up and playing at soldiers in the garden. Most of the work of running the farm fell on his mother and a young woman called Olwen, brought in to help. After eighteen months his mother collapsed and spent some months in hospital, where it was found she had *encephalitis lethargica*, or 'sleepy sickness'. Since the effects of this might make her a lifelong invalid, and the Captain had now to sell the farm and find another occupation, it was decided to send Keith away to boarding school. With the help of a loan from friends, he was enrolled at a small prep school in Guildford, Edgeborough School, in September 1926. Mentally and physically precocious – he was tall and well-built, as well as bright – he seems to have taken easily to his new life, and was soon leader of his own peer group. Meanwhile his mother moved around to a variety of addresses, and his father simply vanished. Eventually, when he was ten, Keith discovered that the Captain had left his mother for good and was going to marry Olwen.

There is not so much as a single photograph of Keith's father in Graham's biography, so all we know about him arrives at second and third hand. In an early autobiographical story his son says 'Keir [Keith] liked his father better than his mother, who fondled him a deal too much and cried sometimes,' whereas his father, who 'did not spend very much time with him ... would speak to him of war and boxing and shew the boy his great muscles' (*PM*, p. 13). Later in the story he describes his mother as looking 'pretty but tired out, and [she] smiled at Keir who was a consolation to her for many things'. In another early story Keith describes his father as 'a hearty playmate whom he secretly feared and wholeheartedly admired' (*PM*, p. 16). These suggestive comments evoke very well the world of an only child, torn between an overprotective invalid mother and a remote but exciting

[2]

father. They are also astonishingly objective for one so young.

There are, on the other hand, several photographs of his mother Josephine, or Jo. In one she sits on the lawn with the eighteen-month-old Keith on her lap, wearing a summer hat and dress, looking very beautiful and calm, while the chubby infant straddles her like a young colossus, staring pugnaciously at the camera. In the background stands a blurred figure, possibly Keith's father or grandfather, looking on from a distance. All his mother's features – strong nose, wary eyes, wide sensitive mouth – are masculinized and parodied in the child's forceful-looking stare. She looks Raphaelesque, he altogether more burly, ready to break out of the icon at any moment.

At school Keith was more than adequate, when he tried, but often accused of truculence and non-conformity. He played rugby with zeal, drew for his own pleasure, and struck out routes of his own devising in Latin and mathematics, drawing down the immemorial schoolmaster's complaint that he was trying to be too clever. His first extant poem, written at ten, was on the subject of Waterloo:

> Napoleon is charging our square,
> with his cavalry he is attacking;
> let the enemy do what he dares,
> our soldiers in braveness aren't lacking.
>
> But naught can his charging avail,
> he cannot do anything more;
> for not one heart does fail
> e'en when 'tis at death's door.
>
> 'I have you!' Napoleon cries!
> but he has a great mistake made;
> for every French soldier flies
> and is caught by a fierce cannonade.

[3]

Napoleon is charging our squares,
but only in memory now;
we remember his charging mares;
and we always will, I trow.

Throughout this period, and indeed his whole childhood
and adolescence, money was in short supply; the family
was genteel but decidedly impoverished. It was only
through the headmaster's kindness and support that
Keith continued at Edgeborough and sat the entrance
exam for Christ's Hospital, the famous Blue-coat school
attended by Coleridge and Lamb. He passed easily and
went off with friends for his first ever holiday in
France, and moved to the new school in September
1931.

The eleven-year-old was one of 700 schoolboys dressed
in the long blue Tudor-style coat (plus knee-breeches
and yellow stockings) which gave the school its popular
name. It had moved from the City to the Sussex
countryside in 1902, so he was not pent mid cloisters
dim in the manner of his famous predecessors; but the
rituals baffled him at first, even though the institution
lacked the snobberies practised at many public schools.
Christ's Hospital was founded for boys from poor
families and the sons of 'persons distinguished' in the
arts or sciences or in public service. The school
cultivated serious academic study, as well as the usual
diet of classics and games, and only 'Grecians' – those
destined for university – made it to the top of the
hierarchy. Douglas quickly adapted and soon became a
leading figure in his year. His drawing and model-
making was much admired; he was picked for the
under-fourteen rugby team, swam for the school, acted
in *A Midsummer Night's Dream* (as Theseus); wrote
and published poems in the school magazine. His
physical size and strength made him respected even by
those who disliked him.

Meanwhile his mother's health, and finances, continued to deteriorate. Both her parents died, and her husband was gone; she survived on the kindness of friends and what money she could make by letting the house to holiday-makers. Eventually she obtained a position as companion to an old lady, which kept her out from 7 a.m. to 9 p.m. every day. Keith never knew where he would be spending his holidays until the moment arrived. His father remained silent, and the son appears to have regarded him as permanently missing, presumed dead. (When he left school in 1938 his father wrote suggesting they should meet, but Keith ignored his letter. See *KD*, p. 26.) On his sixteenth birthday he wrote out a new poem in his English exercise book:

Strange Gardener

> Over the meadows,
> framed in the quiet osiers, dreams the pond,
> region of summer gnat-busyness,
> where, in the afternoon's blue drowsiness,
> fish plop among the water-shadows:
> and the cool trees wait beyond.
>
> A young man dwelt there,
> with a swift, sad face, and full of phantasy,
> repeating, as he heard it,
> the alliterative speech of the water-spirit;
> smoothing his pale hair
> with automatic ecstasy.
>
> This was his garden,
> uncultivated, (order hated him)
> whence, in a winter-madness,
> (whose scourge filled him with recklessness,
> seeing the frost harden),
> the water-spirit translated him.

This is followed by a highly detailed 'Explanation' analysing and explicating the poem's prosody, rhyme scheme and meaning. He names specific influences, such as Frederick Prokosch and the novelist Henry Williamson, C. Day Lewis and T. S. Eliot, confessing that the last two lines of the middle stanza are imitated from *The Waste Land* (see III, 255–6). He concludes with a general comment: 'This explanation is intended to shew that although the main idea of the poem was spontaneous, and the poem itself is short, the scheme behind it is lengthily and carefully thought out. The lapses in metre are put in purposely, in an attempt to make it less stereotyped and more interesting' (*PM*, pp. 18–20).

The 'lapses in metre', or rather the deliberate breaking-up of the pentameter line, packing it with reversed stresses and feminine endings, and the liking for rhyme schemes which work inwards towards a centre (ABCCBA – in this case he transposes the last two rhymes: ABCCAB), are already typical of some of his mature poems. The Pre-Raphaelite languors of subject and diction suggest that he may have been reading early Yeats and the Rhymers' Club as well as Eliot; but the dying falls are resisted both by word-play ('gnat-busyness') and syntax, whose burly parentheses resist pathos and self-pity. This Narcissus doesn't mean to go altogether quietly.

In the summer of 1935 Douglas had his second holiday abroad, this time staying with relatives in Gorizia, on the border between Italy and Yugoslavia. He was instantly attracted to the landscape and climate, as he was later to the Mediterranean and the Middle East. Back at school he grew increasingly rebellious, openly bored with masters and rules. At home he said 'I don't agree' so often that his mother suggested he record the expression to save wasting his breath. Graham says the school at one time suspected him of homosexuality, though his friends thought the charge ridiculous. He pilfered two of the art master's paintings, and, more seriously, stole an old rifle from the armoury to take home and clean, which led to visits from the War Office and the police. He was removed to another house in the school, and sternly watched. In the midst of these rebellions he became a fanatical member of the school's Officer Training Corps, with a particular love of drill. He enjoyed jazz and tap-dancing; and argued that grace and beauty belonged exclusively to the upper classes.

Eventually he became a 'Grecian' with a small study of his own. He drew and painted continually, acted, rode, drilled, studied, swam, footered, and published poems and drawings in the school magazines *The Blue* and *Outlook*. After several rejections he also achieved publication in Grigson's *New Verse*, at the age of eighteen, with a poem called 'Dejection'. (Ironically, it is by no means as good as some of Douglas's other juvenilia.) Meanwhile he was reading Hopkins, Owen, Sassoon, Sitwell, Dylan Thomas, and such thirties luminaries as Auden and Day Lewis. In December 1937 he sat his entrance exam for Merton College, Oxford, and won an Open Exhibition in History, with an option to read English. He wrote a valedictory sonnet, 'On Leaving School', threw away all his exercise books,* and left the institution that had been his only real home for the past seven years.

For some time now Douglas had worn glasses, his sight weakened by an attack of measles. He was also asthmatic, and suffered in the summer from hay fever. These symptoms of stress suggest that, beneath his tough exterior, he was more affected by the insecurity of his family background than he cared to show. Two letters written in 1940, looking back at his childhood, contain revealing comments. 'I lived alone during the

---

* His housemaster H. R. Hornsby found a bundle of them stuffed into a wastepaper basket and, with remarkable foresight, rescued them, presenting them to Douglas's biographer thirty years later. See *KD*, p. 64.

most fluid and formative years of my life, and during that time I lived on my imagination, which was so powerful as to persuade me that the things I imagined would come true.' And: 'I shall never get over the idea of the world in general as a powerful force working for my hurt . . . this conception of things saves me many disappointments' (*KD*, p. 89; see also his poem 'Sanctuary'). At Oxford he steered a middle course between aesthetes and hearties, wearing a red shirt and cravat with labourer's corduroys, or a gown with plimsolls. Switching to English, as expected, he secured Edmund Blunden as his tutor. Blunden was not only a distinguished poet and memoirist but himself an ex-pupil of Christ's Hospital, with a special interest in other 'old Blues'.

Douglas plunged into *Beowulf* and early British poetry, exalting Henryson above Dunbar, and happily mining the Anglo-Saxon word-hoards. An early girl friend described him as 'a very opinionated young man, but not unpleasantly so, because he has a lot of sense. He is remarkably mature and confident . . . looks quite twenty or twenty-one . . . tall and long-legged . . . athletic looking, and evidently fond of sports.' This portrait is supplemented by his younger contemporary Michael Meyer. 'Keith was a strange, very abrasive character; my main memory of him, when I was his sub-editor on *Cherwell* in 1939–40, is that he always seemed to have sticking-plaster over some cut, and a girl on his knee. He was very pugnacious, a good wing-forward and always willing for a fight, on or off the field. Great fun, though. He had a dry voice, with a marked though not exaggerated public-school accent. Very mature for his age, or so he seemed to me, who was a year younger and very gauche' (letter to the author, December 1985). He joined the Mounted Section of the university OTC, for the riding, continued to play rugby, and became a member of the Labour Club and the China Society. It was at the latter that he met Yingcheng, its Secretary,

whose father had once been Chinese Ambassador to
Washington. During the Easter vacation he took a cycl-
ing holiday in France with Hamo Sassoon, the poet's
nephew, riding from Dieppe to Amiens, Soissons, and
then returning via Paris. As the year progressed he saw
more and more of Yingcheng, and wanted to become
engaged to her. She wore a ring he gave her but was less
involved than he, and finally broke off the relationship
in the summer of 1939. All this took place against the
background of imminent war with Germany, which was
declared on 3 September. Within three days Douglas
had reported to an army office. He announced that he
would join a cavalry regiment and 'bloody well make my
mark in this war. For I will not come back' (*KD*, p. 67).

Like others of his age he was not called up immedi-
ately, so settled back as best he could into another year
at Oxford. He bounced from Yingcheng to a younger
friend of hers called Antoinette, and was very soon
engaged to her; but 'there is no prospect of getting
married for at least three years, by which time the thing
will obviously have gone up in smoke, so I'm not really so
very tied down, or up' (letter to another friend, Jean
Turner; *KD*, p. 82). With Blunden and another student
he co-edited an Oxford miscellany called *Augury*, design-
ed to affirm the university's continuing presence in
time of war; and contributed frequently to its magazine
Cherwell, eventually becoming editor. It was a difficult
but productive year. In May he wrote his charming
valedictory poem 'Canoe':

> Well, I am thinking this may be my last
> summer, but cannot lose even a part
> of pleasure in the old-fashioned art
> of idleness. I cannot stand aghast
>
> at whatever doom hovers in the background . . .

By the end of the month, however, Antoinette had
broken off with him too, tired of his jealousy, and in all
probability afraid of his unconventionality. Douglas

[9]

threatened to shoot himself. Instead he deposited all his
finished poems with Blunden, and on 17 July went off
to Edinburgh hoping to find a place in the famous
cavalry regiment the Royal Scots Greys.

The twenty-year-old who stares confidently out at us in
his cadet's uniform (*KD*, p. 105) was highly intelligent,
highly imaginative, highly impulsive and highly in-
secure. He functioned well in closed, hierarchical
societies both because he had to, or go under, and
because they provided him with a sort of family, and
the family's twin possibilities of conformity and revolt.
He loved acting, ballet, and all forms of dramatization.
He swung wildly between self-sufficiency and a strong
desire to be loved and settled into a family of his own. A
bohemian of sorts, he despised aesthetes, and had no
affinity either with the generalized leftist humanism of
Auden or the nostalgic pastoralism of the Georgian old
guard. Siegfried Sassoon may have provided one role
model, and Eliot perhaps another – the latter is
certainly an influence on his evolving poetry. There is
no doubt, however, that he leapt into a cavalry saddle –
and thence into its modern equivalent, a tank – with
something of the alacrity that Brooke's swimmers leapt
into the waves, not in order to cleanse himself of some
hypothetical dirt but because the war would give him
something unequivocal to be and do. The 'vast disturb-
ance which has broken in on your university career', as
Blunden quaintly put it, (*PM*, p. 41) was a stage on
which he would suit the action to the word, and
discover how to act. There was an element of boyish
adventurousness in this which later commentators
have been all too eager to interpret as militarism, thus
fulfilling the poet's own acute predictions in 'Simplify
Me When I'm Dead'.

After some initial training at Edinburgh and the
Equitation School in Northamptonshire Douglas
moved to Sandhurst and transferred to the mechanized

cavalry, exchanging his sword for a set of spanners. He was less at home with tanks than with horses but persevered, learning wireless drill and morse code, and just passing the course. His mood veered between bravado and resignation. 'I can see nothing more attractive than active service and final oblivion, to which I quite look forward . . . I am trying to get East as soon as possible: and when I get there I shall make for the nearest harem and leave the rest to Allah' (*KD*, p. 109). He took a gunnery course at Lulworth Cove, then passed out from Sandhurst on 1 February 1941. Oxford friends gave him a belated twenty-first birthday party during his leave, and he was posted to the Second Derbyshire Yeomanry at Ripon. Most of the regiment's senior officers 'hunted, shot, or fished and brought with them . . . their local social hierarchy . . . Douglas had a commander . . . who always carried a shotgun on manoeuvres, firing it from the turret of his armoured car whenever he saw game' (*KD*, p. 112). After six weeks he moved again, to Wotton-under-Edge in Gloucestershire, and was billeted in nearby Wickwar. Douglas joined in some of the social activities of the county set in which his fellow officers naturally moved, but also held aloof, chiefly because of his lack of money. During these months he came to full maturity as a writer, composing such memorable poems as 'Time Eating', 'The Marvel', and – his last statement before leaving England – 'Simplify Me When I'm Dead'. On a brief course in Birmingham he met a sixteen-year-old called Diana, fancied himself in love, and got engaged yet again. They spent his last leave in Oxford together, and even went to the Register Office for a marriage licence, but it was closed. The relationship came to nothing, but Diana was there to see him off at Southampton, with his mother, when he sailed for the Middle East in July 1941.

After a leisurely voyage on 'an almost luxury liner' and a pleasant stop-over in South Africa he fetched up at a depot near Cairo, and was posted to the Nottingham-shire (Sherwood Rangers) Yeomanry. He moved around for several months between Palestine and Egypt but saw no action as the regiment was not fully mechanized. As in his previous visits abroad, Douglas was immedi-ately captivated by his surroundings. 'There are people who keep saying you can't beat English girls – but for sheer beauty, no English face or figure can compare with almost any Arab child, any Egyptian or Syrian girl . . .' (*KD*, p. 139; in a slightly later letter he writes: 'England will never be my home country').

By one of the flukes of army life Douglas was now made a Camouflage Staff Officer and posted to the divisional headquarters of the Tenth Armoured Division in Palestine. This was a safe job, and promotion too. Many subalterns would have been delighted with their luck but Douglas was furious, for his own regiment was preparing to be sent into battle, and he was determined not to miss that experience. He wrote to his commanding officer, trying to get himself recalled, and badgered everybody up to and including the general. For three months, however, he got nowhere, and spent much of his time sightseeing in Cairo and Palestine. At a bookshop he met a Latvian-Jewish woman called Olga, and prepared to launch his affections on her. 'If I tell you between kisses that I love you more than anyone in the world – you can believe me. But not for long – love comes in waves, it can't be kept burning at the same pitch for years, or it just burns you up altogether' (*KD*, p. 146). He also made contact with the many good writers living in and around Cairo at the time – Lawrence Durrell, Bernard Spencer, George Seferis, Olivia Manning, G. S. Fraser, Terence Tiller, Robert Liddell and others – and the magazines they ran, *Personal Landscape* and *Salamander*. Back in England his friend J. C. Hall had found a publisher interested in new poets and was preparing a selection of the poems of Douglas, Norman Nicholson and himself for the press. Douglas also published in *Citadel*, a monthly edited by his friend David Hicks, whose flat was Douglas's Cairo base. The city was an immemorial pleasure dome, full of beautiful women of every nationality; Douglas spent his time dining, drinking, partying, and swimming out at the Mena House Hotel by the pyramids. In a letter to Olga, now a friend and confidante rather than lover, he wrote: 'The question of the Turkish Delight still is not solved . . . she expects me to sleep with her, even if I only visit her for an afternoon . . . but I hate the idea of "using" her . . .' (*KD*, p. 149).

In mid-June Rommel entered Tobruk, and the Allied forces gathered in strength at El Alamein. Douglas's regiment moved out closer to the war but still took no part in it, having been relieved of their tanks. In July he was abruptly moved to Alexandria, still as a camouflage expert, and still with nothing much to do. Here he continued his pleasurable existence and met the highly attractive and cosmopolitan Milena Pegnas, who spoke four languages and worked at the offices of Saccone & Speed, the liquor company. Desmond Graham suggests that Milena became the real successor to Yingcheng; and, true to form, Douglas soon persuaded her to become the latest in what was now a long line of fiancées. 'If they broke up . . . he would go off and get himself killed' (*KD*, p. 154). Alas, this new love was to be even briefer than the others: returning unexpectedly to Alexandria after a short spell at Wadi Natrun he found that Milena had become involved with a friend of his called Norman Ilett. There was an explosive scene, followed by a resigned acceptance of his loss, which led to one of his best love poems: 'I listen to the desert wind / that will not blow her from my mind . . .' It is worth noting that Douglas was 'betrayed' or severely hurt by virtually every woman he ever seriously gave his heart to. He was often hasty in disposing of this article, it is true, and no doubt his insecurity did not help; none the less it is impossible not to sympathize with his youthful suffering. This in turn made him all the more eager to fling himself into the war.

In a letter to Blunden of March 1942 we get a further glimpse into his contradictory nature. His current boss was a General Clarke who had known Blunden in the First World War. Douglas writes: 'Mon general is one Clarke, who says you were his Intelligence Officer in the last show – "Marvellous feller, always bringin' me reports in astonishin'ly neat handwritin', astonishin'ly neat. And then he'd dish in a bit of astonishin'ly good poetry, too. Well, you'd better write and tell him I'm still tickin' over, what? Good."' This is followed by an account of an accident in his lorry, and his reactions to the locals:

> I had an accident last time I was in Cairo and killed an Arab – he did the usual chicken-crossing-the-road stunt, at the double, from behind a stationary vehicle. I was exonerated but somewhat shaken. It is curious how doll-like a broken up body looks, in spite of blood. A pity it's not so odourless as a doll. (*PM*, pp. 88–9)

The extraordinary unpleasantness of this is hard to explain. Within a few lines of parodying Clarke he has himself taken over the blimpish, xenophobic, arrogant tones of the class he affects to despise. It is this posturing streak in his character, perhaps, which accounts for the dislike reported by some of his contemporaries, who found him cold and insincere. In a letter to Olga some time later he says: 'neither of us can suffer fools gladly, and we are both hemmed in by them . . . I suppose the war will eventually end, but the trouble is that all these idiots live on when one would have thought there was a golden opportunity to liquidate them' (*KD*, p. 190). This recalls the foolish statements to be found in some of Owen's early letters, before he discovered what killing really was.* Similarly Douglas's callous description of

* 'While it is true that the guns will effect a little useful weeding . . .'
See *Wilfred Owen* by Jon Stallworthy (OUP, 1977), p. 109.

the dead Arab pre-dates his first encounters with dead soldiers in the desert. In both poets, the posturing evaporated on contact with reality.

As preparations speeded up for the offensive at Alamein, Douglas loitered still at Divisional HQ, in charge of nothing more than a two-ton truck. He heard the guns booming twenty miles away but was stuck in his safe job at base. One day he could stand it no longer and, leaping into his truck with his batman and a fitter (to drive it back), drove off west to rejoin his regiment and take a real part in the war. His batman said '"I like you, sir. You're shit or bust you are." This gratified me a lot' (AZZ, p. 17). Fortunately Douglas's commanding officer welcomed him back without asking too many questions, and he was posted to 'A' Squadron as a troop leader, in charge of two or three Crusader tanks (depending on their current mechanical strength), each with a crew of three. Within forty-eight hours he was engaged in his first battle; then, after a short rest, the regiment was ordered into action again. 'The landscape [was] littered with derelicts and the signs of earlier fighting ... Everywhere there were unburied dead, Germans, Italians, Libyans, New Zealanders, High-landers, and English, some in unbelievable postures, covered with flies, others reclining in trenches as if asleep. Moving, except under heavy fire, with head and shoulders above the turret top for a better view, it was necessary to scan each trench and weapon pit for possible snipers and it was there the dead lay' (KD, pp. 166–8).

For most combatants the desert war consisted of short sharp bursts of fighting interspersed with long periods of waiting, while forces were regrouped, or moved overland on huge transporters. There were leave periods too, on the Mediterranean coast. The juxtapositions were bewildering: one minute Douglas found himself in a desert minefield, at the mercy of snipers and the German barrage; the next drinking and sunbathing like a wealthy tourist. All this is graphically described in *Alamein to Zem Zem* and the poems: 'By a day's travelling you reach a new world / the vegetation is of iron / dead tanks, gun barrels split like celery / . . . a man with no head / has a packet of chocolate and a souvenir of Tripoli' ('Cairo Jag'). The regiment advanced over nearly a thousand miles of North Africa, sometimes fighting for its life, sometimes hanging around for weeks at a time with nothing significant to do. Douglas was no Yossarian but saw clearly enough the mad logic underlying army life. One part of him resented its absurd artifice, another and perhaps larger part was relieved to find that he had withstood the initiation rites of mechanized warfare. His courage under fire was no longer in doubt. Tanks, he soon discovered, were hellishly noisy and unpredictable, forever shedding their tracks, overheating, jamming gears, or running out of fuel. He survived four months of active service, until he stepped on a tripwire and was injured by a mine. He was hit almost everywhere by some of the hundreds of ball-bearings such mines released, and spent his twenty-third birthday on a hospital train bound for Cairo.

Fortunately none of his wounds were major ones. He spent six weeks in hospital, and during his convalescence wrote some of his finest poems, including 'Dead Men' and 'Desert Flowers'. An essay also written during this period, 'Poets in this War', gives us his view of his contemporaries, and what he conceived his own function as a poet to be. After further convalescence at Port Said, and two enjoyable leaves in Tel Aviv (with Olga) and Alexandria (with Milena and her family), Douglas rejoined his regiment. By now the North African campaign was reaching a successful conclusion. The German regiment they had fought across hundreds of miles surrendered on 13 May 1943, and the Italian army followed suit the next day. In the lull that followed, Douglas continued to write poems and began setting down *Alamein to Zem Zem*. 'Reading about war,' he says, 'cannot convey the impression of having walked through the looking-glass which touches a man entering battle.' Maybe not, but his classic narrative comes very close.

He now enjoyed six months of peace, insofar as life in the army is ever peaceful, writing, travelling, and awaiting the next phase of the war. In June he was promoted to captain. A friend wrote of him: 'while detesting all war stood for, he seemed to me . . . mentally and emotionally invigorated by the life of action . . .' (*KD*, p. 213). Back in England the *Selected Poems* of himself, Norman Nicholson and J. C. Hall was published and reviewed; and Tambimuttu, the eccentric but enterprising editor of *Poetry (London)*, was keen to print anything Douglas sent. He also wanted to publish a volume of Douglas's poems. In his correspondence with Hall, who was not very complimentary about his recent work, Douglas vigorously defended the absence of 'lyricism' in his poems, setting out his position in the most vivid statement of his aims he ever made (see chapter II). He liked Tunisia very much, and (despite many complaints) Egypt too, and enquired at the British Council about the possibility of securing a lectureship there after the war.

In December 1943 the regiment returned to England to prepare for the opening of a second front in Europe – the D-Day landings on the beaches of Normandy. Given three weeks' leave he hastened home from camp at Chippenham to see his mother at East Grinstead, where she now kept house for a Colonel Baber and his family. He revisited Oxford, and told a friend that he would like 'cigarettes and Baudelaire' for his birthday. He also met Tambimuttu, in London, signed a contract for a volume of poems, and continued work on *Alamein to Zem Zem*, including the preparation of line drawings to illustrate the text. Tambi's editorial assis-

[17]

tant was a young woman called Betty Jesse, to whom
he was immediately attracted. They spent a little time
together in war-torn London. In response to his
apparently cynical wit, she called him her *bête noire*.
This struck home, and Douglas commenced the poem of
that name which he never managed to finish to his
satisfaction. (He also planned to use it as the title for
his collection of poems.) Meanwhile Tambimuttu read
and approved his prose memoir, and contracted to
publish that too. The regiment moved to Sway, in the
New Forest. Spring was so beautiful Douglas ordered
three of his men to pick primroses and decorate the
huts. For two months he bombarded Betty with letters
and proposals for meetings. He was in love again, and
she, though married (unhappily), seemed to recipro-
cate. They snatched occasional days together but the
camp was out of bounds to civilians, and Douglas was
caught up in the 'big flap'. The army was in a whirl of
preparations for the Normandy landings. He was
convinced that this time he wouldn't survive – 'time,
time is all I lacked / . . . as the great collectors before
me.' This is from his last completed poem, 'On a Return
from Egypt', which ends:

> The next month, then, is a window
> and with a crash I'll split the glass.
> Behind it stands one I must kiss,
> person of love or death
> a person or a wraith,
> I fear what I shall find.

In the last letter he wrote to Blunden, Douglas
expresses his increasing dislike of the things he was
supposed to be fighting for. '. . . I've been fattened up
for more slaughter and am simply waiting for it to start.
. . . I am not much perturbed at the thought of never
seeing England again, because a country which can
allow her army to be used to the last gasp and be paid
like skivvies isn't worth fighting for. For me, it is

simply a case of fighting *against* the Nazi regime. After that, unless there is a revolution in England, I hope to depart for sunnier and less hypocritical climes' (*PM*, pp. 152–3). The logic behind this outburst is not altogether clear. No doubt it has partly to do with his mother's (and his own) continuing financial difficulties. The gentility of much English social life stuck in his throat. Perhaps, too, his political sympathies were moving leftwards, like those of most thirties writers. Above all, however, the letter is a cry of youthful pain. He had survived the entire North African campaign and fought bravely; now he was having to risk his life all over again in the invasion of Europe. Louis Simpson describes the self-same mixture of anger and war-weariness in his poem 'The Runner':

> He had been there; his courage had been proved
> To his own satisfaction . . .
> . . . And it seemed unjust
> That he should be required to survive
> Again. The sound increased. The battleground
> Looked ominous. Visions of a huge mistake
> Struck at his heart. (*Selected Poems*, Harcourt Brace and World Inc., 1965, p. 57)

The invasion fleet sailed at midnight on 5 June 1944. The weather was bad, and the German bombardment of the beaches worse. Douglas's tank got clear of the mines and anti-tank guns and made inland. They reached Le Hamel, then Bayeux, of tapestry fame, and finally high ground near the villages of Saint-Pierre and Fontenay Le Pesnel. On their third day, 9 June, they came under heavy fire from German defenders. After a skirmish by a river Douglas and a fellow officer drove back to report to their senior officers. 'Douglas had climbed down from his tank to make his report, when the mortar fire started. As he ran along the ditch one of the shells exploded in a tree above him. He must have been hit by a tiny fragment, for although no mark was found on his body, he was instantly killed' (*KD*, p. 256). He was twenty-four years and four months old.

II
Prose

Douglas's prose may be summarized as follows:

1 Juvenilia – stories and articles written at school and at university.

2 Three short stories written in 1941 and 1943, 'Death of a Horse', 'The Little Red Mouth', and 'Giuseppe'.

3 Literary criticism.

4 Correspondence.

5 *Alamein to Zem Zem.*

   The categories are not mutually exclusive. Some of his best criticism, for example, is contained in his letters to J. C. Hall; two of the three 'mature' stories come out of material also used in *Alamein to Zem Zem*, and all three are based on army experience; the juvenile stories and articles are of literary-critical as well as fictional interest; and so on. For present purposes, I shall confine myself to remarks on some of his stories and literary criticism, before going on to a more extended consideration of *Alamein to Zem Zem*.

Fiction

There are signs that, had he lived, Douglas would have
written excellent short stories, memoirs, perhaps even
novels. What was actually accomplished, however, is
apprentice work, whose main interest is in the light it
throws on Douglas's character and poems. At the same
time 'everything he wrote', as Graham rightly says,
'carried the impress of his vitality of mind' (Introduc-
tion to *PM*, p. 9). It was a mind which moved with
perfect ease between poetry and prose, bookish but not
in awe of what it admired, equally adept at reproducing
and analysing physical and metaphysical appearances.
His signature is boldness of apprehension and design.
The fact that he ended up in command of an armoured
vehicle is one of those symbolic coincidences that
illuminate character; there he was relatively invulner-
able, crouched behind the big guns of his intelligence
and ambition. But, as he was well aware, such armour
could readily become a tomb. Like Rosenberg, he was
an artist as well as a poet (though his graphic skills
seem to me much inferior to his poetic ones); and like
him too there is a density and thrust in his language
which shoulders aside convention in an attempt to
grasp essences in a single trajectory of the pen. There is
also an aggressive hunger towards experience, and a
sardonic humour in his treatment of it, which some-
times reminds one of the Russian short-story writer
Isaac Babel. Those who find Douglas cold and posturing
are reminded rather of Hemingway. It would be foolish
to deny Douglas's real interest in war, but I can see
nothing of Hemingway's inflationary machismo either
in the poetry or the prose, nor of his incipient
sentimentality. Douglas's great virtue, like Babel's, is
his honesty about what he sees and what he feels,
regardless of his public 'image'. No doubt this dual
integrity, as man and as artist, is what all writers
aspire to. Unlike Hemingway, however, he did not go

looking for wars, nor did he regard them as the ultimate test of character.

These remarks have a more obvious application, perhaps, to the mature poetry and prose than to the juvenilia, but the early work too is strikingly accomplished. The first extant story is an autobiographical piece about his childhood, untitled (*PM*, p. 13). After a highly confident opening – 'As a child he was a militarist, and like many of his warlike elders, built up heroic opinions upon little information, some scrappy war stories of his father' – it draws swift and convincing portraits of his father and mother and two grandparents, and ends abruptly with the mysterious phenomenon of his mother's illness. The most notable feature is the self-confidence with which it exhibits and analyses character, his own included. Within the communal family structure each individual manoeuvres for space and gratification. The competitiveness between Keir (Douglas) and Billy is continued in his relations with his father and grandfather. The one 'teased his son, and pinched and tormented him sometimes', the other is 'almost unaware of the existence' of any other class and lifestyle than his own. Keir himself is equally selfish and self-absorbed, overturning his grandfather's card table when impatient to be told a story, then feigning penitence when he sees that it will bring quick returns. Traditional male and female roles are assigned to the grown-ups: men are absent, working, or at home, playing; women cook and shop. Only when Keir realizes that there is something the matter with his mother does he lose control: 'Someone he had never seen took him back to his bed with some unsatisfying explanation, and locked the door on him. He began immediately to scream and beat upon it, but they had all gone and he was alone, locked in. He became frantic, fell on the floor and shouted curses . . .' Grandfather comes up to explain to him that his mother has something called Sleepy Sickness, and 'With that, for the moment, Keir was content.'

Just as the *Collected Poems* opens with an astonishingly precocious poem, so this is an amazingly good story for a twelve-year-old – Graham dates it 'c.1932'. I am tempted to think that it was written, or perhaps revised, at a somewhat later date than this, c.1936–7, which is the date of the next piece in *A Prose Memoir*. Either way, it is the work of a born writer.

The stories and fragments that follow do not warrant extended comment. Most of them are autobiographical in cast, and continue to explore the growing-pains of youth. 'Drunk' employs an obvious metaphor for the poet's intoxication with language, just as 'A Present for Mimi' offers Van Gogh's severed ear as a plangent symbol of *angst*. Such romantic postures gradually give way to the maturer humour of some of his *Cherwell* articles and editorials. It is noticeable that romanticism of this sort is hardly present at all in the poems contemporary with the early prose. In a piece 'On the Nature of Poetry' written for *Augury*, Douglas himself makes an absolute distinction between the two forms: they are not to be compared any more than pictures and pencils, for the one is instrument and the other art (*PM*, p. 44).

Of the three later stories, 'Death of a Horse' is the most interesting. ('The Little Red Mouth' uses material from *AZZ*; 'Giuseppe' is a hasty and unconvincing war-yarn.) It describes a vet's killing and dissection of a lamed horse, in front of army students. It is based on one of Douglas's experiences at the army Equitation School in Gloucestershire, and possibly owes something to Orwell's 'Shooting an Elephant':

'I draw a line from here to here,' said the vet. And he drew a line with the chalk, diagonally across the horse's forehead: from the base of the left ear, more or less towards the right eye. Then he drew another line, diagonally the other way. The horse stood still.

'You never want to go lower than this,' said the vet,

pointing to where the lines cut. The orderly moved forward holding something, a sort of tube, which he put against the intersection of lines on the horse's forehead. The horse still stared in front of it. Someone said: 'The old hammer type.' Simon stiffened. But he was ready to see the horse's stagger, desperately trying to stand, and the death agony. The orderly's hand fell, he struck the tube and there was a small report.

The horses's knees gave way at once, so instantaneously that the eye could hardly mark its fall, and so silently that Simon might have been watching it through binoculars. It only stiffened and relaxed its legs once. The suddenness and silence of its death defeated his preparations to be unmoved. (*PM*, pp. 137–8)

In Orwell too there is a reference to 'where one would shoot' – 'an imaginary bar running from ear-hole to ear-hole'; but Orwell's is a much more elaborate and extended account than Douglas's swift sketch. It is noteworthy that the moment of death is accomplished 'so silently that Simon might have been watching it through binoculars': both fact and image presage the circumstances of Douglas's later encounters with death in the desert. At the moment of greatest intensity the experience is seen as through a lens, and removed to a great distance. The vet proceeds to his dissection:

. . . presently the horse lay stretched out into a diagram, to which the vet pointed as he spoke. The colours were brilliant, but not wholesome, and now a faint sweet sickly smell came . . .

'The horse has a small stomach,' said the vet. 'Look!' And he flapped the stomach in front of him, like an apron. The stench was unbelievable. Simon began at last to feel sick; his hand searched frantically for his pipe, but it was not in his pocket. He looked firmly at the wreck of the horse, the crowd of spectators, some craning their necks for a better view. The horrible casualness of the vet's voice grew more and more apparent; the voice itself increased in volume; the faces merged and disintegrated,

the wreck of the horse lay in a flurry of colours, the
stench cemented them into one chaos. He knew it was
useless. His one thought, as he felt himself falling, was
that he had let the horse down.

There are a number of clichés and tired phrases dotted
about in this, but overall it is a potent and moving
creation. No matter how much the vet tries to turn the
horse into a 'diagram', it remains – to borrow Law-
rence's phrase – one of the lords of creation, brilliantly
present throughout its sacrifice: 'the wreck of the horse
lay in a flurry of colours, the stench cemented them
into one chaos.' It is like a shipwreck or a sunset. There
is a passive verb for the splendours of the first sentence,
and an active, material one ('cemented') for the hypos-
tatization of the second; and the syntactical identity
underlines the force of the juxtaposition, as does the
declension of 'colours' into 'chaos'. The notion that
chaos might be cemented heightens the air of paradox;
and the story ends with the narrator re-enacting the
horse's fall. As so often in Douglas, absence and
presence are the dominating polarities; the horse is
abstracted and distanced into a diagram, yet simul-
taneously a living, interior spirit whose extinction
diminishes us all. The defeat of Simon's 'preparations to
be unmoved' is an exact diagnosis of what happens in
some of Douglas's best poems.

Literary Criticism

Douglas's best criticism is that which is written
directly in defence or explanation of his own poems.
The two most substantial statements he made are
'Poets in This War' (*PM*, pp. 117–20), written in the
summer of 1943, and a long letter to his friend and
fellow-poet, J. C. Hall (*PM*, pp. 127–8). Two things
emerge very strongly from the essay: first, that he was
hyper-conscious of his predecessors, the soldier-poets of
the First World War; and second, that only those with

first-hand experience of war could even begin to write about it. 'The Great War was entered upon by us in a spirit of terrific conceit and was the culmination of a complacent period ... The retreat from Mons, the aggregate of new horrors, the muddling generalship, the obsolescence of the gentleman in war demanded and obtained a new type of writing ... Rupert Brooke ... appeared superannuated in a moment ... Instead, arose Owen, to the sound of wheels crunching the bones of a man scarcely dead; Sassoon's tank lumbered into the music hall in the middle of a patriotic song, Sorley and Isaac Rosenberg were hypnotized among all the dangers by men and larks singing.' Interestingly, he mixes up Owen and Rosenberg for a moment; the 'wheels crunching the bones . . .' are surely those at the end of Rosenberg's 'Dead Man's Dump'. I say interesting because I think it is Rosenberg, the more 'difficult' and unEnglish of the two poets, who had the greater impact on the young Douglas.

Turning to the present, he says 'I do not find even one [poet] who stands out as an individual. It seems there were no poets at Dunkirk; or if there were, they stayed there. Instead we have had poetic pioneers and land girls in the pages (respectively) of *New Writing* and *Country Life*. There have been desperately intelligent conscientious objectors, RAMC orderlies, students. In the fourth year of this war we do not have a single poet who seems likely to be an impressive commentator on it.' He goes on to dismiss Henry Treece and his school, 'of what kind I am not sure', and his friend John Hall's 'very involved verses with an occasional oblique and clever reference to bombs or bullets'. Tambimuttu's *Poetry* (*London*) and John Lehmann's *Penguin New Writing* are similarly scanned and found wanting, the latter merely 'encouraging the occupants of British barrack rooms to work off their repressions . . .'. Sidney Keyes and the wartime Oxford poets 'are technically quite competent but have no experiences worth writing of'. John Heath Stubbs is even worse. 'The poets who wrote so much and so well before the war, all over the world, find themselves silenced, or able to write on almost any subject but war. Why did all this happen? Why are there no poets like Owen and Sassoon who lived with the fighting troops and wrote of their experiences while they were enduring them?'

There is an element of self-righteousness in all this, a clearing of moral and poetic space for his own man-oeuvres; but the judgements are accurate enough. The only new thing about this war, he goes on, is its 'mobile character'; that apart, everything has been already said. 'Almost all that a modern poet on active service is inspired to write, would be tautological.' The change into the conditional tense is eloquent of his dilemma. He concludes: 'it seems to me that the whole body of English poetry of this war, civil and military, will be created after war is over.' This prediction turned out to apply much more accurately to the novel than to poetry; Alun Lewis, Roy Fuller, Norman Cameron, F. T. Prince and others wrote most of their best poetry while the war was still on.

It is clear that Douglas both welcomes, and yet feels constrained by, the 'war-poet' label. His acceptance of the role of officer and (some sort of) gentleman shows similar tensions. He welcomed discipline, in life and in art, yet despised the bad faith that such games-playing seemed to engender. Hence, in part, the obsession with artifice that runs through the poems, early and late. 'I don't like this dance', the concluding line of his early poem 'A Ballet', becomes an epitaph on all the ways in which 'choreographer / and costumier combine' — that is, to put it in summary terms, the ways in which form devours content. He had witnessed this at close quarters all his life: boys became blue-coated scholars, young men became uproarious or pompous Oxford undergrads, older men became officers and gentlemen. In all these cases a uniform was ready and waiting, literal and social, and the majority were happy to slip it on and act out their allotted role. This denial of self-consciousness, a species of bad faith, contrasts with the animal and vegetable life that impinges on the desert, the flies and mosquitoes and wild dogs finding 'meat in a hole' ('Dead Men', *TCP*, p. 96). A letter of June 1943 to Hall shows him reacting against these human and formal (poetic) constraints: 'With regard to your criticisms of my stuff, I think you are beginning to condemn all that is not your own favourite brand, and are particularly anti-reportage and extrospective (if the word exists) poetry – which seems to me the sort that has to be written just now, even if it is not attractive' (*PM*, p. 121). Douglas tartly summarizes what I have called 'bad faith' as 'Bullshit' in his important letter to Hall of the next month. (*PM*, pp. 127–8). It is the finest statement he ever made about his own character and poetry, and needs to be read in full:

> . . . Incidentally you say I fail as a poet, when you mean I fail as a lyricist. Only someone who is out of touch, by which I mean first hand touch, with what has happened outside England – and from a cultural point of view I wish it had affected English life more – could make that criticism. I am surprised you should still expect me to produce musical verse. A lyric form and a lyric approach will do even less good than a journalese approach to the subjects we have to discuss now. I don't know if you have come across the word Bullshit – it is an army word and signifies humbug and unnecessary detail. It symbolizes what I think must be got rid of – the mass of irrelevancies, of 'attitudes', 'approaches', propaganda, ivory towers, etc., that stands between us and our problems and what we have to do about them.
>
> To write on the themes which have been concerning me lately in lyrical and abstract forms, would be immense bullshitting. In my early poems I wrote lyrically, as an innocent, because I was an innocent: I have (not surprisingly) fallen from that particular grace since

then. I had begun to change during my second year at Oxford. T. S. Eliot wrote to me when I first joined the army, that I appeared to have finished with one form of writing and to be progressing towards another, which he did not think I had mastered. I knew this to be true, without his saying it. Well, I am still changing: I don't disagree with you if you say I am still awkward and not used to the new paces yet. But my object (and I don't give a damn about my duty as a poet) is to write true things, significant things in words each of which works for its place in a line. My rhythms, which you find enervated, are carefully chosen to enable the poems to be *read* as significant speech: I see no reason to be either musical or sonorous about things at present. When I do, I shall be so again, and glad to. I suppose I reflect the cynicism and the careful absence of expectation (it is not quite the same as apathy) with which I view the world. As many others to whom I have spoken, not only civilians and British soldiers, but Germans and Italians, are in the same state of mind, it is a true reflection. I never tried to write about war (that is battles and things, not London Can Take It), with the exception of a satiric picture of some soldiers frozen to death, until I had experienced it. Now I will write of it, and perhaps one day cynic and lyric will meet and make me a balanced style. Certainly you will never see the long metrical similes and galleries of images again.

Your talk of regrouping sounds to me – if you will excuse me for exhibiting a one-track mind – like the military excuse of a defeated general. There is never much need to regroup. Let your impulses drive you forward; never lose contact with life or you will lose the impulses as well. Meanwhile if you must regroup, do it by re-reading your old stuff.

Of course, you will never take my advice nor I yours. But in these tirades a few ideas do scrape through the defences on either side. Perhaps all this may make it easier for you to understand why I am writing the way I am and why I shall never go back to the old forms. You may even begin to see some virtue in it. To be sentimental or emotional now is dangerous to oneself and to others. To trust anyone or to admit any hope of a better world is criminally foolish, as foolish as it is to stop working for it. It sounds silly to say work without hope, but it can be done; it's only a form of insurance; it doesn't mean work hopelessly.

'... my object ... is to write true things'; 'I see no reason to be either musical or sonorous about things at present'; 'perhaps one day cynic and lyric will meet and make me a balanced style'; 'Let your impulses drive you forward'; 'To be sentimental or emotional now is to be dangerous to oneself and to others' – the letter bristles with Douglas's tough-tender personality, casting aside attitudes and brilliantly feeling a way forward. Poetry is no less subject to bullshit than any other area of human endeavour. What is required now is 'extrospection', a careful attention to the facts. Poetry must still draw conclusions, as he says in his essay on Leigh Hunt, but such conclusions must emerge from observable reality rather than from poetic tradition or wishful thinking. Technique ('My rhythms ... are carefully chosen') must serve not itself but a 'true reflection', which means desert warfare on the one hand, and, on the other, 'the careful absence of expectation ... with which I view the world', which is not to be confused with cynicism or apathy. Eliot's and Hall's criticisms of his poetry were in fact doubly obtuse, for his recent work was fine in itself, and also a perfectly logical development from his earlier style and preoccupations. Lushness of any kind was utterly foreign to his nature; emotion in his poetry – even in the early lyrics – is almost always implicit. This is a masculine trait, perhaps, but is certainly not to be confused with coldness or impersonality, as it sometimes has been. The pressure of feeling in Douglas's best poems is enormous – as it is, indeed, in this classic letter – but is never dissociated from his restless honesty.

[31]

Alamein to Zem Zem

*I look back as to a period spent on the moon
almost to a short life in a new dimension*

'As a child he was a militarist . . .' Douglas's self-characterization makes a neat epigraph, but tells only a part of the story. As we have already seen, a Cairo friend reported that, though he seemed to thrive on a life of action, he actually detested the war. An editorial written for *Cherwell* in 1940 shows also that he was extremely alert to the sort of propaganda that always accompanies war. 'It has taken but a short time for the superstition to take hold again, that we are fighting a race of submen, of whom every member from birth is certainly a brutal moron . . . the words pacifist and coward will soon be as synonymous as they were a quarter of a century ago. In no time at all it will be once more *de rigueur* to put nearly everyone against a wall: and the Englishman with his traditional modesty will consider himself the salt of the earth and the saviour of it' (*PM*, p. 45). Pacifism was not an option Douglas ever considered possible for himself – temperamentally and intellectually he was a combatant – but it is clear that he was no blind enthusiast for war. His position was much like that of other thinking men of his generation, for example Roy Fuller, who wrote: 'The poets who *were* called up felt by and large that the war was necessary to destroy fascism, but they had no enthusiasm or confidence about the governments who were to be the instrument for this. Patriotism was absent, but so too was indignation about horrors. Pacifism was an untenable position: equally so was a crusading spirit . . .' (*Professors and Gods*, pp. 128–9).

Moreover, the opening page of *Alamein to Zem Zem* is perfectly clear-sighted about 'the great and rich men who cause and conduct wars. They have so many reasons of their own that they can afford to lend us some of them . . . They are out for something they want, or their Governments want, and they are using us to get it for them.' For himself, however, 'there is nothing unusual or humanly exciting at that end of the war. I mean there may be things to excite financiers or parliamentarians – but not to excite a poet or a painter or a doctor.'

Douglas writes, he tells us, 'not . . . as a soldier' but as an observer at an 'exhibition', or 'like a child in a factory.' He wants to describe 'more significant things than appearances; I still looked – I cannot help it – for something decorative, poetic or dramatic.' The parenthesis is interestingly double-edged, part self-accusation, part self-justification. He links the child's-eye-view with the artist's, both committed to wonder; and this hardly consorts with the soldier's commitment to action. The word 'decorative' sounds damagingly aesthetic, but he allies it with 'poetic and dramatic', and sets it over against 'appearances'.

There are some confusions and obliquities in these opening paragraphs, but they arise out of Douglas's characteristic honesty. In fact he *was* a soldier, and a good one, legitimately proud of his record. The down-grading of 'appearances' is questionable because it is precisely in them that 'significance' is to be located and pondered (as his own best prose and poetry demon-strates). Partly he is grappling with the writer's perennial problem of how he shall approach and order his material; and partly he is determined to be truthful about his own motives, which go wider and deeper than king and country.

His self-examination culminates in the assertion: 'I never lost the certainty that the experience of battle was something I must have . . . it is there [the battlefield] that the interesting things happen.' Like the earlier statement 'I cannot help it', the phrase 'something I must have' is again ambiguous, simul-taneously active and passive, conjuring some ultimate experience he both fears and desires, like sex or

[33]

marriage. The language is that of some ordeal or
initiation he must undergo – and the compulsions are
psychological as well as social. Like the hero of Crane's
The Red Badge of Courage, a novel Douglas admired,
he would find himself, perhaps, in the very act of facing
death. The word ticks throughout his poetry like a
metronome.

It is a commonplace to compare a man's character to
a battlefield but none the less true for that, and the
image is a perfect one for the dramatic conflicts
apparent in Douglas's make-up. At bottom, whatever
its rights and wrongs, war was 'humanly exciting'. It
was 'exciting and amazing to see thousands of men,
very few of whom have much idea why they are
fighting, all enduring hardships, living in an un-
natural, dangerous, but not wholly terrible world,
having to kill and be killed, and yet at intervals moved
by a feeling of comradeship with the men who kill them
and whom they kill, because they are enduring and
experiencing the same things. It is tremendously
illogical – to read about it cannot convey the impres-
sion of having walked through the looking-glass which
touches a man entering battle.'

Illogic was home ground to Douglas; the syntax of his
long sentences beautifully captures the sweep and the
jolting conflicts of battle. 'Touches', we might note in
passing, picks up the old word for someone who is
simple or slightly mad, 'touched'. At the same time, a
reflection is precisely something that *cannot* be
touched. In his last sentence the subject, 'battle', is
deferred and refracted through the phrases which lead
up to yet also distance it: 'read about . . . convey the
impression . . . having walked . . . which touches . . .'
etc. The looking-glass reminds us of the 'dial of glass' in
one of his best poems, 'How to Kill': 'Now in my dial of
glass appears / the soldier who is going to die.' Literally
the dial of glass is a gunsight, metaphorically it is a
mirror reflecting his own face: killing another, he kills

himself. In stepping through the mirror, like Alice, he enters the kingdom of death, which paradoxically resembles the kingdom of childhood, where inexplicability is the order of the day.

Within a couple of paragraphs of this profound paradox Douglas shifts from the Alice-image to 'the sort of little-boy mentality I still have' (in running away from his safe Staff job to rejoin his regiment); 'A little earlier, I might have wanted to run away and be a pirate.' His candour undercuts the *Boys' Own Paper* heroics of bravery, and his batman's reported response: '"I like you, sir," he said. "You're shit or bust you are." This praise gratified me a lot.' It is typical of Douglas that he acknowledges both the gratification and the schoolboy Achilles-fantasy that lurks among his motives.

After this preliminary self-analysis, which explains the circumstances of his personal entry into the war and introduces us to our narrator, Douglas vividly sets us down in the chaos of the western desert, where the battle of El Alamein is under way. ' . . . I drove up the sign-posted tracks until, when I reached my own place in all this activity, I had seen the whole arrangement of the Army, almost too large to appreciate, as a body would look to a germ riding in its bloodstream . . . huge conglomerations of large and small vehicles facing in all directions, flags, signposts and numbers standing among their dust. On the main tracks . . . lorries appeared like ships, plunging their bows into drifts of dust and rearing up suddenly over crests like waves . . . Every man had a white mask of dust in which, if he wore no goggles, his eyes showed like a clown's eyes . . . even with a handkerchief tied like a cowboy's over nose and mouth, it was difficult to breathe.'

Reporting to his colonel, whom he names Piccadilly Jim, Douglas agonizingly waits to discover whether he will be welcomed back to his regiment or cashiered for leaving his previous post without permission. Fortun-

[35]

ately the incident passes off with British understatement. 'The Colonel, beautifully dressed and with his habitual indolence of hand, returned my salute from inside the fifteen-hundredweight, where he was sitting with . . . the Adjutant . . . "Well, Keith," stroking his moustache and looking like a contented ginger cat, "we're *most* glad to see you – er – as always. All the officers in 'A' Squadron, except Andrew, are casualties, so I'm sure he'll welcome you with open arms. We're probably going in early tomorrow morning, so you'd better go and get him to fix you up with a troop now."'

As in a good novel or narrative poem, the double drama of these opening pages – Douglas's own personal escapade, and the 'big push' at Alamein – takes us effortlessly through the looking-glass in his Ford two-tonner, which is no more adapted to desert life than he is. Made troop leader of two Crusader tanks, he stows his gear, which includes 'a small cricket bag with shirts, slacks, washing and shaving kit, writing paper, a camera and a Penguin Shakespeare's Sonnets' and a revolver and flask of whisky. The list, especially the cricket bag, reminds one of certain continuities; it was a different war, but it might almost have been written by Owen. Thereafter we begin to meet the people Douglas will live and fight with, including his driver Mudie, who 'would wake up talking, as birds do', and his gunner Evan, who was taciturn and selfish. After a meal he lies down to reflect on the dramatic change in his circumstances. 'I had exchanged a vague and general existence for a simple and particular (and perhaps short) one . . . I had that feeling of almost unstable lightness which is felt . . . after putting down a heavy weight. All my difficult mental enquiries and arguments about the future were shelved, perhaps permanently.' When he goes to bed that night, 'I suddenly found myself assuming that I was going to die tomorrow . . .'.

Woken at four the next morning, and told they will move out at five, he prepares for his first engagement.

'In the half-light the tanks seemed to crouch, still, but alive, like toads. I touched the cold metal shell of my own tank, my fingers amazed for a moment at its hardness . . .' Already the dialectic between interior and exterior realities is in full play: darkness and dawn, poetry and war, the moon and the multi-coloured tracer bullets, the tanks crouching like toads yet hard and cold to the touch. (Touch, as we shall see in the poems, is the crucial confirming sense when it comes to life or death.) A little later he describes yet another paradox, in which the eternal noise of the tank engine produces silence: 'The view from a moving tank is like that in a camera obscura or a silent film . . . since the engine drowns all other noises except explosions, the whole world moves silently . . . I think it may have been the fact that for so much of the time I saw it without hearing it, which led me to feel that the country into which we were moving was an illimitably strange land, like the scenes in *The Cabinet of Doctor Caligari*.' The remainder of this impressive paragraph could be set out as verse:

> Silence is a strange thing to us who live:
> we desire it, we fear it,
> we worship it, we hate it.
> There is a divinity about cats,
> so long as they are silent: the silence
> of swans gives them an air of legend.
> The most impressive thing about the dead
> is their triumphant silence,
> proof against anything in the world.

Douglas would never have permitted himself such abstract discursiveness in a poem; but no less than six of the nine lines fall naturally into pentameters (not all are regular, but neither are the ones in his poems). Once again it is the strangeness of the experience that haunts him, and which is emphasized by the imagery of silent films and the camera obscura – both associated

[37]

with a dreamlike visual beauty. We note also the frequent conjunction in Douglas's writing of mirrors, screens, dials, binoculars and telescopes with heightened moments of experience. It is as if that which is most real demands the interposition of some medium of detachment and control, which is to say some form of art. (Cf. Coleridge's '... balance or reconciliation of opposite or discordant qualities' in *Biographia Literaria*, chapter 14.) This is sometimes construed as a pose on Douglas's part, a facile adoption of the stiff upper lip. It seems to me rather that the distancing images come into play at precisely those moments of greatest personal emotion.

In chapter 4, out near the front line now and looking for the enemy, Douglas and his tank get separated from the regiment, and he provides a memorable account of his confusion

> Andrew now began to call me impatiently over the air. 'Nuts five, Nuts five, you're miles behind. Come on. Come on. Off.' Speeding up, we saw the shape of a tank looming ahead of us again, and made for it. As we came nearer, it was recognizable as a German derelict. I had not realized how derelicts can complicate manoeuvres in a bad light ... we rushed eagerly towards every Crusader, like a short-sighted little dog who has got lost on the beach. Andrew continued to call up with such messages as: 'Nuts three, Nuts three, I still can't see you. Conform. Conform. Off.' I perceived that two other tanks of the squadron had attached themselves to me and were following me slavishly about, although the other tank of my own troop was nowhere to be seen ...

The farce is compounded by the fact that his first 'victim' is a man who is already dead. Instantly the subject goads him into detailed description. The 'man in black overalls ... leaning on the parapet', who is also black himself, is his 'first dead man', symbol and fact. The other dead scattered about are mediated by 'photographs' – once more the reality is distanced by memory and medium. Then he sees a dead Libyan soldier in a gun-pit:

> He was a big man: his face reminded me of Paul Robeson. I thought of Rimbaud's poem: 'Le Dormeur du Val' – but the last line . . . was not applicable. There were no signs of violence. As I looked at him, a fly crawled up his cheek and across the dry pupil of his unblinking right eye. I saw that a pocket of dust had collected in the trough of the lower lid. The fact that for two minutes he had been lying so close to me, without my noticing, was surprising: it was as though he had come there silently and taken up his position since our arrival.

A plethora of personal pronouns ushers himself into close contact with the fact of death. The macabre quality of the last sentence fuses the *memento mori* of a morality play with the magical queerness of the sort of silent film Douglas has previously evoked. The juxta-positions, as ever, set up their own shock waves: 'no . . . violence' is followed by a fly crawling on the dead man's eye; this 'unblinking . . . eye' is instantly followed by 'I saw . . .'; he has 'no . . . arms' (weapons) but his 'arms' are 'flung out'. As in other examples we have looked at, memory and art (Paul Robeson and the Rimbaud poem) come quickly into play. This experience, and others like it, are the source of his most anthologized poem 'Vergissmeinnicht' – which in turn contains more emblems of art.

Shortly after this episode there follows a brilliantly graphic account of the capture of enemy snipers in and around a derelict German tank:

> 'There they are!' cried the infantryman suddenly. A few yards from the left of the tank, two German soldiers were climbing out of a pit, grinning sheepishly as though they had been caught out in a game of hide and seek . . . men now arose all around us. We were in a maze of pits. Evan flung down the Besa machine-gun, cried impatiently,

'Lend us your revolver, sir,' and snatching it from my hand, dismounted. He rushed up and down calling 'Out of it, come on out of it, you bastards,' etc. The infantry officer and I joined in this chorus, and rushed from trench to trench ... The figures of soldiers continued to arise from the earth as though dragon's teeth had been sown there ...

The element of ludicrousness and games-playing which instantly succeeds the serious fighting is beautifully caught. Douglas's honesty authenticates every detail, just as his imagery lights up the narrative with imaginative precision – e.g. the soldier cowering to the ground like a scolded puppy, which is crowned by the linking image of the tank following their excited activities 'like a tame animal'. Best of all, perhaps, is the wonderful mythopoeic tenor of: 'The figures of soldiers continued to arise from the earth as though dragon's teeth had been sown there.' This fuses past and present wars in an endless cycle of recurrence; and in the case of the present war, provoked in part by the punitive Versailles Treaty, this is historically as well as psychologically accurate. Douglas's language is briskly colloquial, yet easily accommodates such biblical locutions as 'arise from the earth'. (Substitute 'rise', which would perhaps be the more obvious word to use, and the allusive ricochet is lost.) It also echoes the earlier sentence 'But now men arose all around us. We were in a maze of pits.' I hesitate to reach for the word 'symbolic' too often, but one of the pleasures of the passage and the whole book is the way in which large issues are made so richly concrete. Conversely, the unique muddle of this particular time and place are suggestive of an altogether timeless allegory.

Moving towards the end of his first, memorable day on the battlefield, Douglas confesses: 'These were the intensest moments of physical fear, outside of dreams, I have ever experienced.' The qualification confirms the actual turmoil of his inner life, which was kept hidden from his friends but publicly anatomized in the poems, another paradox to bear in mind when estimating his character. 'Simplify me when I'm dead . . .'

'I shall remember that day as a whole,' he says, 'separate from the rest of my time in action, because it was my first, and because we were withdrawn at two o'clock that morning for a four days' rest. My last sensations were of complete satisfaction in the luxury of sleep, without a thought for the future or the past.'

Stephen Crane said that he learned about battle on the football field. Much the same might be said of Douglas, who had been a keen rugby player, horseman, and member of the OTC. Like Crane's hero, he 'felt that in this crisis his laws of life were useless. Whatever he had learned of himself was here of no avail. He was an unknown quantity. He saw that he would again be obliged to experiment as he had in early youth. He must accumulate information of himself, and meanwhile be resolved to remain close upon his guard lest those qualities of which he knew nothing should everlastingly disgrace him' (*The Red Badge of Courage*, chapter 1). Douglas's apprehensions about going into battle were very similar. Like Henry Fleming, he first exults in his ability to function as a soldier and not disgrace himself by cowardice; then grows sick of the fact that this is an ordeal he must re-submit himself to as long as the war lasts. It is one thing to risk your life for the first time, and another to turn that risk into a way of life. The information Douglas needed to accumulate is nowhere more apparent than in his descriptions of the dead, which are frequent and obsessive. Dead men are to a battle what goals or runs or points are to a game. The analogy may seem facetious or disgusting but it is one that is employed relentlessly, albeit implicitly, by Douglas's fellow-officers. All the extended descriptions of death occur fairly early in the narrative; as Douglas grows battle-hardened, such sights absorb less of his attention. (In addition, 'his' war was fiercest in the early months.) For ease of discussion, I will bring together some of his descriptions of dead men from various parts of the book.

In chapter 6, Douglas takes us 'into the minefield' by way of an anecdote about their first sight of some new tanks: '. . . we passed . . . three monstrous tanks, the first Churchill tanks we had ever seen. They were being sent into the battle on test: unfortunately, whoever arranged these tests . . . had omitted to inform the combatant troops, and one of the three was destroyed neatly and ruthlessly by our own anti-tank gunners.' Shortly after this classic idiocy he passes 'an area of weapon pits where British and Italian corpses lay together.' As his tank moves slowly forward to engage the enemy, he begins to look carefully into such pits and trenches as they pass by:

> . . . I looked down into the face of a man lying hunched up in a pit. His expression of agony seemed so acute and urgent, his stare so wild and despairing, that for a moment I thought him alive. He was like a cleverly posed waxwork, for his position suggested a paroxysm, an orgasm of pain. He seemed to move and writhe. But he was stiff. The dust which powdered his face like an actor's lay on his wide open eyes, whose stare held my gaze like the Ancient Mariner's. He had tried to cover his wounds with towels against the flies . . . This picture, as they say, told a story. It filled me with useless pity.

This is the same incident which Douglas expanded into his short story 'The Little Red Mouth'. The body's 'stare' meets Douglas's 'gaze' with reciprocal incomprehension; and yet, like the Mariner's, it tells an immense story. Throughout this and similar passages the appearance/reality theme is mirrored or echoed by Douglas's prose. He takes aim, as it were, with a variety of rhetorical and poetic devices (including assonance, pararhyme, pun), and bombards the dead

[42]

man with phrases, syntactical repetitions, and allusive images, ending with an echo of Owen's famous sentence 'The Poetry is in the pity.' I don't wish to suggest that Douglas's responses are not first-hand. Patently they are. But those responses are instinct with the tyrannies of language, from ordinary cliché ('belching inky smoke') to the definitive rhythms of the First World War poets that Douglas grew up on. There are no elements in the scene that have not been drawn with consummate skill by his predecessors. Hence one part of his struggle is with the linguistic and poetic paradigms that work to determine his responses in advance. At the same time there is comfort to be had in sheltering beneath the propriety of the canon. When a wounded New Zealand officer asks him, shortly after this episode, whether a comrade in a nearby tank is dead:

> 'Dead as a doornail,' said my voice. The words blundered out without any intention. God knows what made me say them. I had meant only to nod. I saw him wince and felt dumb with embarrassment.

It is a finely human moment, encapsulating all Douglas's problems as a soldier-writer: how to achieve the correct dumbness, and nod in words. Intend is a transitive verb, which is here shorn of its object ('. . . without any intention' – full stop), yet we know exactly what he intends; so that the curtal-sentence embodies the very tact he accuses himself of lacking. The hallowed Dickens phrase (from the opening of *A Christmas Carol*) is followed by 'God knows . . .' so that he blunders from one ready-made formula to another; and this linguistic stumbling has its own eloquence too. It says everything and nothing.

A little later in this extended episode Douglas looks into another pit:

> The bodies of some Italian infantrymen still lay in their weapon pits, surrounded by pitiable rubbish, picture post-

[43]

cards of Milan, Rome, Venice, snapshots of their families, chocolate wrappings, and hundreds of cheap cardboard cigarette-packets . . . The Italians lay about like trippers taken ill.

The epithets – 'pitiable rubbish', 'cheap cardboard', etc. – are readily transferable, bouncing about as between bodies and artifacts. The postcards and photographs, as well as functioning in ways I have already analysed, suggest also the mechanical and transitory nature of this world; everything seems to be two-dimensional and hence easily portable, so that it could all be folded away like the scenery of a play, or cut short like a vacation, or crumpled up and thrown away like the wrappings on a chocolate bar. Nothing is properly grown-up and *serious*. And yet it is as serious as death can make it.

The details are eloquently present in the poem Douglas made out of this scene, 'Cairo Jag': 'you can imagine / the dead themselves, their boots, clothes and possessions / clinging to the ground, / a man with no head / has a packet of chocolate and a souvenir of Tripoli'. Douglas's prejudice against Italians, which was common throughout the Eighth Army, does not feature in the poem but is very evident in the prose. Commenting on their alleged practice of leaving booby-traps behind them, he refers to them as 'little beasts, who combined underhand cruelty with cowardice, and servility when we caught up with them. The Italian attitude of "we never wanted to fight" was true enough, with its corollary: "We only wanted to tie bombs to wine-bottles and corpses, and leave them for you to find."' His animus recurs in a later description of German and Italian war-graves. The German ones are 'neat' and 'surmounted by their eagle-stamped steel helmets'; the Italian ones are 'more hastily dug' and occasionally surmounted by 'the ugly green-lined Italian topee'.

The last of his detailed descriptions of dead men

occurs in chapter 8, after the end of the successful
battle of Galal Station. It comes immediately after a
vivid account of the climax of the battle, and Douglas's
dressing himself up in the spoils of the victor:

> I approached a brand-new-painted M13, with no sign
> of any damage . . . It was dark in the turret, and I leant
> over the manhole first, trying to accustom my eyes to the
> darkness . . . A faint sweet smell came up to me which
> reminded me of the dead horse I once saw cut up for our
> instruction at the Equitation School.
>
> Gradually the objects in the turret became visible: the
> crew of the tank – for, I believe, those tanks did not hold
> more than two – were, so to speak, distributed round the
> turret. At first it was difficult to work out how the limbs
> were arranged. They lay in a clumsy embrace, their
> white faces whiter, as those of dead men in the desert
> always were, for the light powdering of dust on them.
> One with a six-inch hole in his head, the whole skull
> smashed in behind the remains of an ear – the other
> covered with his own and his friend's blood, held up by
> the blue steel mechanism of a machine gun, his legs
> twisted among the dully gleaming gear-levers. About
> them clung that impenetrable silence I have mentioned
> before, by which I think the dead compel our reverence. I
> got a Biretta from another tank on the other side of the
> railway line.

It is a compelling passage, which moves between
humour and pathos and awe and a near-brutal relish in
his own survival. The games-playing – 'like . . . boys in
a shooting gallery' – leads on to self-beautification in
the enemy's clothes. Then, 'feeling hugely pleased with
myself', he encounters darkness, an alarming smell,
and the dead men, whose 'clumsy embrace' goes back
through the Owen and Rosenberg to the Jacobean and
Elizabethan dramatists. By now there is something
frenetic, it seems to me, in the studied detachment of
Douglas's description, making believe that the disposi-

tion of smashed limbs is a problem in anatomy or life-class. The hypotactic syntax and phonic chaos of the language – 'his legs twisting among the dully gleaming gear levers' – accurately mimic his horrified response. Yet the final paragraph is a little too literary for comfort. The semi-archaic inversion of 'About them clung . . .' for example, which reintroduces the topic of silence, is less than compelling, and so is the assertion of 'reverence'. Earlier the silence of the dead had been 'triumphant'; now it is 'impenetrable'. In context this is another ghastly antinomian joke, since both tank and crew have clearly been penetrated by what they most feared. And Piccadilly Jim's ritual swear-words ('look to your BLOODY procedure') are grotesquely instantiated in the covertly erotic procedures of death, which cover a man with 'his own and his friend's blood'.

Douglas's poem 'Landscape with Figures' (which was one of the provisional titles for *Alamein to Zem Zem*) brings together many of the features common to these micro- and macroscopic slides of death. '. . . You who like Thomas come / to poke fingers in the wounds' is as much Douglas himself as it is his reader. There is the ubiquitous desert dust, part biblical ('dust to dust'), part reductive, suggestive of powder and make-up; there is blood, another item of 'maquillage'; the figures are actors, mimes, waxworks, Ancient Mariners, trippers, lovers; the 'décor' is of iron torn into 'fronds' and 'celery' and other parodies of the vegetable world; the 'backdrop' is the neutral desert (neutral also, as Desmond Graham has pointed out, as between England and Germany) – and the product of it all is silence, which is the strong 'proof' Douglas reaches for in his poetry and his life.

As well as guns and shells, Douglas had to come to terms with his fellow officers, and one of the pleasures of *Alamein to Zem Zem* is the skill with which he sets down their characters and conversation. Typically, he finds himself torn between admiration and disgust, a mixture of feelings admirably summed up in his poem 'Aristocrats'. Early on he notes that the officers' 'origins and ideas were beautifully standardized'; for the most part they are the direct descendants of the officer-and-gentleman types familiar to us in the memoirs of Graves, Blunden and Sassoon. Being members of a cavalry regiment, Douglas's senior officers were probably as snobbish as any in the army. Many of them knew more about horses than they did about tanks, and tended to look down on the newer officers who had specialized mechanical knowledge. 'These new officers were not gentlemen, in the sense of *gentilhomme*. Very few of them could ride, and very few of them could afford to hunt or shoot, or knew any of the occupations or acquaintances of "the boys". This made it difficult for "the boys" to find anything to talk about with the new arrivals . . .' These 'had . . . mechanized training and knew their work reasonably well. Yet it was obvious to the cavalrymen that newly joined subalterns could not be allowed to tell the regiment what to do.' The usual class distinctions were further exacerbated by the regiment's history: all the 'old boys' had served together in Palestine, whereas the new ones were either fresh out of training or transferred from other regiments. It was, says Douglas, 'an unbridgeable gulf' (chapter 15).

The subalterns (junior officers) with whom Douglas worked were Tom, 'with his filthy pipe and rakish air of being in the know', a careerist who had dealt in horses before the war and hence had something in common with his senior officers; Edward, a shy and somewhat ineffectual county type governed entirely by the notion of 'good form'; and Raoul, voluble, half-French, and disliked both by officers and men. Only Douglas takes the trouble to find out his history, and ends up finding him 'likeable and well-meaning'. Their immediate superior is Andrew, 'a hardened and embittered soldier' who had once been a colonel but is now, through no fault of his own, only an acting Major; 'second in command of a squadron whose squadron leader had been a subaltern under him before'. He is small, 'brick-red with sun and wind, the skin cracking on his lips and nose', and evil-tempered. The colonel, whom we have already met, is Piccadilly Jim, an 'old boy' *par excellence*, and in civilian life a Tory MP. Douglas's names are all invented ones; the colonel's is a small triumph of characterization, suggesting dandyism, raffishness and flair. After Douglas himself, he is the most vivid presence in the book. The officers' almost parodic insouciance is brought out in an incident in chapter 6. Douglas is refuelling and brewing up a drink, when he looks up to see an 'odd sight':

> It was a Sherman, right enough, but as it came towards us in the beginning of twilight, a red aureole about the turret top proclaimed that the inside was blazing. The immediate effect was of something supernatural, as though the dead or mangled crew were bringing in the remains of their tank . . . The tank stopped about a hundred yards off, as I finished my coffee, and a figure emerged from the driver's manhole and came a little unsteadily towards our fire. It was Nick, a lieutenant out of 'C' Squadron whom I had only once met before, at Division when he was sent up there on a liaison job. His pleasant face was as black as a Christy minstrel's and lit up into a nigger smile as he said: 'Hullo old boy, I've just brought my Sherman in; I wonder if you'd mind giving a hand to put the fire out?' and sniffing – 'I say, is that coffee?'

This is British understatement with a vengeance, the stiffest of stiff upper lips, straight out of a Pinewood film; and the supernatural weirdness of the blazing tank, conversely, is like something out of *The Ancient Mariner*, though Douglas himself likens it to one of the macabre fantasies of Bierce. The 'supernatural' effect is one that he will return to in 'Vergissmeinnicht'.

Other officers include Sweeney Todd, 'tactless, good-hearted, and perfectly unimaginative', disliked by the men but devoted to the regiment. 'His upbringing as a member of the English upper classes seems to have been rigidly typical, and has left him with fixed inherited views on life . . . He mistrusts jokes . . . and . . . is afraid of intellectual conversation, of music and of painting.' Then there is Guy, who

> was older than Piccadilly Jim and had been in the regiment . . . longer than anyone . . . a figure straight out of the nineteenth century. He was charming and entirely obsolete . . . He seldom, if ever, wore a beret . . . he had a flannel shirt and brown stock pinned with a gold pin, a waistcoat of some sort of yellow suede lined with sheep's wool, beautifully cut narrow trousers of fawn cavalry twill, without turnups, and brown suede boots. On his head was a peaked cap with a chinstrap like glass, perched at a jaunty angle. His moustache was an exact replica of those worn by heroes of the Boer war . . . He chafed at having to keep out of the enemy's range when he might have charged the guns in line, and found the matter of writing a report afterwards very tedious.

Sweeney Todd and Guy are both 'types', and Douglas's set-piece descriptions are not altogether free of tiredness and the conventions of the genre. The sketch of the former moves self-consciously into the present tense; and Guy calls up phrases as well-worn as his social attitudes. However, both are convincing enough for the purposes of the narrative. So too are the vignettes of some of the men, for example the young tank-driver whose tank has been hit:

> He did not appear very shaken: a young North Country-man, stocky built with a square red face and tow-coloured hair. 'I didn't seem to be getting any orders, like, sir,' he said in explanation, 'so I had a look at George – Corporal Wood. He were sitting in his seat and at first I

thought he were all right. But then I see he were dead. Then I had a look at Bert, like, and *he* were all over blood; so I come out of it jildi.' (chapter 6, p. 54)

Compared with Nick's 'Hullo old boy, I've just brought my Sherman in . . .' quoted earlier, the driver's brand of understatement, 'Bit mucky in the turret' (chapter 6, p. 54), is engagingly unaffected. Douglas was not oblivious to such distinctions, and on the whole seems to have felt more at home with the men than with the officers. A prickly character at the best of times, the fact that he was also a poet and an artist clearly made him a peculiar fish for Guy and Edward and Piccadilly Jim. Douglas was alternately charmed and exasperated by their 'stupidity and chivalry' and 'famous unconcern' ('Aristocrats').

Just occasionally he is a prisoner of his own social attitudes. The comment on Billy in chapter 15, for example, hitches an easy ride on stereotypes: 'Billy, like many NCOs, had learnt a lot of long words for the purpose of impressing squads under his charge.' The word in question is 'incorrigible'. One can't imagine Douglas ascribing such motives to commissioned officers, or to himself.

The episode comes from the weakest and flattest chapter in the book, which attempts to record mess talk. This record of the interminable yarns of army life, told to while away the time, is stilted and second-hand, owing more to middle-brow literature than to Douglas's normally acute ear. The failure contrasts sharply with his rendering of the 'idiom of our wireless traffic', which he likens to 'that of a wildly experimental school of poets' giving a 'vivid, inimitable running commentary' on the course of any deployment or battle.

Piccadilly Jim, however, jumps off the page at us with Dickensian brio. After some brief references to him early on, we meet him again in chapter 6 where, after Sunday morning service, he is 'giving a last twirl to his moustache and regarding his suede boots' preparatory to making a little speech to the troops:

> The laces of these boots were tied in reef knots, with exactly equal ends hanging symmetrically on each side of the foot, ending at the welt of the boot. 'Tomorrow,' he said, 'we shall go forward to fight the second phase of the battle of Alamein. The first phase, the dislodgement of the enemy from his position along the whole of his line of battle, is complete. In that phase this Division, this Brigade, did sterling work. The Divisional General and the Brigadier are very pleased.' Here he interposed some acknowledgement to the efforts of individuals, somewhat like an author acknowledging indebtedness in a preface, adding 'But you all did your jobs, in a way of which you can be proud. In the action at dusk on Tuesday, you stuck to your guns, you didn't give way, and you were extremely successful. When it was possible to investigate the position it was found that we had knocked out five enemy tanks, without casualties to ourselves, and at the price of one lorry. That was most excellent. Bloody good. Couldn't be better.
>
> 'Now this time, in the second phase, we shall not have quite so much dirty work to do; other people . . . er . . . are to be allowed to look in . . . When General Montgomery is ready we shall move in behind them, to administer the *coup de grâce* to the German Armour. That is a great honour and you can take credit to yourselves that it has been granted to this Brigade. When we've destroyed the enemy's armour and routed his forces, we shall then go back to Cairo, and . . . er . . . have a bath, and leave the other buggers to do the chasing for us.' (chapter 5, pp. 46–7)

Piccadilly Jim is no less a type than Edward or Guy or Billy, but the detail brings him perfectly to life, from the symmetrical boot-laces to the comical hesitations and stock phrases of his speech. Douglas is charmed but undeceived by its 'nice mixture of parliamentary and colloquial terms, in magnifying what we had done, half belittling what remained to be done ... It was exactly the right speech, in exactly the right words. It put everyone into a good fighting temper ...' The next episode of any length in which we meet the colonel is when he is in a bad temper over the loading and unloading of tanks from their huge transporters. Both operations were tricky ('The tank was lined up and gingerly approached ... the whole incident was like the mating of two immense creatures, mythical and prehistoric'), and Piccadilly Jim issues a stream of contradictory orders. Unfortunately Douglas's tank accidentally plunges off the road, and Piccadilly Jim dresses him down in front of the entire army. Deciding that 'if I accepted this rebuke tamely, Piccadilly Jim would despise me,' and wondering privately whether his colonel isn't 'getting a sort of Agamemnon complex', Douglas writes a letter of explanation and offers to leave the regiment, which provokes the following reply:

Dear Keith,
   It is a great mistake ever to refer to matters which are already forgotten and done with. Napoleon once gave this advice to a friend. Never complain. Never explain ... I am liberal with my praise, of which you have had your fair share. I am equally outspoken in my criticism, and this you must, I fear, accept. In conclusion, may I recommend to you this advice which Theodore Roosevelt gave to the undergraduates of Harvard – Keep your eyes on the stars, but your feet on the ground. (chapter 12, p. 90)

It is a small classic of sententiousness, worthy of Piccadilly Jim's political training. The quotation in the third line belongs to Disraeli, but 'Napoleon' has a finer ring to it. (Douglas tells us he had heard the same quotation handed out to Raoul.) Once past the first sentence – 'as near an apology as he would go,' remarks Douglas – the letter manages to say nothing whatever, whilst maintaining an air of grand pro-

[52]

fundity. One can almost hear Douglas collapsing into laughter as he read this species of the higher bullshit. The 'of which' constructions, (common to this letter and the speech to the troops), at once archaically 'correct' and orotundly pompous, are the perfect linguistic complement to his suede boots and impeccable reef knots.

Throughout the campaign Piccadilly Jim continues to inspire and infuriate his regiment. In the final chapter, when Douglas is sitting at a pavement café in Tel Aviv recovering from his wounds, he picks up a paper and reads with disbelief of Piccadilly Jim's death – 'killed . . . typically, while he was standing up in his tank, shaving under shell-fire':

> It was impossible to realize it. The whole moment and everything in it . . . seemed suddenly part of a dream. Piccadilly Jim, with all his faults of occasionally slapdash and arbitrary conduct, had been a brave man and a Colonel of whom we could be proud. Of whom, I discovered, somewhat to my surprise, I had been proud myself. He was an institution: it seemed impossible that in a moment a metal splinter had destroyed him . . . I was amazed to find, reading of his death, that I felt like a member of the old régime who looks on at a bloody revolution. ('Zem Zem', p. 147)

It is as fine an elegy as anyone could wish for. By a stroke of imaginative empathy, the concluding analogy puts Douglas literally in the shoes of the 'old boys' he stood at such a queer angle to himself. Such empathy finds a linguistic counterpart too: in the act of remembering he echoes the very locution ('a Colonel of whom . . .') that was Piccadilly Jim's voiceprint. Finally, the 'bloody' of 'bloody revolution' picks up one of his favourite swear-words and the literal substance of war. He was an institution and, as Douglas presciently implies, the régime in England would never be quite the same again after 1945. He learns that Tom is dead

[53]

too, and also Guy, the most aristocratic officer of all.* 'The plains were their cricket pitch / and in the mountains the tremendous drop fences / brought down some of the runners . . .' ('Aristocrats').

The boy-scout side of Douglas relished the camaraderie and the improvisatory nature of the soldier's existence in the desert. There are excellent accounts of meals lovingly prepared from unpromising materials, of impromptu fraternization with German prisoners, and of the intricacies and exhilarations of moving at speed across the desert, which is more than once compared to the excitements of the hunt. As the narrative goes on, however, the fighting becomes increasingly dangerous, reaching a climax in the long chapter 18, which is crammed with action. After a great deal of skirmishing and lucky escapes Douglas's tank finally gets hit:

> I heard the Corporal say: 'Get out, sir, we've been hit' as though from a long way off, and simultaneously I was able to move, as if his voice had broken a spell . . . I was able to open my eyes for a second but they closed themselves and tears poured out from under the lids. I realized the wireless was still working and said: 'King Five, my horse has copped it. Wireless OK, but we shan't be able to take any further part in the show. I'll just have a look at the damage and tell you the extent.' 'King Five, that's the second time. You MUST NOT say such things over the air,' said Piccadilly Jim . . . I'm sorry you're dizzy. But you really must not say these things. Now take care of yourself. Off.' (chapter 18, pp.126–7)

This is the first and last time Douglas mentions tears, and the description is as impersonal as may be, as

* Desmond Graham tells us that 'Guy' was probably Lt-Col. J. D. Player, who 'left £3000 to the Beaufort Hunt, and directed that the incumbent of the living in his gift should be a "man who approves of hunting, shooting, and all manly sports, which are the backbone of the nation"'. See KD, p. 199.

though they cried themselves. There is something of the 'manly', public-school ethos about this, no doubt, but also an admirable honesty. His shock is such that physiology takes over the function of the will. Prior to this, some of his phrases ('. . . as though from a long way off . . . as if his voice had broken a spell') belong to the world of schoolboy adventure fiction.

His driver had been badly wounded. Douglas gets him out and into the shelter of a pit, and runs off to fetch a morphia syringe from a fellow officer. '. . . the needle was very blunt and a good deal of the stuff flowed out of a crack . . . and dribbled on the skin. Dunn did not seem any better for the injection. It later turned out that we had been given by mistake a preparation for waking people up under anaesthetic.' An episode worthy of *Catch-22*. Failing to move his damaged tank, Douglas drops to the ground and suddenly realizes that the flow of battle has left him and the other men dangerously exposed:

> 'Capture,' I thought suddenly. 'I shall be captured.' . . . I walked forward blindly and almost tripped over a man on the ground. He was a 'C' Squadron corporal, and his right foot was not there: the leg ended in a sort of tattered brush of bone and flesh. He said something which I could not hear, or which my mind would not grasp. After he had said it twice, I realized he was asking me not to leave him behind. To carry him seemed to my tired muscles and lungs impossible. I looked ahead and saw the sandhills stretching out for an eternity, without a sign of life. 'Kneel down,' he said. 'I can get on your back.' I got on my knees and he fastened a grip on me like the old man of the sea. I tried to stand up, and at last achieved it, swaying and sweating, with the man on my back; his good leg and his stump tucked under my arms, his hands locked at my throat. (chapter 18, pp. 129–30)

Douglas carries him half a mile over open ground and into the shelter of another pit, where an officer and more men are sheltering. He then starts back for his own lines, with three of the men, to try and find a vehicle in which to rescue the others:

> Presently I saw two men crawling on the ground, wriggling forward very slowly in a kind of embrace.
>
> As I came up to them I recognized one of them as Robin ... His left foot was smashed to pulp, mingled with the remainder of a boot. But as I spoke to Robin saying, 'Have you got a tourniquet, Robin?' and he answered apologetically: 'I'm afraid I haven't, Keith', I looked at the second man. Only his clothes distinguished him as a human being, and they were badly charred. His face had gone: in place of it was a huge yellow vegetable. The eyes blinked in it, eyes without lashes, and a grotesque huge mouth dribbled and moaned like a child exhausted with crying. (chapter 18, pp. 130–1)

The 'two men crawling on the ground, wriggling forward ... in a kind of embrace' (cf. the dead Italians in their tank) are similar to those in the poem 'Landscape with Figures': 'On scrub and sand the dead men wriggle / in their dowdy clothes.' The description of the second man on the ground is perhaps the most horrific in the book. There is no suspicion of fine writing here, nor of exaggerated detachment, and the passage is all the better for it. The lashless eyes take us back to Douglas's description of his own shock earlier ('I was able to open my eyes for a second ...'), and to all the other eyes of dead men encountered in previous descriptions. Eliot's 'Eyes that last I saw in tears / ... Here in death's dream kingdom ...' may also be somewhere at the back of Douglas's mind. The image of the face as a 'vegetable' immediately summons up such images in 'Cairo Jag' and 'Vergissmeinnicht'. The man is recognizable as a human being only by the charred remains of his clothes, which are in marked contrast to Robin's 'fleece-lined suede waistcoat and polished brass shoulder titles'. The more Douglas struggles to identify

[56]

what is specifically human, the more he is driven to images of costumed dolls and 'meat in a hole' ('Dead Men'). One of Owen's controlling images is that of butchery and carcasses ('earth set . . . cups / . . . for their blood') – the trenches were a horrific mulch. Douglas's desert, by contrast, is a neutral backdrop or stage, on which the actor's highest art is to act out and to express futility and silence. There is next to no Christian symbolism; only mines are 'capable of resurrection' ('Dead Men'). Nor is there any travellers' mysticism about the healing emptiness of the locale. All the desert manufactures is dust and flies and sores and a bizarre crop of iron, which parodies the vegetable world of nature, just as the dead and dying parody the natural world of lovers and families. Douglas's awareness of the doubleness of *acting* – to pretend, and to do in earnest – is almost Hamlet-like. '. . . I was ashamed: my own mind accused me of running to escape . . .' In the poems this same obsession with appearance manifests itself again and again. 'A yard more, and my little finger / could trace the maquillage of these stony actors' ('Landscape with Figures'). To 'trace' is to copy, which distances him even further from the bodies, as does the gallicism. The final line reminds one of another last line, 'And our wheels grazed his dead face' (Rosenberg, 'Dead Man's Dump'). A yard more, that is to say, in one direction or another, and Douglas could merge his identity with the dead, victim of a shell or a bullet. A yard more and he too might break free of self-consciousness and simply live or die, free of the compulsion to observe and bear witness. In his later poem 'On a Return from Egypt' he speaks of standing 'here in the wings of Europe'; but where death is concerned he is always in the wings, waiting to go on, even in the thick of battle, forever rehearsing his unknowable part. There is a continual rage to 'split the glass' and 'kiss / . . . love or death, / a person or a wraith' (with a pun on wreath), either to rise above or wriggle out underneath the unreality that surrounds him. Sincerity is at a premium. How should he face the facts, about the war and about himself? Or, putting it the other way round, how should he avoid all the varieties of bullshit, interior and exterior? It was precisely the same question Alun Lewis, his most gifted contemporary, faced in Burma; and it seems that he took his own life.

The chapter ends – fittingly, I almost said – with his own near-approach to death. He has regained his own lines, with a lieutenant, but then steps onto a trip-wire:

> I remained standing, numbed. It seemed impossible that anything could hit so hard and leave me on my feet: and as feeling came back, I shrank from movement. But the explosion of a second mine suggested to me that I ought to throw myself down, and I toppled forward and sprawled on the sand. A third mine went off, further away. I was aware of the new subaltern lying on the other side of the trip wire, which stretched between us as taut as ever. It was a bright new wire strung through wooden pegs: I realized that I had seen it and discounted it because of its newness, and because subconsciously I had come to expect such things to be cunningly hidden. People ran towards us from Mousky's scout car. I shouted to them: 'Look out for mines. Don't explode any more.' One of them said mistakenly as he came up, '*You're* all right, sir,' in a soothing sort of voice. I found I could raise one arm and waved it at Bert Pyeman whose attention the bang had attracted. He swung his little beetle of a car round and came across to us. 'Don't try to get up, Keith,' he said.

Everything in *Alamein to Zem Zem* leads up to the trip-wire. Men either rush and blunder about, or wriggle and writhe ('Poetry is like a man . . . in such a posture . . . you can hardly believe it a position of the limbs you know' – *Augury*); action takes place at a distance, seen through a lens, or in monstrous close-up, scarcely seen at all. The combatants are 'Perched on a great fall of air' ('Landscape with Figures'). In addition to the paradoxes already noted, and those spelt out in his unfinished poem 'Bête Noire', there are a myriad juxtapositions in the narrative which dizzy the mind. Bouts of bombardment alternate with silence, or reading 'a libraryful of novels'; one minute he is stalking the enemy, the next he has himself become the prey; similarly in his private life he is first beneficiary then victim of Milena's predatory charm. The lunatic explosions and burnt-out derelicts are succeeded by a desertful of flowers. The landscape itself is made up of ridges and hollows, heat and cold, flowers and scorpions. The tanks they ride in are their only protection and, when hit, perfect death-traps.* He frequently mistakes the enemy for his own side, and vice versa. He often gets lost, both when at rest ('One night it took me nearly three hours to find my tank') and when in battle: the front line shifts so fast that pursuer becomes pursued before he even knows he is in danger. No one can perceive when or why or how the balance changes. At a critical moment Douglas shouts instructions to his driver and finds that he is yelling to the whole regiment because he has forgotten to switch wireless channels; his driver can't hear a word. As in other intense records of experience, the literal becomes of its own volition symbolic.

Back at a first-aid station Douglas is examined by a Medical Officer, who cuts away his uniform with 'a huge Struwwelpeter pair of scissors' to reveal comprehensive, but not lethal, wounds.

* 'Losses were heavy and the tanks acquired a bad name for vulnerability . . . The main enemy of the Crusader was the anti-tank gun and against such a weapon the two-pounder (40-mm) was of little use' (Eric Grove, *World War II Tanks*, Orbis Publishing, 1976, p. 84). The Crusader II, introduced in 1942, had a six-pounder (57-mm) gun in a redesigned turret, but was still much more vulnerable than the heavier Shermans and Grants.

He is transferred to a series of ambulances on the long drive back towards a railway station, not knowing yet where his destination will be. In one he records the following:

> A man on the stretcher opposite moaned all the way, talking to himself, or to us, I don't know which. I was beginning to be accustomed to the regularity and monotony of wounded men's moaning. This man said: 'Oh. Oh. I didn't want to fight. Oh. I didn't want to fight. Oh. I didn't want to fight,' every four seconds, I judged, for ten lurching miles. Then he altered it suddenly to: 'Had a good job. Had a good job,' and, changing quickly again: 'Bags o' money. Bags o' money. Oh. Oh. Oh. Bags of money. Packets of money.' But in the end he came again to: 'I didn't want to fight . . .'

Like a music-hall song or Brechtian poem, the wounded man's chant sums up a whole world of feeling, somewhere between *Oh What a Lovely War* and *Catch-22*. Douglas is taken all the way back to Cairo, where he is at first admitted to the wrong ward. '"I thought you was an other rank," says a warrant officer; "You've got other rank's pyjamas on."' We are back in the world of Henry Reed's 'Naming of Parts'.

Douglas skips over his hospitalization and convalescence, which lasted about six weeks, and writes a last chapter called 'Zem Zem', which is an epilogue to his Middle East experience, the 'battle . . . I must have'. There follow the elegiac memorials to Piccadilly Jim and Guy already quoted, and the story of the final, anti-climactic days of the North African campaign. He rejoined the regiment at Enfidaville, and the poem of that title is a notably tender one, perhaps reflecting his chastened mood after so many deaths and his own near-fatality. Much of the chapter recounts a long expedition in a lorry in search of food and drink for the regiment, and a comical drinking bout with a group of French Tunisian officers. '"Was it a fact," they asked, "that in the British army we ate things out of tins?"'

Within a short time both the Italian and German armies surrendered. The immense convoy of defeated men and vehicles parallels earlier convoys in the narrative, as the letting-off of coloured Verey lights is a reminder of the multi-coloured tracer bullets at Alamein, at the start of things:

> But the distant booms and thuds which had been a background to all this for so long were gone. We repeated over and over again in our thoughts and our conversation that the battle was over. The continual halting and moving, the departure at first light, the shell-fire, the interminable wireless conversation – and the strain, the uncertainty of tomorrow, the fear of death: it was all over. We had made it. We stood here on the safe side of it, like swimmers . . .
>
> And tomorrow, we said, we'll get into every vehicle we can find, and go out over the whole ground we beat them on, and bring in more loot than we've ever seen.

The final short paragraph attempts an up-beat ending, but is not too convincing, though it is undoubtedly honest. The real loot lay in his head.

Alamein to Zem Zem is a work of art, fully comparable with the three classic prose accounts of the First World War, Sassoon's *Memoirs of an Infantry Officer*, Blunden's *Undertones of War*, and Graves's *Goodbye to All That*. When one considers that it was written in a few months while the war was still on, whereas the elder writers had had long years of peace in which to compose and revise, its achievement appears all the more remarkable. Unlike the poems it has never lacked admirers (see chapter V), though it seems to me that precisely the same rare qualities are discernible in both. Perhaps the most eloquent tribute to the book's enduring honesty is the Hebrew translation published by Israel's Ministry of Defence in 1972.

III

The Early Poems

Despite the brevity of his life, Douglas's poems reveal the sort of unity Eliot thought a significant characteristic of all good poets. Both Hughes and Hill have commented on the way he returned obsessively to certain constellations of objects, feelings and ideas, never letting go of the disparate elements ('detail and horizon') of his experience. 'Poem after poem circles this idea [the doomed man in him or his dead body], as if his mind were tethered' (*SP*, Introduction, p. 13). 'It would seem that he possessed the kind of creative imagination that approached an idea again and again in terms of metaphor, changing position slightly, seeking the most precise hold' (Geoffrey Hill, 'I in Another Place: Homage to Keith Douglas', *Stand*, vol. 6, no. 4, p. 6). Tethered, yet forever changing holds and position – both images offer a way in to the paradoxes that are such a prominent feature of Douglas's character and poetry.

As a schoolboy and undergraduate he was capable of astonishing things, such as 'Encounter with a God', 'A Ballet', 'Villanelle of Gorizia' and 'Poor Mary', all written in his teens. And, it must be added, of failing honourably later on, as in 'Bête Noire' and 'Actors Waiting in the Wings of Europe'. The important transitional period is that of the early army poems, written during his training in 1940/41, culminating in 'Time Eating', 'The Marvel' and 'Simplify Me When I'm Dead'. These mark the beginning of his full maturity as

a poet. I have therefore treated 'The House' and 'Song:
Dotards Do Not Think' as the terminus for his
apprenticeship and this chapter.

The early poems are best seen as a series of
skirmishes and try-outs in which he exercises and
explores his talent, rather than as a body of work which
calls for extended comment. I have thought it best
therefore to provide a brief commentary on the more
interesting poems as an introduction to his subjects and
techniques, and as a starting point for further discus-
sion. It is designed to be read with *The Complete Poems*
to hand.

'Mummers'

Most beginners betray their anxiety to conform to the
rules, and fall into rhythmic monotony. The precocious
technical assurance of this poem is therefore all the
more startling. Douglas uses a six-line stanza rhyming
AABCCB, and an octosyllabic line, with mostly femi-
nine endings. This is handled with considerable skill,
for example in the opening stanza: 'That sable / Doff'
where the enjambement and reversed stress act out the
sense, putting stresses on 'Doff' and 'brighter silks'.
Similar means are used at the end of the last stanza –
'and ancient rusted / Blade' – to place a heavy stress on
'Blade'; and then a pause, enforced by the comma,
which fills the missing syllable so that the line reads
like normal iambic tetrameter.

The rhymes are good and sometimes enhance mean-
ing, as in 'Tapestry / artistry' and 'snow-crusted /
rusted'. There are two striking images, and lots of
hyphenated epithets: wind-fluttered, weather-addled,
well-carven, snow-crusted, all signalling gaily from the
ends of lines.

The poem seems to work by the juxtaposition of
imagistic blocks of words, rather than by tracing any
continuous emotion or thought. The woman at her

embroidery and the mummers are as anonymous and thinglike as the gargoyle and its creator, Brother Ambrose. Inside and outside, sable and pearl, starlight and lamplight, mask and stone, saint and Turk: there is a visual and emotional synaesthesia at work in the polarities ('glints of pearly laughter shuttered') which offers parallels between the exterior and interior life. The sources of the poem are probably literary. Brother Ambrose reminds one of Browning, the woman and her bright silks might be a figure out of the medievalizing strain in Coleridge or Keats. Yet already Douglas has stamped this bookish composition with something of his own; there are no nudge-words, no adjectives to cue in a correct emotional response. The mummers who act out the story of the Crusades prefigure the sort of dumb-show Douglas later foregrounds in some of his desert poems, such as 'Landscape with Figures'.

'Love and Gorizia'

Douglas's mother had a half-sister living in Gorizia, with whom he spent a two-week summer holiday in 1935. Aquileia, once the fourth city of Italy, was an agricultural village nearby. Painswick, in the Cotswolds, was visited by Douglas in the school holidays. Birdlip is a small village at the top of a long hill a few miles away. *CP(PL)* and *CP* print the first stanza only, under the title 'Bexhill'. The poem's abrupt transitions suggest the possibility that it may be an amalgamation of previous separate drafts.

As Graham says, the poem celebrates the sensuous pleasures of the south, 'pleasures not only of taste and sound but . . . of the eye, and the eye of the artist' (*KD*, p. 32). It is also Douglas's first (preserved) attempt at a love poem. The small girl with red-brown hair of the third stanza is reminiscent of similar characters in his early stories: 'She was small, with freckles and red-gold hair' ('Misunderstanding', *PM*, p. 28). In the poem, however, she is rather swallowed up in the general aesthetic dazzle. There are traces of Hopkins, perhaps, in the rich diction and packed syntax of the last stanza: and the form of the questions ('how could I mould, / . . . how could I take you?') is reminiscent of Hopkins's question to Margaret in 'Spring and Fall'. The oppositions between south and north, desire and woundedness, are somewhat bald and schematic. And the stanza-form, rhyme royal – the most difficult he had yet attempted – imposes some strain on his resources.

'Villanelle of Gorizia'

Douglas returns to the same locale two years later, this time more successfully. A villanelle (from the Latin *villa*, or farm) was originally a round song sung by farm labourers, or villeins, and is therefore particularly appropriate to Douglas's celebration of sunlight and wine. The great temptation of the form is to write a series of endstopped pentameter lines, which can then be juggled in the required manner.

There are some weaknesses in the poem. 'Eves', for example, is a fairly desperate rhyme-word in the fourth tercet, even if it does carry the bonus of a pun on 'eaves'. Similarly 'weaves', in the second tercet, belongs with sunlight rather than with the kite's string; Douglas is perhaps remembering Eliot's 'Weave, weave the sunlight in your hair' of *La Figlia Che Piange*. And it's hard to pin down the literal sense of the second line. Are the oxen hitched to a cart, which is collecting leaves? Or munching fallen ones? The general drift is clear – it is so hot that even something as light as a leaf will tire an ox – but the specific reference vague.

Such flaws are more than compensated for in the poem's successes, which are substantial. The bringing together of sunlight, flutes and wine achieves a verbal and emotional synaesthesia expressive of delight in the relaxed pleasures of the Italian town. Assonance, alliteration, internal rhyme ('street . . . repeated', 'street . . . sunlight', 'noon . . . sound . . . wine', 'Oxen . . . even') all work to heighten the musical sense of repetition. The feminine ending of the ubiquitous 'sunlight' gives the pentameter a light, echoic touch, and links metrically with the other compound, 'wineshop'. The poem also plays sophisticatedly with notions of absence and presence: its constituent nouns (sun, wine, flute) are vividly concrete, yet conjure up ineffable abstractions which may be intuited but not grasped – heat, distance, music, grief.

TCP alters the punctuation and capitalization of *CP(PL)* and *CP*, and substitutes two inferior lines in the last stanza, which the earlier editions printed as follows:

> All this the bottle says, that I have quite
> poured out. The wine slides in my throat and grieves.
> Over and over the street is repeated with sunlight,
> the flutes sound in the wineshop, out of sight.

In this much stronger version, we may note the first line's anticipation of a similar line in 'The Marvel': 'All this emerges from the burning eye.'

'Famous Men'

The poem is so pared-down and compacted as to make interpretation difficult, yet its intriguing and powerful ending invites attention. The title does not say what kind of fame, but the mention of 'dactyls', and the imaginative grandeur invoked in stanza three, suggest famous poets, though without ruling out other sorts of fame. There is an Eliotic note, once more, in the 'seas / they smote, from green to copper', which reminds one faintly of the 'Huge sea-wood fed with copper / Burned green and orange' of *The Waste Land*, II, 94–5. The Websterian skulls of 'Whispers of Immortality' may also be relevant in the final stanza.

The skulls of the close are 'licked clean' metaphorically, perhaps – by art and art's consumers, or by action and its admirers – as well as literally. The poem points forward in some ways to 'Simplify Me When I'm Dead' and the skulls that litter the desert writings, but here it is the nexus of fame and creativity and death that takes all Douglas's attention. Such extraordinary men are complete and completed, the last line suggests, yet somehow unappeased; past thinking yet teasing us out of thought ('And think . . .'), satiated but insatiate even in death.

A variant title was 'Epitaph'. Desmond Graham comments: 'Varying the pace of his diction, withdrawing sensory detail until the third stanza's celebration, and forcing home the grim image of his final stanza, Douglas displays his supreme indifference to everything but the poet's power.' 'Grim' does not seem quite the right adjective here; the last stanza displays rather a Metaphysical or Empsonian wit, made all the sharper by unusual syntax. The words provide us with material for simile and metaphor but the logical connectives have all been excised, leaving powerful grammatical stumps. The last line, for example, reads: verb/noun; adverb; present participle, and the tense moves from past ('licked') to present. All this reinforces, as Graham rightly says, a sense of the poet's disturbing power to straddle different worlds, that of the living and the dead. The comma in the last line interrupts, yet also strengthens, the reciprocity of thought between the two modes of being (triumphantly mediated by art); and the unstressed syllables of 'beautifully, staring' counterpoint the certainty of bald statement with the uncertainty of near-silence.

'Encounter with a God'

This is one of the best of the schoolboy poems, as delightfully imaginative as it is self-assured. Douglas made a linocut to accompany the poem when it was published in *Outlook* (the school magazine) under the title 'Japanese Song', which is reproduced in *KD*, p. 44.

Lady Ono Komachi (834–80) was one of the 'Six Poetic Geniuses' who served at the imperial court in Kyoto in the middle of the ninth century (Geoffrey Brownas and Anthony Thwaite, eds., *The Penguin Book of Japanese Verse*, p. xiv). Daikoku is a guardian deity (Sanskrit name Mahākāla) who is usually portrayed with an angry or aggressive face.

The opening stanza, with its formulaic repetitions and delicate rhythms ('the perception of the intellect is given in the word, that of the emotions in the cadence' – Pound), sets the scene. The three opening lines are all of nine syllables, but the poem keeps to no metrical or syllabic pattern; the five-line stanzas are in rhyming free verse – an odd but effective combination. The rhymes disappear in stanza 4, a humorously deliberate comment on the god's words: 'I am not beautiful . . . and I will not be in a poem.'

Douglas's habitual irony sits well with the tonal limpidity of the Japanese mode, and this says much for his poetic tact. The 'slight / tendency to angles' of stanza two, for example, presumably refers to the god, the rule, and to the poetess herself. Similarly the 'greenish gods of chance and fame' makes a sly dual reference both to the god and to his representation in art and mythology. The 'rule' has various applications: gods are gods, and must be praised according to the conventions of worship, as well as to those of poetry, which celebrates beauty. The incongruous 'angles', on the other hand, hardly fit the carp or the waterfall or Daikoku's round belly, so perhaps they refer punningly to the poet. There is an angle to be found on everything, including the gross conduct of the gods themselves. In the lightest possible way, the poem is an affectionate little treatise on art and life, each with its own rules and unruly contingencies.

'Pleasures'

Returning to memories of his holiday in Gorizia – Monte Nero was fifty kilometres away – Douglas creates an unusually sophisticated persona in this poem, recalling lost latin pleasures as from a cosmopolite's or Alexandrian eye. Occasionally the sophistication rings hollow; the Yeatsian peasant girl 'fashioned for love and work', for example, is a piece of literary posturing, like his own inflationary identification with princes and princely halls. But the poem carries indelible marks of real imagination, especially in stanzas two, three and four, and looks forward to the later mastery of 'The Marvel', 'Enfidaville' and 'Behaviour of Fish in an Egyptian Garden'.

Like Bernard Spencer and Lawrence Durrell, whom he was to meet later in Cairo, Douglas was irresistibly drawn to the pleasures of the Mediterranean and the Near East. The clarity of light, the clear warm seas, the superabundance of wine and fruit, the sloe-eyed inter-racial beauty of women and children, and the immemorial association of all this, in the western mind, with high ideals and uncomplicated pleasure, were perfect antitheses to the puritanism, boredom and hypocrisy of English middle-class gentility. There one might worship the 'splendour and silence' of sun and moon without being thought freakish, and pursue the 'bright fish ... about their business' even if, or precisely because, they led him to the 'jewelled skulls' of absolute pleasure and pain.

CP(PL) and *CP* have slight variants, mispunctuate, and print the poem under its earlier title 'Forgotten the Red Leaves'.

'Poor Mary'

Graham tells us that the subject of the poem is Mary Oswin, a girl Douglas knew and quarrelled with at

Oxford (*KD*, pp. 72–3; there is a photograph of her on p. 70). He 'published it to annoy her.' However that may be, the poem easily transcends its petty origins, and seems to me one of his finest early achievements.

'Made up', in the opening line, means both invented and made up as for a part in a play, which latter sense is reinforced by 'costume' and 'impersonate' (cf. the 'maquillage' of the 'stony actors' in 'Landscape with Figures'). The second and third stanzas are straightforward, and introduce the governing metaphor of the house. The travellers of the next stanza are the living, going about their business, who question death but can obtain no answer. 'They have lost their breath' (i.e. they need not have bothered asking) punctures the periphrasis with its grimly literal meaning. Death, somewhat surprisingly perhaps in this context, is masculine: 'His quiet hand'; 'he will not answer', suggesting that death is her true lover or bridegroom; suggesting too that the poem moves outward from Poor Mary to embrace a whole class or type, not just one individual.

She is like a bird trapped in a house, desperate to fly out of the window, gibbering incomprehensibly. 'Effigy' intensifies the earlier images of impersonation; the bird (emblem of the soul) is already starved and paper-light. The powerful ending objectively and yet compassionately traces out the ramifications of these images. Mary is stripped of spirit, song, colour, breath; 'no answering song' and 'he will not answer' are in fact answered by silence, not 'the triumphant silence of the dead' of *Alamein to Zem Zem* but the silence of nothingness. The poem is made up entirely of simple statements, hammering repetitions of 'you' and 'your', and each one invests the grammatical person with absence, inability, imitation. Precisely what Mary's make-up looks like ('Death has made up your face') we never learn: she is made up of abstractions embodied in concrete metaphors, 'house of sorrow', 'halls of your heart', etc. Her 'starling speech' (incorporating the near-homophones 'starveling' and 'staring'?) is the alien but unignorable language of a dead spirit, which comprehensively 'falls down' on the stage of the living.

If the opening phrase of 'Poor Mary' looks back to the skulls of 'Famous Men', its development points forward to the complex bird-imagery of 'Adams'. There too we meet someone who seems to rob the world of colour and of thought:

> Till Rest, cries my mind to Adams' ghost;
> only go elsewhere, let me alone
> creep into the dead bird, cease to exist.

Douglas's leading images – stone, mask, bird, cave, etc. – never function in a simple tabular way, merely endorsing or recoiling from the subjects they seek to describe and evaluate, or rather incarnate. In fact the word 'image' is itself inadequate, suggesting something appliquéd, stuck on from the outside, whereas in his best poems such images are primary pieces of ontology, locked in with the *is* of identity rather than the *is* of predication. Mary and Adams are not 'like' effigies or birds, the hovering male presences in 'Behaviour of Fish . . .' are not 'like' fish, they actually are those things, submerged in the various forces and modes of being that make up the world's sensory and spiritual possibilities. Which is perhaps simply to say that Douglas's imagery constantly aspires to the condition of metaphor. As such, it becomes isometric with, and permeated by, the self-same contraries and paradoxes that so often make up his subject-matter.

'Stranger'

A love poem, dedicated to the (westernized) Chinese girl Douglas fell in love with at Oxford, Yingcheng Sze. Graham suggests that the 'alert Audenesque explorer of the school poems' has quite vanished from this piece;

[71]

instead we find 'an openly romantic poet who transforms the magic and shipwrecks he had found in Shakespeare's last plays into a landscape of love' (*KD*, p. 72). *The Tempest* may well be one source of allusion, and the *Odyssey* is pretty obviously another, but it seems to me that Auden is still very much present as an influence, both in phraseology ('And call on you, the strange land, to save') and in the extended parallelism of love and place.

Too much in the poem is arbitrary or vague. 'Stand' in line four is there only for the sake of the rhyme; at first one takes it for a noun. And why is the secret 'venerable' when the subject is youthful beauty? Because love is old, regardless of any particular instantiation? Because Chinese faces suggest ancient wisdom? Maybe, but the adjective remains uncomfortably vague. Similarly there is a vein of grandiosity in the repeated personifications, 'your beauty's land', 'you, the strange land', 'you . . . the whole continent of love.'

Good love poems are hard to write. Douglas's accompanying letter to Yingcheng (reproduced in *KD*, p. 73) is perhaps more playfully eloquent:

> Perhaps you would like Ophelia for your name? Ophelia Sze; perhaps not. Personally although I admit Margaret isn't good, Marguerite Sze sounds well enough . . .
>
> Do you remember which piece of wall we sat on, where for 10 seconds you became one of the world's great heroines? I shan't bother to go and sit there but my shadow will be on duty for me. When you have given me up and spoilt the few good bits there are left in my heart, you will see that shadow every time you come past late at night. Maybe it will come and block the way of whatever man is with you, like the angel standing in the donkey's path.
>
> I suppose you have read A. E. Housman. If you will take as from me the saddest and most moving love poem he ever wrote, and read it well, you will have much better what I want to say than I could tell you . . .

It is easy to forget how young Douglas still was, beneath his apparent maturity. Half way down the letter he converts an ink blot into a drawing of a heart.

'Pas de Trois'

Whether or not Douglas's love of ballet predates Oxford is hard to tell. From this time on he enjoyed shocking Oxford hearties and army veterans with demonstrations of ballet's extreme physical difficulty.

The poem shows him experimenting still with metaphor and diction, trying out prose rhythms ('strength such as grass has') alongside poetic ones ('gently to divide the strength of stone'), seeing where his images will take him. Here they remain similes, tentative and heterogeneous: 'like plants', 'such as grass', 'like gods' etc. The prosody, too, is variable, exchanging his opening pentameter stanzas for a middle section which plays a syllabic variation over an octosyllabic norm, and doesn't reach regularity until its ninth and last line ('intent on every jewelled space'). The model may be some of Eliot's early poems, such as 'Preludes' and 'Rhapsody on a Windy Night', which are similarly intent on deconstructing received rhythms. Douglas's poem is nothing like so accomplished, but works hard at reproducing (to quote the poem's close) the 'ordinary face' of language.

'Haydn – Military Symphony' and 'Haydn – Clock Symphony'

The first of the two Haydn poems shows Douglas responding light-heartedly to the music with a fiction of his own, the two scarlet and tall grenadiers, seen first through a child's admiring eyes, and then more sceptically. 'All authentic heroes are unreal', are 'men of air', figures of 'dead romances', 'madmen'. Yet the 'painted backcloth' (an image Douglas imports from theatre or ballet; they are seldom present at symphony concerts) may 'quicken and be alive', the 'fantasy' might just come true if sufficiently believed in.

Douglas's obsession with theatricality was of long standing, and went with him into the real fighting that was to come, as did the early Auden's experiments with sinister charades.

The second poem also employs an extended conceit, whose stately archaism ('Consider, Sir . . .') is partly deliberate, partly forced (e.g. the inversion at the end of the second stanza). Alliteration ('enchantment . . . tune . . . Detained') and Douglas's typical use of enjambement ('enchantment of the tune / Detained') effectively act out the neo-classical gravity and polish of the Jane Austen-like scene. The music and the dance constitute another 'brilliant game' (like war?) that quizzes reality and mimes our dreams, which perform a similar function. 'Polished', in the last line, is a pervasive attribute of things and people, the dance-floor and the eighteenth-century dancers; and also takes us back to the mirror (or rather 'glass', itself a pun on hour-glass) of the first stanza. There is a further suggestion that the ground is polished by dreams, so that the dancers move in an infinite regress of mirrors (glass, moon, 'oval countenance', mind, dream) and an infinite motion between timelessness ('eternity') and time.

The poem's movement and diction are still a bit stiff – sometimes Douglas dictates to the stanza, and sometimes it dictates to him – but the obsession with art and artifice, enchantment and panic, is one that will bear increasingly rich fruit, pointing forwards to 'Landscape with Figures' and 'Vergissmeinnicht'. Notice in both poems the changing viewpoint of the anonymous, omniscient narrator: he looks up like a child at things larger than life, or down like a god, seeing things *sub specie aeternitatis*; is a madman or a dreamer. Only in the middle stanza of each poem does he stand briefly 'opposite', on a level with the soldiers or his dancing partner; elsewhere he shrinks to insignificant smallness, or swoops up to a great height, or penetrates behind and into the 'recesses' of what he sees. These swift changes in perspective, with their dis- and re-orientations, are typical of the best of the desert poems.

TCP relegates an interesting fourth stanza of 'Haydn – Clock Symphony', given in *CP(PL)* and *CP*, to its Notes.

'Sanctuary'

'Sanctuary' is one of the most personal and revealing of all Douglas's early poems. Like 'The House', written a year later, it dramatizes some of his own deepest fears, emotional and physical. The war was now a fact and he knew that he would be fighting in it sooner rather than later. Hence the 'desperate fence' marks off civilians from servicemen, as well as children from adults. 'The world will lance at every point / my unsteady heart ... subjugate my tired will' recalls his remark in a letter that he tended to think of 'the world in general as a powerful force working for my hurt ...' Both poem and letter confess to a sort of vulnerability not often seen in Douglas's work. It would seem that his fear of emotional wounds was at least as strong as his fear of literally losing his life. No doubt this connects with the attitudinizing Ian Hamilton and some other critics have accused the poems of, which I discuss in the last chapter.

The middle stanza suffers from inflation and vagueness: he becomes a St Sebastian, or Christ after the crucifixion. 'Anoint' is there partly for the sake of the rhyme, which is then blurred by an extra syllable – a practice Douglas occasionally uses elsewhere. 'Fence', in the last stanza, is also slightly incongruous, since its domestic or surburban connotations sit oddly with the previous image of a castle under siege.

[75]

The spatialization, as it were, of the mind and heart is a favourite strategy of Auden's, and one which Douglas was quick to learn. The weaknesses in this poem are reflected in its confusing geography. The most interesting crux is that represented by 'the line between indifference / and my vulnerable mind'. That makes good intuitive sense but is impossible to visualize in the terms proposed by 'wall', 'barrier', 'fence'. It is the wall erected by himself against further hurt that really interests him, and what will happen if it is breached not by some hypothetical 'they' but by himself. The last two lines could be construed as an anticipation of the unambiguous cry of 'Simplify Me When I'm Dead'; or as a prediction, made in the form of a threat, of the soldierly brutality he will have to adopt in order to survive.

'Russians'

In a letter to J. C. Hall from the Middle East Douglas later disowned this accomplished satire because it was written before he had had any personal experience of war. He got the idea from something he read, as he reported to a friend: 'During the Russian campaign against Finland, a Russian regiment was reported to have been discovered frozen to death, the soldiers still holding their rifles ready to fire' (*TCP*, Notes, p. 130). His preoccupation with soldiers, dating back to early childhood and his father's profession, is very evident. The poem's vigour springs from its confident colloquialism ('That's never a corporal'), which shapes the pentameter line to its own ends, and from its cool mockery of the military virtues. The soldiers are 'properly stayed' on parade forever – or at least until it thaws; their 'line of sight' is now reduced to a childish game ('they won't look') of grotesque ineptitude and irrelevance; 'coming home' is precisely what they will never do, nor be 'struck' by any thought but death.

[76]

They are nothing more than dummies got up to look like soldiers, whose 'mazed minds' have been frozen by their own training manual. The rhyme on 'artist/ smartest' makes its own comment on this make-believe world, which is later likened to a sinister fairy tale ('struck / with a dumb . . . spell').

TCP prints a slightly different and superior text to *CP(PL)* and *CP*. The latter reproduces a small drawing by Douglas.

'Canoe'

This companion piece to 'Farewell Poem' might be read as a Song of Innocence to set against the Song of Experience. Douglas's 'last summer' is a hedonistic last supper, his last at Oxford and possibly his last anywhere. The girl in question may be Yingcheng, or Antoinette, or possibly someone else. Whichever, his mood is now entirely different. 'I cannot stand aghast / at whatever doom hovers in the background.' The final stanza replaces the 'thunder' and 'rain' of passion with disinterested and disembodied friendship; his shade or spirit will return to kiss 'your mouth lightly', free now of entanglement or consequence, because in this special place and time love is 'allowed to last forever'.

'A Round Number'

An obsession with time understandably runs through many of Douglas's poems. The round number of the title is presumably 1940, date of the poem's composition, also seen as 'my last existence' as the lover of a 'sacred lady' who is three parts muse and one part Yingcheng, or some other girl he has lost, such as the one mourned in 'Farewell Poem'. We know from other sources that Douglas was determined to be among the English poets after his death. The fact that the lady is 'without art' is a twin judgement on the girl/Muse and on himself. She has preferred an 'idiot' to him; he is an 'idiot' to think his poetry is of any lasting value. Like Cressida, the girl he loved, or thought he loved, 'only lived inside my head'. That idealized figure 'perished with my innocence' – which may refer either to his sexual or to his aesthetic experience, or an amalgam of both.

Note that the 'hope of happiness and renown' go together: his unluckiness in love is part and parcel of his unworthiness as a poet. The 'rank ivy' of the opening stanza, which contrasts with the 'fragrant girl' of the second, is literally time, but also a type of lust for sexual and literary favours. Unlike those who have time to sue for grace and win the bays by years of devotion, Douglas is up against the fast-forward motions of a poet in wartime, for whom last week or month is already 'two hundred years ago'.

A cancelled version of part I of the poem, given in *TCP*'s Notes, p. 131, heavily underlines the element of sexual disgust:

> But I am yours and must
> lie in the very bog where I am anchored
> as low as you, as coarse and cankered,
> fallen to lie with humming lust.
>
> God knows how we shall get again
> the drug of love and the sweet pain.

Whichever way we choose to interpret the girl, as Muse or as changeable and fallen girl-friend, in neither version does Douglas make clear what crime she has committed. The language of the cancelled draft is extravagantly angry ('Foul as a yellow ferret') yet totally unspecific. The tone throughout is anachronistically reminiscent of the Shakespeare of *Troilus and Cressida*, or the sonnets, or Hamlet rounding on Ophelia: 'Are you fair now? . . . oh how you change / flower to animal' etc. All this suggests an access of sexual jealousy occasioned by some rebuff, which Douglas excises from the final text in favour of generalized complaint.

'A God is Buried'

The setting is Gorizia once more, on the border between Italy and Yugoslavia, scene of Douglas's summer holiday in 1935. Monte Nero was fifty kilometres away; closer at hand, alongside the village of Aquileia, lay 'the ruins of the Roman port and town which had once ruled the whole region . . . the fourth city of Italy' (*KD*, p. 32).

Section I, published on its own in *CP(PL)* and *CP* as 'Search for a God', reads as though Douglas originally intended it to be a sonnet, but added another quatrain before the sestet. Section II allies the nameless god, whom even 'high explosive could not move', with the innocence of children and nature, as against the destructive world of men. Section III continues the association, linking the god now with images of fertility and rebirth. The 'murderous plot' refers back to wars ancient and modern, and perhaps to the symbolic murder of a god or a king associated with fertility rites, of the sort discussed in Frazer's *Golden Bough*. Section IV lets the god speak for himself, ending in an image – men as trees – that Douglas will return to in the moving last stanza of 'Desert Flowers'.

Except insofar as it touches on war, it is not a very typical poem; yet it has connections with those early stories and poems which are sensitive to the spirit of place. And the poem's opening – 'Turn your back on Monte Nero, that mountain / to the west' – strongly recalls some lines in 'Dead Men': 'Come// to the west, out of that trance, my heart . . .' In both poems he contrasts the 'white town', and 'white dresses glimmer[ing] like moths', with what he calls in 'Dead Men' the 'sanitary earth', or 'fertile / seed and sap . . . of . . . new earth' in 'A God is Buried'. If it is permissible to

[79]

talk of a poem's subtext, as we do in the case of plays, then the poem seems to be rehearsing some innocent myth of procreation as an alternative to the 'murderous plot' of sexuality, which is inextricably linked with bloodshed and war, empirically and psychically: the 'bright blood and shrapnel' of stanza 3.

'The Deceased'

There was a rash of such ironic epitaphs written by poets about themselves in the 1940s and 1950s, of which the best is probably John Heath-Stubbs's 'Epitaph'. Douglas's witty sonnet of couplets is full of vigour until the last unfortunate line, which abandons satire for self-righteousness. At least, it does in *TCP*, which prints an inferior text to that of *CP(PL)* and *CP*. In the latter 'His hair depended in a noose from / a Corona Veneris', not from 'a pale brow'; and the ending reads

> and appears to have felt a refined pain
> to which your virtue cannot attain.
>
> Respect him. For in this
> he had an excellence you miss.

Here the modulation into a serious case for the defence retains irony ('refined pain'), and, in the last couplet, is free of sententiousness. Douglas's increasing fluency with idiom and form is seen in such constructions as '. . . probably between curses, // probably in the extremes of moral decay': the repetition carries its own vernacular irony; the full line contains twelve syllables and only one regular foot ('decay') but nevertheless reads as a perfectly good iambic pentameter.

Ted Hughes picks out this poem for extended comment. 'At once, and quite suddenly . . . he produces poetry that is both original and adult. Already, in this poem 'The Deceased', we can see what is most important of all about Douglas. He has not simply added poems to poetry, or evolved a sophistication. He is a renovator of language. It is not that he uses words in jolting combinations, or with titanic extravagance, or curious precision. His triumph lies in the way he renews the simplicity of ordinary talk, and he does this by infusing every word with a burning exploratory freshness of mind – partly impatience, partly exhilaration at speaking the forbidden thing, partly sheer casual ease of penetration. The music that goes along with this, the unresting variety of intonation and movement within his patterns, is the natural path of such confident, candid thinking' (Introduction to *SP*, pp. 12–13).

'Soissons'

Douglas spent the Easter vacation of 1939 on a cycling holiday in France with Hamo Sassoon (Siegfried's nephew), to whom the poem is dedicated. 'After spending their nights in chicken houses and by the roadside, at Soissons they put up at a good hotel. For the first time they ate a huge meal and drank champagne, their high spirits leading them to perform handstands and backflips at midnight on the steps of the cathedral where earlier in the day they had watched a stonemason at work.' They also 'heard Daladier announce over the wireless that Germany had betrayed the Munich agreement' (*KD*, pp. 74–5). The imminence of war is alluded to, perhaps, in the concluding lines of both the second and third stanzas.

The opening is full of direct utterance, typical of the maturing style that 'seems able to deal poetically with whatever it comes up against', as Hughes puts it. The bicyclist's-eye-view of the approach to the town is particularly vivid, triumphantly skirting cliché by its syntax and rhythm, which bowl the reader along in a continuous filmic take of subject and object, the road that 'snakes / . . . into the town's heart'. The juxtaposition of snake and devil, gargoyle and cathedral, 'late sunlight' and 'Lights Out' combine to produce an emotional equivalent of the 'sweet-sour' wine clambering in their heads. The final stanza takes up again the casual, elliptical style of the first, both of which contrast with the longer, prosy, static lines of the middle one. But the poem does not really sustain its opening momentum. The movement from medieval simplicity to the 'dark ... country' of the twentieth century, and from sunlight to rain, is believable enough, but remains at the level of a moderately interesting travelogue. (For a kinder estimation, see Rowland Smith's interesting discussion of the poem in his review of *TCP* in *Dalhousie Review*. Smith points out that 'The route from Laon to Rheims ... runs parallel to both the old western front and the new Maginot Line.' He also notes how the gargoyles point forward to similar images in 'Bête Noire'.)

'The Garden'

Published in *CP(PL)* and *CP* as 'Absence' with slight variations in text. The opening bears some resemblance to Auden's celebrated 1933 poem 'Out on the lawn I lie in bed . . .', but Douglas is wholly concerned with emotional solitude and disappointed love. The setting is enchanting and enchanted, part-revealing and part-concealing the dinner party and the lover who waits on the lawn in moonlight. The evening 'discourses', to those alive to its magic, no less than the 'company at dinner'; but though the lover longs to be a part of one or the other gathering he stands outside both, as silly as Cupid on his stone monument, struck dead by disappointment. The identification with Cupid subtly changes to identification with insubstantial 'ghosts' and rustling leaves; the 'traditional splendour' of stanza 2 turns into the equally traditional shadowy grieving of stanza 3 – which, incidentally, alters the rhyme scheme, trying to marry up 'silence' and 'sighing', and ending with the finality of a couplet.

Who is the 'you' referred to in this close? The speaker? But then who has he come 'instead' of? Perhaps this use of the second person is indicative of the lover's 'attitude', implying disbelief in his own enterprise. It is no longer 'I' who waits in the garden but 'you', an unbeliever, for whom nature speaks only of death. In a phrase Geoffrey Hill has drawn attention to, Douglas speaks elsewhere of 'I in another place', in a context which is both erotic and death-haunted, and which gathers in some of the same elements – light and dark, moonlight, action and inaction, desire and death – to be found in 'The Garden'. 'I am the solitary' also takes on an un-self-pitying plangency in this poem, contrasting with the composite voice of the company at dinner and the unifying discourse of nature on a beautiful spring night. For all his 'shit or bust' impatience, in love as in war, Douglas is extraordinarily sensitive to his surroundings, from the sleeping bush nearby to the splendour of the stars leaning nearer to the earth. Time and again in observing and recording his own impulses he seems to fuse the intensity of a shaman with the sardonic objectivity of a behavioural psychologist. The result is a far cry from such a poem as Hardy's 'A Broken Appointment', with which it might be compared. Hardy diagnoses selfishness at the centre of love ('love wrings with wrong' as he puts it in 'Neutral Tones'), and contrasts that with the 'high compassion' of 'pure loving kindness'. Douglas is less interested in apportioning blame than in asking the Blakean, Lawrentian, Hughesian question 'Is it – am I – alive or dead?', which is logically prior to, and perhaps even incompatible with, the sticking on of ethical labels. Thus in the later hurt-love poem 'I listen to the desert wind', written after Milena's defection, Douglas says 'all the elements agree / with her, to have no sympathy / for my impertinent misery / as wonderful and hard as she.' Her behaviour, the poem suggests, and his pain, are as natural and as inevitable as that of the birds skimming the hot and cold sands by night and day. And in the last of the love poems, 'To Kristin Yingcheng Olga Milena', which dispassionately reflects on the four important women in his life, he describes their loss as the operation of 'natural law': 'Here I give back perforce / the sweet wine to the grape / give the dark plant its juices / what every creature uses / by natural law will seep / back to the natural source.' The emphases here, on *creature*, *uses*, *law* and *natural source* all suggest an inexorable cycle of profit and loss which the individual is powerless to influence. In such cases the 'I' necessarily dies or seeks out 'another place' in which to survive; and the whole of creation, revolving on the same axis, is implicated in the outcome.

'A Ballet'

This, like 'Encounter with a God', is one of the most successful of the early poems that concern themselves with art. Like 'Pas de Trois' also, it celebrates the subtle 'craft of quiet', but with great brevity and panache. Douglas's ever-present obsession with death seizes on the transmogrification of the dancers from youthful acrobats to ancient mutilees. Even at the outset their 'grace' is seen as the product of artificial 'effects'. It is when the male dancer is on his stumps, bleeding, that he jumps and prances most energetically, replacing mere cleverness (opening stanza) with a deeper necessity. Such figures, like the mimes and actors I have already discussed, always appear in a context of menace, fear, and unresolved conflict. Here the conflict is implied in the constatation of death and sexuality; after the rites of spring 'he bleeds' but continues energetically to jump; the graceful dance of courtship turns into a grotesque pantomime of lust and survival. The diction likewise moves from a somewhat coy eroticism – 'is this not the fair / young sylph? I declare . . .' – to brute monosyllabic facts: dance into prance, with the ghost of a pun, perhaps, on 'prince'.

'A Speech for an Actor'

Published in *CP(PL)* and *CP* as 'Leukothea' with a slightly different text and a superior ending:

> Last night I dreamed and found my trust betrayed
> only the little bones and the great bones disarrayed.

Another dramatization of the loss of Yingcheng, the poem might also be construed as a dry run for some aspects of 'Simplify Me When I'm Dead'. Leukothea herself, 'my ornament' (the sea-nymph Ino, sent by Athene to save Odysseus from a storm; in *The Bacchae* of Euripedes she is one of the mob who tear Pentheus limb from limb, 'scratching off his flesh'), is hardly particularized at all, beyond the conventional attributes of beauty. Graham characterizes the mad lover, furious to discover the decay of beauty, as 'necrophiliac'. (*KD*, p. 101). His plight also reminds one of Wordsworth's explanation to Catherine Clarkson of the origin of the 'Immortality Ode': 'an indisposition to bend to the law of death as applying to our own particular case'.

'John Anderson'

The poem begins as satire, somewhat in the manner of Sassoon or Ransome, contrasting the futility of random death with the rhetoric of art and elegy, but goes on to invoke the sort of pomp appropriate to the cutting-down of a scholar-hero. Some irony still attends the close, perhaps – in the juxtaposition of the homely name and the 'Homeric tongue' – but it is of a gentler variety than the opening lines seem to promise. 'By the end,' says Graham, 'ironic diction has given way to dignified elegy, the power of poetry performing the ritual move towards peace which Anderson's innocence has deserved. It is an extraordinary and moving change of direction, in which Douglas finds his cynicism no longer ground to be held, but rather, a route to be traversed, to find on the other side a new affirmation' (*KD*, p. 103; Graham also gives an early draft of the opening two stanzas). While agreeing with some of this, I do not find myself as moved by the change of tone as Graham does. The poem looks towards such later and more assured elegies as 'Gallantry' and 'Aristocrats' (entitled 'Sportsmen' in *TCP*), where the Englishness of the supporting mythology is both more telling and more tender than the merely intellectual appropriateness of Anderson's Hellenism.

'The Prisoner'

With 'The Prisoner' and the half-dozen poems that follow, Douglas makes the transition from apprenticeship to full maturity. This is the last and best of the poems exclusively about Yingcheng, though he returns to her again in 'The House' and 'To Kristin Yingcheng Olga Milena'. It begins with the lover's sense of wonder, struck dumb by the beauty and grace of its object. He can only 'gesture' at the mystery, not 'prove' it: only the senses can explore what is incarnated in flesh and bone. His hands flutter like moths near the unreachable flame of her being, 'luminous . . . in a paper house'. The image suggests danger, fragility, vulnerability, as well as capturing the look and feel of Yingcheng's skin stretched taut over her cheekbones: the mere 'paper house' of love beneath which burns the bone flame of death. Characteristically, the stone/bone/death cluster has a more powerful and destructive reality than the 'bright flesh', which is merely a mask. (See my discussion of such images in the next chapter.) The 'mask' derives from the 'paper house' of stanza 2; both register the frightening quality of that which we cannot see beyond, and the alleged 'inscrutability' of oriental faces to western eyes. No doubt the antinomies of the poem – paper and stone, love and cruelty, touching and telling, gods and mortals – owe something to the Jacobean and Metaphysical poets, perhaps as mediated by Eliot, but such paradoxes are central to all Douglas's major poems. That which is most acutely and painfully real – a loved woman, the dead bodies of fellow soldiers – is continually metamorphosed into something *un*real. (The opening line's 'I touched your face' is echoed by 'The wires touch his face: I cry / NOW' of 'How to Kill') Conversely, the unreal takes on the power to devour the real, illustrated in Douglas's drawing of Yingcheng as half face, half skull (reproduced in *KD*, p. 119).

J. C. Hall evidently complained about the unusual syntax of the poem's broken-off last stanza, which is indeed somewhat difficult, but for a good reason. Does the 'urge' to 'escape' belong to the lover, to the beloved, or to the 'ambitious cruel bone' of death itself? Douglas replied in a letter: 'The point of the Prisoner is that the ambitious cruel bone is the prisoner, who wishes to escape the bright flesh and emerge into fulfilment as a skeleton. "There was the urge (to break the bright flesh and emerge) OF the ambitious cruel bone." There is no question of escaping from the bone' (*PM*, p. 123). The poem leaves open the possibility, however, that lovers themselves are cruel too. The 'urge' that follows the two I-statements will naturally be ascribed to the 'I' as well: the urge to tear away the paper mask and find fulfilment in touching death. 'Analysis in worshipping', to recall the last line of the previous poem, reveals how double-edged the nature of love is. The 'prisoner' is both subject and object of the poem's bafflement, a bafflement which is itself imprisoned in endless paradox.

This reading is strengthened by the *CP(PL)* and *CP*

text, which is superior to the one *TCP* adopts.* In the former the last stanza reads 'There was the urge / to break the bright flesh . . .' (not 'escape'), where 'break' clearly suggests the lover's propensity, as well as the bone's.

'Oxford'

Possibly this and the other valedictory poems about Oxford were suggested by Auden's famous tribute of the same title, written just a few years earlier (December 1937). 'And the stones of that tower are utterly / Satisfied still with their weight', says Auden, contrasting them with the 'nervous students' and their 'careless beauty'. Likewise Douglas's poem speaks of the 'stones of the city, her venerable towers', a city both of 'the old, looking for truth' and 'of young men, of beginning, / ideas, trials, pardonable follies'. For once he eschews paradox, addressing himself to Oxford's spirit calling out to the 'spirits of the young', who may in turn become the 'leisurely immortals' venerated by future generations.

'The House'

There are several important differences between the *CP(PL)/CP* text and that in *TCP*. On the whole *TCP* is superior, except for the last two lines. In the former the 'visitor' and 'beautiful stranger' of the closing section are singular, whereas in *TCP* they are plural. The first ends: 'the beautiful stranger, the princess' as against *TCP*'s 'the beautiful strangers, coming to my house'. The singular version underlines the possibility that the

---

* But *CP(PL)* misguidedly changes 'of' to 'from' in the last line, to meet the sort of objection Hall had raised. It also has 'a hundred years' in place of *CP*'s 'a hundred hours', and *TCP*'s 'a thousand hours'. *TCP* prints 'stone-/ / hard face of death' in place of 'stone/ / person of death'. All the variants are Douglas's, of course. My judgements as to which are to be preferred, here and throughout this book, are based on critical, not textual, considerations.

dead or sleeping young lady in the attic is once again Yingcheng.

The poem brings together a number of images that often accompany Douglas's self-explorations, including glass, stone, mask, actors, strangers/visitors, and the controlling image of the house itself, used in such earlier poems as 'Poor Mary' and 'Sanctuary'. The narrator is first a pillar and then a mouse, unnoticed by the 'weightless shadows' that march in and through him (cf. 'the weightless mosquito' and 'shadow . . . man' of 'How to Kill'). The 'queer magnificence' of the house and its 'conjured spectacle' are glasslike, 'thin as air', and also like 'the house that devils made'; and it is apparently in need of 'defence', being invaded by 'substances, shadows', voices and faces and masks. In brief, the profusion of image and metaphor announces that he is a poet, living in the vulnerable but magnificent house of imagination. Section III's eleventh line specifically recalls Theseus's famous description of the poet in *A Midsummer Night's Dream* (V,i,7–17) as being 'of imagination all compact', giving 'to airy nothing / A local habitation and a name'.

The 'creative stone' referred to in the same section suggests an amalgam of the philosopher's stone, which confers immortality, and the poet's Muse, giving substance to shadows, objectifying the interior life. The dangerously obsessive nature of this Faustian pursuit is also glanced at: 'prospecting this is all the care I have'. Section IV moves on to an abstract inventory of the guests and performers who have been invited in, some of them installed in the 'best rooms', and closes with the discovery of a young lady's corpse up in the high attic, among old pictures and hyacinth bowls, which last probably derives from Eliot's hyacinth girl in *The Waste Land* (I, 35–9). The next line, too, is Eliotesque, recalling his Marlovian epigraph to 'Portrait of a Lady': 'but that was in another country, / And besides, the wench is dead'.

In section V the narrator marvels – like the 'necro-philiac lover', in Graham's phrase, of 'A Speech for an Actor' – at the fact that love and beauty will not last forever, noting that 'on death her obscure beauty thrived'. His love for her is 'the most permanent thing / in this impermanent building'; her presence continues to haunt him, deterring both other visitors and lovers ('the beautiful strangers'), and hence the possibility of a new Muse and renewed creativity. In becoming legendary, a princess with jewelled heart, gold hair, marble limbs, she becomes immortal like a work of art, 'fairer now than when she lived'. Moreover she thrives on death, the 'fine stones' of her eyes paradoxically negating the 'creative stone' that was to have turned 'all alive'. Like the legendary heroes of Yeats's 'Easter 1916', her very timelessness casts a deathly chill over the living – 'the stone's in the midst of all'; somehow art and imagination have inverted normal values. Beauti-ful and ugly have changed places, what was most alive feeds sinisterly now on death, real and unreal are fused together in 'natural marble'. Fairy-tale love has turned into insoluble witchcraft.

The extended conceit of the self as house goes back through George Herbert and the Metaphysical poets to the Bible, and has been used by scores of poets. This particular example may be read as an allegory of the poet's imaginative openness and vulnerability, 'trans-parent to the touch' of multitudinous and irreconcilable particulars of life and death. The word 'I' occurs seventeen times in 'The House'. If we add 'me', 'my', 'myself', the number increases to twenty-one. And on five occasions the pronoun is used in the phrase 'I am'. 'I' is a notoriously hard part of speech to analyse. When Hume introspected, he reported that he could find no corresponding mental particular. Descartes identified the self with the act of thinking. Keats abolished the 'poetical Character' altogether – 'it has no self' – dispersing it among the objects of the poet's empathic imagination (Robert Gittings, ed., *Letters of John Keats*, OUP, 1970, p. 95). In another famous letter he speaks of the 'Chamber of Maiden-Thought . . . on all sides of it many doors are set open – but all dark – all leading to dark passages – We see not the ballance of good and evil.' Like philosophers and laymen, Douglas too finds the self bafflingly insubstantial, 'transparent to the touch'; and like Keats, section III of 'The House' finds him lost in a maze of possibilities, unable to strike a balance between 'substances, shadows on their ways / crowding or evacuating the place'. Above all he finds it hard to strike a balance between love and lust, self and not-self (seeing everything and nothing in the 'glass' of himself, which is both a mirror and yet transparent), security and insecurity. The self remains a 'mute invisible audience' to the performers who have marched 'ignorantly in' or been 'chosen by chance'.

In other words, there seems to be a dizzying gap between the subjective feel of first-person experience, our identity to ourselves, and our identity as perceived by others. Its chief 'property', as the poem says, is 'that it is thin as air and hard to see'; yet it is also that round which everything else, for us, revolves. The self may be reinforced when we fall in love, made more substantial and complete, for love 'turns all alive'; and it may also feel invaded and threatened, both by the intrusion and the invitation to assume dependence on another. For Douglas glass and stone are always radically ambiguous images. Having gone beyond the 'rampart' of childhood ('Sanctuary') to independence, he is now a 'pillar' of his own adult house, strong and impervious, yet constantly 'scrutinizing' and 'prospecting' for love and creativity, which demand that he become a 'bright portico' for inspiration to enter, 'whether to speak, to sing, to play, or dance . . .' In poem after poem he plays variations on *stone* (which relates to *jewel* and hence *glass*) and *wall*. In 'Devils', for example, he speaks of the 'insubstantial wall' of the self: 'there'll be an

[91]

alliance of devils if it falls'. In 'Tel Aviv', another love
poem, he says 'We . . . can never lean / on an old
building in the past / or a new building in the future,'
and tries to preserve 'our walls of indifference' in case
they explode into flame. 'Landscape with Figures 3'
says 'I am possessed, / the house whose wall contains
the dark strife / the arguments of hell with heaven'.
Fragment A ii of 'Bête Noire' says the 'monster . . .
walks about inside me: I'm his house / and his landlord.'

In 'The Two Virtues' the 'drowned heart' is likened to
something 'made into a marvel by the sea, / that stone,
that jewel tranquillity'. In 'To a Lady on the Death of
Her First Love' death is 'like a secret jeweller' attend-
ing a 'Despoiled princess'. In 'How to Kill' stone is a
'gift', yet one that is 'designed to kill'. Likewise glass is
either to be looked in, at a safe distance from what it
reflects, or something to be crashed through (cf.
Alamein to Zem Zem, p. 16, and 'On a Return from
Egypt'). Both have miraculous properties, at once
benevolent and sinister, keeping the self safe from
harm, objectifying the intangible, yet also raising a
barrier between it and further experience. Poems too
are built of stone and glass, metaphorically speaking.
In raising a monument the poet simultaneously
entombs himself, erecting a cenotaph to the sterile
magic of memory and art.

I do not mean to suggest, by the length of this
analysis, that 'The House' belongs with Douglas's
major poems; plainly it doesn't. But I do think it
provides significant clues to his psychology, and to the
tangled roots of the creative and sexual drives in his life
and poetry. The peculiar mixture of self-confidence and
uncertainty apparent in his relations with women is
reflected in the somewhat confused egotism of this
poem. Such parallelisms and confusions, however, are
by no means exclusive to him. The poem's final
reference to a 'princess' calls up the legend of Sleeping
Beauty, lying in a glass case or coffin, who may be

awakened with a kiss. Douglas knows that such a consummation, in the case of Yingcheng, is unlikely, yet cannot 'exorcize' her from the house of his heart. Once through the looking-glass into the land of love everything goes into reverse, including alchemy. She is the jewel who has turned into a stone.

Two uncollected poems

The Heart's Prison

The marble pillars contain oblique cracks.
The wild briar has taken possession of the pediment;
The rose-petals float slowly down to the yellow grass.
Mosses and lichens creep round the pillars from below.
As we proceed up the broad steps we see the grass
Springing through the broken places where the soil has
    drifted.
The entrance-hall is deserted, like an old woman.
We look through the door-way into the great hall.
Horror of horrors! we see priceless manuscripts

Strewn on the floor, and mouldering to dust.
A pillar snaps, and the left wing of the building collapses.
From the top of the steps we see a row of broken columns
And blood streams from the top of each like so many
    truncated figures.
There is a statue of Venus to the right.
For no apparent reason it totters and falls forward.
The plaster of which it was made crumbles to a powder.
In the base were jumbled sundry articles of clothing
Far, far, over the horizon.

Published in *Cherwell* 9 March, 1940, unsigned, when Douglas was assistant editor. Yingcheng later sent a copy of this to Desmond Graham, saying that it was Douglas's. As Graham remarks in his thesis, the style is not very characteristic; but the subject-matter is. The extended central image recalls 'The House'; and there are one or two internal rhymes (yellow/below, crumbles/

jumbled) of the sort Douglas might have written; but in general both the writing and the organisation of the poem are slack, and the ending is notably feeble. It has the feel of a travelogue or tourist's effusion: 'As we proceed up the broad steps we see . . . We look through . . . From the top of the steps we see . . .'

Sandhurst

This severe building and barracksquare
with the guns of Waterloo exactly as they were
whence officers and gentlemen would go
to seek their fame a century ago

should make me copy in the end
the lieutenant who cried Floreat Etona to his friend
and at once tumbled heavily in the dust
bravely to die, precisely as he must.

But how could I achieve that grand moustache
or such élan without a sabretache
or dying, leave that fervent glare, or at
the sudden cue, have all my last words pat?

Then, whatever will restrain
the coward closely reasoning in my brain?
I think only that I must try to see
the whole performance and what the end will be.

The poem was written during his army training as an officer, and is partially quoted in Graham's biography (*KD*, pp. 116–17). Clearly it anticipates 'Gallantry' and 'Aristocrats', sometimes with astonishing closeness as in the second stanza, which prefigures the fate of 'Peter'. 'And when I prepare to die behind my gun / I shall not glow with fervour like a sun' runs an alternative version of the last couplet in stanza 3. There is an alternative draft of the close too (Graham's unpublished thesis, p. 418):

> I think it will be that I am mad to see
> the whole performance and what the end will be.

The pun on 'mad', offering two radically opposed meanings, and the revealingly colloquial diction of the first line, oscillating between hesitancy and assertion, as between tenses, make this a superior ending. The poem's tone is cheerfully deflationary until the last stanza, where the word 'coward' opposes and questions the ironic attitude taken up towards the 'officers and gentlemen' manufactured by Sandhurst. This dialectic is not resolved. 'I am mad to see / the whole performance' echoes the introductory words of *Alamein to Zem Zem*: '. . . the experience of battle was something I must have'. The word 'performance' too echoes the 'something decorative, poetic or dramatic' he talks of in *AZZ*, and the theatrical metaphors and images that throng the war poems. If there is no resolution of the problem of what attitude to adopt towards the war and its putative heroes, however, there is a characteristic honesty in his closing confession which forbids easy judgement, either his or ours.

IV

The Major Poems

The two poems that stand at the beginning and end of
Douglas's brief maturity, 'Simplify Me When I'm Dead'
and 'On a Return from Egypt', both reflect his lifelong
fear of an early and unproductive death. Of course he
was not alone in experiencing these intimations of
mortality; the theme runs, unsurprisingly, throughout
the poetry of the period. But in his case it goes back to
his earliest writings, long before war and his part in it
became inevitable. Skulls, skeletons, bones, shades,
spirits, effigies, ghosts throng the early poetry and
prose in Websterian profusion. 'Death is the season and
we the living / Are hailed by the solitary to join their
regiment' ('Dejection'). All young men are death-
haunted to some extent, no doubt, but Douglas's case is
different, for the subject takes on the character of an
obsession, partly perhaps because of the very depth of
his vitality. As Ted Hughes has said, 'Poem after poem
circles this idea [the doomed man in him or his dead
body], as if his mind were tethered' (*SP*, Introduction,
p. 13). Like others before him, he seems to have sensed
that he would either have to mature quickly, or not
mature at all.

To say, as he said of himself as a child, that he was a
militarist, and that 'war was his ideal subject', as
Hughes does, is to tell only part of a complex truth. In
the first place some of Douglas's best poems such as
'The Marvel', 'Behaviour of Fish . . .', 'Egypt', 'Syria',
'Adams', 'The Sea Bird', 'Time Eating' and 'Enfidaville'

have nothing, or very little, to do with war at all. It is
clear from these, and from his early poems, that
Douglas would have been a good poet whatever his
subject-matter. In the second place we have to remem-
ber what an unusual psychological mixture he was,
taking pleasure in confounding the categories and
expectations of his friends. The swimmer-horseman-
athlete who delighted in drill and bulling his kit was
also a balletomane, tap-dancer and jazz-lover. The
hyper-efficient young subaltern admired by his batman
as 'shit or bust' was also a bookish solitary poet-painter
reared on de la Mare and Jefferies who liked nothing
better than executing water-colours on long country
walks. The narcissistic young womanizer worried about
pimples and the size of his nose – 'I have the face of a
parrot' (*KD*, p. 51) – and proposed marriage to almost
every girl he ever kissed. The man-of-action despised
aesthetes and bohemians just as much as the poet
despised hearties and philistines and immemorial
English snobbery. By turns ebullient and suicidal,
competitive and indifferent, arrogant and serene, he
threw himself on the mercies of friends and school-
masters, supercilious undergraduates, elderly dons,
sixteen-year-old Diana from Birmingham, and his
superior officers, cutting a dash wherever he went but
continually searching for stability and reassurance in a
world that seemed at best hostile, at worst dedicated to
his particular destruction. In short, he was a prickly
high-flier in search of immortal fame and a secure
domestic base.*

* 'The record he played – became almost a Douglas signature-tune –
was "It Ain't Necessarily So": that was his favourite . . . when I . . .
saw him writing, and read his poetry, he made it quite clear – "I'm
going to be a major poet" end of message . . . "There are lots of people
who dabble with poetry, they don't really understand it, but I insist, I
am going to be a . . . poet come what may." ' Lt-Col. John Stubbs, 'A
Soldier's Story: Keith Douglas at El Ballah', recorded by Desmond
Graham, *PN Review* 47, vol. 12, no. 3, pp. 26–9.

Such a mixture of appetites and contradictions is not peculiar to Douglas, but their number, variety, intensity and volatility warns us off the temptation to make easy generalizations about his character. This is precisely the burden of 'Simplify Me When I'm Dead':

> Remember me when I am dead
> and simplify me when I'm dead.
>
> As the processes of earth
> strip off the colour and the skin
> take the brown hair and blue eye
>
> and leave me simpler than at birth,
> when hairless I came howling in
> as the moon entered the cold sky . . .

There are any number of models for this theme, such as Shakespeare's sonnet 81 ('No longer mourn for me when I am dead') and C. H. Sorley's untitled poem beginning 'When you see millions of the mouthless dead', but the two that Douglas probably had in mind are Christina Rossetti's famous sonnet 'Remember' ('Remember me when I am gone away, / Gone far away into the silent land') and Rupert Brooke's equally famous elegy 'The Soldier' ('If I should die, think only this of me: / That there's some corner of a foreign field / That is forever England . . .'). All these are gravely formal sonnets, wringing whatever comfort can be got out of saying one thing and meaning another, or rather infusing one sense vividly with its opposite. Thus Christina Rossetti's ending – 'Better by far you should forget and smile / Than that you should remember and be sad' – makes sure that the remembering and the sadness get into that last crucial line, where we are least likely to forget them. Similarly, John Carey argues, Douglas's poem 'amounts to a request to have his complexities put on record' (*The New Review*, vol. 1, no. 5, August 1974, pp. 72–4; Carey's further witticism,

'It's not the simple that want simplifying,' rather misses the point of the poem). Douglas also begins with a sonorous first line, but swiftly undercuts it with line 2, which repeats yet varies the opening, and by eliding 'I am' to 'I'm' acts out in little the simplifications that will follow his death. Next he describes the brute facts of decomposition, so much less comforting than Brooke's 'rich . . . dust' pulsing in 'the eternal mind', and in doing so also moves to irregular stresses and a more offhand diction and grammar ('As the . . .', 'Of my . . .', 'not by . . .'), closer to scientific notation than to elegiac rotundity; yet one which can encompass the grand gesture of lines 7 and 8, with their echo of Lear's 'We came crying hither.' Once again death is viewed through a 'lens', this time a 'wrong-way telescope' that reduces instead of magnifying, collapsing time (with a pun on 'minute') and space into one of two polar opposites: 'substance or nothing'. The withholding of any punctuation mark between stanzas 8 and 9 is puzzling at first, but has three possible effects: first to dizzy us a little, next to underline the double enjambement of 'oblivion / / not', and lastly to mime syntactically the double movement of unity and disjunction, forcing us to read what looks like one sentence as two, or two as one. This dizzying effect is compounded by the pun – 'see if I seem' – and a sort of parody of logic-chopping discourse, full of truth-table particles such as 'if' and 'not' and 'or'. Apart from the opening and closing refrain, which rhymes inertly on itself, the triplets employ chain-rhyme (ABC, ABC, DEF . . . etc.), rhyming *world* with *hurled* and *oblivion* with *opinion*.

The memorable comparison of birth to the moon entering the cold sky introduces an image that recurs frequently in later poems, often related to images of stone and death. Here it personifies the self as a *tabula rasa* of pure energy and apetite (cf. the 'planetary love' of 'Dead Men'). Is it a new moon, as befits the subject of birth, or a full one? We cannot tell, and in a way it does not matter, because within a line that self is a 'skeleton' stripped down from substance to nothing. The subjective pleading of the first line abruptly gives way to objective appraisal. As in 'The House', Douglas seems to be grappling with the irreconcilability of first-person and third-person descriptions of the nature of experience. The telescope may tell us something about the moon but our knowledge is radically simplified by distance. This one is 'wrong-way' (with a pun on one-way?), shrinking what it should magnify. We have all the time in the world to investigate his character and poetry; yet the forces which governed his actions will remain forever conjectural, like the history of a star.

'He is a renovator of language,' Hughes says of this poem, who 'has invented a style that seems able to deal practically with whatever it comes up against. It is not an exalted verbal activity to be attained for short periods' but a 'utility general-purpose style . . . that combines a prose readiness with poetic breadth', one that encompasses 'intensity and music . . . with clear direct feeling, and yet in the end is nothing but casual speech' (*SP*, Introduction, pp. 11–14). This is well said. Yet for all its undoubted power 'Simplify Me When I'm Dead' seems to me a harbinger of things to come rather than a fully achieved poem. Stanzas 4 and 5 ('Thus when . . .') are flatter and less convincing than what surrounds them. 'The long pain I bore', for example, does not quite square with sudden and early death, and carries an inappropriate echo of Pope's famous reference to 'this long disease my life' (*Epistle to Dr Arbuthnot*). The last line of stanza 5 is both vague and questionable. And the speech rhythms do not quite mesh with the formal structure, which arguably pulls his syntax into some knobbly shapes. None the less the linguistic freshness and emotional drive of the poem are admirable, even though Douglas cannot yet hold the components of his talent fully together.

No such qualifications apply to 'The Marvel', which is

a marvel of Hughesian power and delicacy, leavened by a detached yet wholly engaging wit. It opens with a trumpet-blast: not 'like' a baron, but 'A baron of the sea, the great tropic / swordfish . . .', using the *is* of identity and three strong stresses in the last three words to underline his power. The swordfish's eye, removed by the sailors who catch it, is 'forged in semi-darkness', midway between the 'dim country' of the sea's depths and the hot sun above. He is 'a lord' in his domain (like Lawrence's snake), but has in turn been preyed upon by the lordly sailors, whose 'enquiring blade' has been turned upon his own. Like Hughes after him, Douglas is fond of using 'eye' in such a way as to suggest a pun on 'I', fusing the self with its strongest sense; this prepares us for the union of multiple identities at the poem's close. Eliot objected, somewhat pedantically, to the adjective 'enquiring', noting that it might be used of a surgeon's blade, and asking what propriety it had when applied to a sailor's knife.* The answer is self-evident. The sailor is enquiring into the nature of creation, specifically that of another 'strong traveller' like himself, and by extension that of everything under the sun.

The eye 'taken from the corpse' – a macabre act, yet one which is described with a complete absence of grisliness or sensationalism – becomes a 'powerful enlarging glass': death itself is an 'instrument' for investigating life, instrumental, indeed, in dictating the shapes that life will take (compare Hughes's 'Pike': 'a life subdued to its instrument'), including the further predatory act of having 'a harlot in his last port'. The impersonality of 'harlot' (even though the sailor writes

* *PM*, p. 76. Cf. his own lines in 'East Coker', IV: 'The wounded surgeon plies the steel / That questions the distempered part', which he had written the previous year (March, 1940). Eliot also queried the adjectives in 'dim water' ('was the water dimmer than most sea-water?') and 'interesting waves' ('Why?'). The last query is reasonable, though answerable; the others seem a little dim.

her name, or rather *burns* her name, on the wooden deck) matches the detached vocabulary that runs through the whole poem until we reach the penultimate word 'marvel', which casts its warmth and wonder back over the entire chain of events leading to its utterance. The characteristic juxtaposition of 'corpse' and 'glass' is given a new resonance by the introduction of the sun and the sea and the prostitute. All are seen as 'curious devices', not least because of their power and interdependence. To this litany of bizarre yet compelling events is added 'the querulous soft voice / / of mariners who rotted into ghosts'. The 'sailors' have become 'mariners'; and mariners, we know from Coleridge, have marvellously pertinent stories to tell. With 'ghosts' we circle back to the 'corpse' of stanza 3; yet again a predator has been preyed upon by something stronger than itself. With a sudden magical change of perspective the poem now converts depth into height and death into hospitable life: 'Let them be your hosts' –

> and take you where their forgotten ships lie
> with fishes going over the tall masts –
> all this emerges from the burning eye.

'Emerges' merges the burning eye/I with the whole dazzling array of events and experiences that spill down the terza rima triplets like a fountain, only to shoot back up again in an endless cycle of recurrence. Similarly 'engrave' puns on the mariners' grave deep in the sea. There is a wonderful reciprocity in the poem between high and low, inner and outer, darkness and brightness; everything writes and is written upon, burns and is burned, forges and yields. The 'baron' swordfish is seized and instantly 'spreadeagled'. The sailors travel and fornicate and then rot into their 'last port' as ghosts, where the fishes go over the tall masts of their once stately egos. The 'unusual sun', 'interesting waves', 'gluttonous tides' are first useful instruments and then killers in their turn. Likewise the eye is both predator and prey, active and passive, 'burning' with its own energies and with those of the larger chain of being it is caught up in. All the contraries are finally reconciled in 'that word' of the final stanza, engraved not by the sailors or the barons of upper or lower creation but by the sun, writing a name which is now everybody's name, harlot's, sailor's, sea's, sun's and all their ghostly opposites, in this world and the next. 'Energy is eternal delight', as Blake's famous proverb says. The last main verb, 'writing', is in the present tense; and the poem ends appropriately on the word 'too'.

Images of submarine life recur throughout Douglas's poems, culminating in the masterly 'Behaviour of Fish in an Egyptian Tea Garden'. 'Encounter with a God' has the poetess 'Thinking of the rock pool / and carp in the waterfall at night'; 'Pleasures' speaks of 'tall seas where the bright fish go like footmen / . . . The jewelled skulls are down there'; in 'News from Earth' there are 'Limber monsters of the deep', 'sea nymphs and mermaidens . . . / jewelled from the depth'; in 'The Two Virtues' sorrow is a 'lagoon' in which 'the lost, / the drowned heart is wonderfully recast / and made into a marvel by the sea, / that stone, that jewel tranquillity'. 'The Marvel', as we have seen, assimilates sexual energy into the elemental natural forces urging us on towards death. The very last poem, 'On a Return from Egypt', refers to the heart as a coal 'growing colder / when jewelled cerulean seas change . . .' Most of these images occur in an erotic context, and that in turn is linked to strong forebodings of death, 'an atmosphere of Juliet's tomb', to quote Eliot,* where Romeo dies spreadeagled across Juliet in a grotesque parody of coitus. Sex is 'jewelled', multi-

* 'Portrait of a Lady', I,6. Douglas's images of sea-change and sea-enchantment may owe something to Eliot's fascination with *The Tempest*. Similarly I think the traces of seventeenth-century wit are Eliot-influenced.

faceted, the 'philosopher's stone' that will turn all alive' ('The House') or conversely into the 'jewelled skulls' of the dead ('Pleasures'). Related images of caves/fissures/recesses often accompany this singular use of stones and jewels and sea-change as metaphors of desire. Thus we read of the 'recesses of your eyes' in 'Poor Mary'; the 'cool red cave of lips' in 'Stranger'; the 'deep / Recesses of your mind' in 'Haydn – Clock Symphony'; the eyes 'dumb' in 'cavernous slots' in 'The Deceased'; the 'forgetful caves' of shadowy waters in 'Shadows'; the eyes as 'mouths of caves' looking out on a 'blessed sea' in 'The Knife'; the 'charms through fissures where the eyes should be' and 'teeth . . . parted in a stare' of 'Behaviour of Fish . . .' The caves and recesses are all properties of the flesh, which are determined by the geology of the skeleton and the skull; to explore the first is necessarily to be drawn into the mysteries of the second. The 'crustacean old man' of 'Behaviour of Fish . . .' has already become a living skull, a Websterian emblem of death-in-desire; the cotton magnate 'with great eyepouches' is well on the way to the same fate.

On the battlefield these metamorphoses are seen in brutal and ambiguous close-up. The literal wounds are a mirror-image of the psychic wounds inflicted by desire. The 'burst stomach like a cave' of 'Vergissmeinnicht', for example, or the figures 'poking in the debris' ('Enfidaville'), the reader/writer who comes to 'poke fingers in wounds' ('Landscape with Figures'), the inventory of split gun-barrels and 'steel . . . torn into fronds' that runs through much of *Alamein to Zem Zem* and the desert poems. Pierced and battered and twisted into strange shapes by explosives, the iron 'vegetation' is a metallic analogue or parody of the submarine images of fecundity and libidinous force; and of fissures and recesses in the minds of the lovers and killers who execute these deadly manoeuvres. Douglas constantly draws parallels between 'men's . . . cruel wish / for love' and its perverse realization in the impulse to kill. (Cf. the 'ambitious cruel bone' of 'The Prisoner'.) Thus the 'mimes' who crouch and 'wriggle' impotently on desert sand, 'at a queer angle to the scenery', have gone clean through the looking-glass into a world ruled only by destructive egotism. There is no reciprocity, no accommodation between men and their environment, or between man and man, except in the Darwinian struggle to survive. No women participate in this theatre of war (the time-honoured metaphor is one Douglas brings vividly back to life); they exist only as photographs, cardboard dummies who can't answer back, or as whores to be visited on brief periods of leave. The dream of love turns into the 'nightmare ground' of naked appetite; sexual organs become nothing more than weapons or wounds; lovers are transmogrified into necrophiliac 'combatants' whose courtship results only in death. 'Returning over the nightmare ground / we found the place again, and found . . .' ('Vergissmeinnicht'; cf. Edmund Blunden's 'I must go over the ground again,' *Undertones of War*, Penguin Modern Classics, 1982, p. 8): the obsessive return, the mental picking at the exact time and place, the coincidence of 'soldier . . . gun . . . demon . . . dishonoured girl' constitutes a meticulous taxonomy of this Faustian world of good and evil, in which roles are instantly reversible and all the complexities of normal behaviour are reduced to a series of binary oppositions, reconcilable only in death.

In 'Vergissmeinnicht' (forget-me-not), Douglas's most anthologized poem, all these antinomies are brought to a head. The thunderclap with which the demon king arrives onstage in a pantomime is a strange image for the deafening clang that occurs when a tank is hit or pierced by a shell (see the graphic account in *Alamein to Zem Zem*, chapter 8). Here it evokes the terrors of childhood in the face of uncontrollable events. This devilish figure's name caps a series of obsessive rhymes: *gone, sun, gun, on, demon*, whose

similarity may be merely accidental, or may function-
ally suggest that the next word, *Look*, is the beginning
of the devil's own commanding speech. The 'entry of a
demon' is into the speaker's own mind and heart, as
well as his armoured vehicle, the 'beast on my back' of
'Bête Noire' come to take possession of what is
rightfully his, the damned sorcerer of 'How to Kill', the
evil spirit summoned up in Faust's 'gothic script'.
(Coincidentally, Alun Lewis reaches for the Faust story
when describing his own regiment's tank training: 'it's
about time I . . . made my Faustian pact with the great
armour-plated monster of Today.' Letter to Robert
Graves, *Anglo-Welsh Review*, vol. 16, no. 37, 1966,
p. 11.)

Notice how it is a 'she', the 'dishonoured girl' of the
photograph, who 'would weep' to see death, just as it is
the mother who is associated with tenderness and
compassion in 'How to Kill'. What does 'dishonoured'
mean, literally or figuratively? Has someone scrawled
sexual graffiti on the photo, drawn in genitalia?* Or is
it dishonoured by its presence in the 'gunpit spoil' and
its owner's defeat?' 'Spoil' itself is both vivid and
ambiguous: the spoils of war – something worth having,
traditionally – or the spoilt mess of items enumerated
in *Alamein to Zem Zem* and 'Cairo Jag', souvenirs,
chocolate, cartridges, etc.? The pararhyme on spoil/girl,
and the sexual symbolism of the scene – a soldier
sprawled dead beneath the 'overshadowing' barrel of
his gun; a girl dishonoured in a 'gunpit' – suggest a
metaphorical rape of both by the destructive forces
unleashed by the 'lover and killer . . . who had one body
and one heart'. Here the parallelism between impulses

* In an alternative draft (see *TCP*, p. 140) Douglas replaces
'dishonoured' with 'soiled', and appends a fuller version of the
'copybook gothic script': 'Mein mund ist stumm, aber mein Aug'es
spricht / Und was es sagt ist kurz – Vergissmeinnicht. Steffi.' (My
mouth is dumb, but my eye speaks / and what it says is brief –
forget-me-not.)

is explicitly underlined; and the syntax suggests a further parallelism between lover/body and killer/heart, while the rhymes simultaneously tighten the screw of paradox: mingled/singled, heart/hurt.

This distribution of guilt, as it were, between the enemy and the self (which is its own enemy) is prepared for in stanza 4: 'We see him almost with content / abased . . .'* The 'content' is clearly shared by victor and vanquished; and the other meaning of the word, as in form and content, is glanced at in the 'burst stomach' of the next stanza, where the adjective chimes alliteratively with 'abased' and its ghostly pun on 'based'. Similarly 'his own equipment' hints at sexual and instinctual drives as well as the literal hardware that outlasts his decaying body: both mock the vulnerability of flesh, living and dead. In poetry of great flexibility and skill Douglas combines the 'casual speech' Hughes speaks of with a grave formality:

> But she would weep to see today
> how on his skin the swart flies move;
> the dust upon the paper eye
> and the burst stomach like a cave.
>
> For here the lover and killer are mingled
> who had one body and one heart.
> And death who had the soldier singled
> has done the lover mortal hurt.

The burly rhythms of the first three stanzas give way to a hymnlike regularity and monosyllabic tenderness, which encompasses and partially atones for the hungry mortality of the mutilated corpse. How much more effective 'swart' is than 'black' would have been, picking up connotations of evil ('wicked, iniquitous' –

---

* *TCP* prints a comma after 'content', thus undermining Douglas's double reference. Neither *CP(PL)* nor *CP* has the comma, nor has the variant draft given in *TCP*'s Notes. Douglas's practice elsewhere is strongly against its retention.

SOED) and the word's Common Teutonic etymology 'sweart', so that the flies become an instantiation of the 'gothic script' in stanza 3, writing their own black postscripts on the skin and the 'paper eye' / I of the decaying body. 'Bur*st st*omach' has its own 'dynamic assonance', as Edna Longley notes, mimetically breaking up the iambic line with a heavy spondee. 'Lover', 'killer', 'mingled' and 'singled' are all trochees, also reversing the iambic flow. Even the feminine endings are functional, mingling paradox and simple truth in a rhythmical dying fall. Notice too how it is impersonal death that does the killing, just as it does in 'How to Kill' ('Death . . . has made a man of dust / of a man of flesh'), not the 'I', a pronoun that never appears in the poem at all.

The effect of the whole is of an elegiac song which refuses any trace of sentimentality yet provides whatever comfort is to be got out of such rigorous truth-telling. How different a poem it is, as Longley notes, from Owen's 'Strange Meeting', which it superficially resembles (Edna Longley, 'Shit or Bust: The Importance of Keith Douglas', *The Honest Ulsterman*, no. 76, Autumn 1984, pp. 13–31). Whereas Owen's homoerotic tenderness turned outwards into fury at the barbaric indifference of generals and politicians, and inwards towards Christ's passion, Douglas, having no such 'other' to hit out at or assuage, confines himself to the behavioural patterns observable in and through his own agnostic eyes, the gnostic become internalized and ghostly. Thus the fly's-eye-view, with its multifaceted lenses, like a jewel's, or the hungry dog's finding meat in a hole ('Dead Men'), or the tiny mosquito's, piercing the skin with its demonic sting (mirror-image of the tank-piercing shell, or the sniper's bullet piercing flesh), is as valid and compelling in this neutral desert landscape as any other. It is the perfect backdrop for this twentieth-century re-run of the allegory of love, starring knights in camouflaged armour and faraway ladies whose favour is a fading snap. The tanks were even called 'Crusaders'. 'Three lives hath one life / Iron, honey, gold' said Rosenberg, who richly allegorizes almost everything he touches ('August 1914'); and Douglas's view of things is closer to his than to Owen's, as he openly acknowledges in 'Desert Flowers'. Both locate the causes of disaster firmly in the antinomian nature of man's own make-up, a psychic maquillage removable only by death. Hence the impulsion towards the skull's uncovering, 'to poke fingers in the wounds'; or the related ambition to become stone-like, at one with 'the triumphant silence of the dead'. Douglas sums up a part of his own bafflement ('these curious identations on my thought') in the last two stanzas of 'Negative Information':

> For as often as not we meet
> in dreams our own dishevelled ghosts;
> and opposite, the modest hosts
> of our ambition stare them out.
>
> To this there's no sum I can find –
> the hungry omens of calamity
> mixed with good signs, and all received with levity,
> or indifference, by the amazed mind.

The 'modest hosts' who stand 'opposite' their own dreams and ghosts and terrors are like the dancers who 'step opposite' their partners in 'Haydn – Clock Symphony', walking the 'corridors and . . . deep / Recesses of your mind'. There is no 'sum' to such information because the signs and omens never cease, and because they simply don't add up. The 'polished ground' of love turns constantly into the 'nightmare ground' of death.

'Well I have been walking beside the sea waves,' Douglas wrote to Jean Turner, an Oxford friend, in October 1941, 'and have rather unoriginally been inspired, presumably by the waves etc. to produce three rather unoriginal poems' (*KD*, p. 131). He was convalescing, recovering from an ear infection at a Palestine hospital on the coast of Nathanya. The three poems were 'The Hand', 'Adams' and 'The Sea Bird', and his flippant judgement couldn't have been further from the truth. 'The Hand' is to some extent an exercise, albeit an interesting one; the others are his first major Middle East poems. In fact they are two versions of a single poem, both of them compelling and 'difficult'. 'The Sea Bird' begins as a description of the brilliantly coloured birds he had seen on his walks along the coast, and tells his mother about in a letter home: 'There is a sort of sea-kingfisher here, brilliant blue on the back and orange underneath, with a long black beak. They appear by themselves, and always sit very upright' (*KD*, pp. 132–3). Prompted partly, perhaps, by the bird's sharply divided coloration, and by his own restless apprehension of paradox in everything about him, the poem quickly turns the excitement of the bird's electric presence into a metaphysical excursion:

> Walking along beside the beach
> where the Mediterranean turns in sleep
> under the cliff's demiarch
>
> through a curtain of thought I see
> a dead bird and a live bird
> the dead eyeless, but with a bright eye
>
> the live bird discovered me
> and stepped from a black rock into the air –
> I turn from the dead bird to watch him fly,
>
> electric, brilliant blue,
> beneath he is orange, like flame,
> colours I can't believe are so,
>
> as legendary flowers bloom
> incendiary in tint, so swift he
> searches about the sky for room,

[110]

> towering like the cliffs of this coast
> with his stiletto wing
> and orange on his breast:
>
> he has consumed and drained
> the colours of the sea
> and the yellow of this tidal ground
>
> till he escapes the eye, or is a ghost
> and in a moment has come down
> crept into the dead bird, ceased to exist.

The poem consists of a single extended sentence, in which the 'I' is confronted with 'a dead bird and a live bird': 'I see', 'I turn', 'I can't believe', yet believe he must for the evidence is there in front of his own eyes. The central paradox is prefigured in the dividing lines between land and sea, rock and air ('the cliff's demiarch'), sleeping and waking, sense and thought. The first main verb, 'I see', is deferred by the piling up of clauses in lines 2, 3 and 4, so that *what* he sees is thrice-mediated, by the sea turning in sleep, by the half-arch in the rock, and by 'a curtain of thought'. This introduces a conceptual dizziness and variety which is mirrored both by the outer events and objects the poem describes, and by its tactical shifts of hold and perspective. Just as the bird 'searches about the sky for room', so the poem searches for a foothold or point of view from which to make sense of this experience. 'Beside', 'under', 'through', 'beneath', 'towering', 'escapes', 'come down', 'crept' – the auxiliaries are as changing as the metamorphoses of the bird and the poet's corresponding flight of imagination. 'Demiarch' appears to be Douglas's own coinage, meaning literally half-arch, but also strongly suggestive of 'demiurge', which *SOED* defines as the Maker of the World, in Plato's scheme of things, or 'in the Gnostic scheme of things . . . a being subordinate to the Supreme Being, and sometimes . . . the author of evil'. The binary possibilities mesh perfectly with the poem's exploration of the relation between live bird and dead bird, incendiary flame into motionless ghost.

The hypotactic verbal/visual/conceptual mirrorings are reinforced by a further metamorphosis of subject into object, the poet's discovery of the bird giving way to the bird's apprehension of him: 'the live bird discovered me / and stepped . . . into the air.' I take it that the adjective in 'dead bird' is a *façon de parler*, descriptive of motionlessness; an expression of astonishment at the disparity between the bird at rest and the bird in flight. How can the eye or brain reconcile near-invisibility at one moment with incendiary flame the next, something rock-like with the 'stiletto wing' of pure dangerous energy? The kingfisher has taken on all the colours of his environment (stanza 7) and so 'escapes the eye', meaning that he blends in perfectly with his background, which is in some sense the author of his existence, and further that the ego is distributed to the point of abolition (I-less), whereupon it is 'a ghost / and in a moment has come down / crept into the dead bird, ceased to exist'. The ending suggests various possibilities: (i) as quickly as it 'stepped . . . into the air' it steps back into inanition, quicker than any eye can follow; (ii) phoenix-like it consumes its own life, blooms and dies in a cycle of recurrence; (iii) halcyon-like it calms the sea, and just as that ocean 'turns in sleep' so the bird turns into a 'ghost'; (iv) it escapes from itself, exactly as the soul leaves the body.

Like 'The Marvel' the poem has a swift, confident movement from beginning to end, impatient to disclose some metaphysical key to its cabinet of vivid and apparently irreconcilable appearances. One notable feature is its handling of diction, syntax and prosody through the eight terza rima stanzas, hovering between but never quite settling into octosyllabic and pentameter lines, blending colloquial speech with a highly complex reconnaissance of sensory and intellectual impressions. Another is the exclusive concentration on the visual sense. Elsewhere in Douglas's poems birds figure quite often as emblematic messengers, but nearly always by virtue of their (intelligible or unintelligible) speech. Thus in 'Caravan' the wise speaker is 'speaking the tongue of the swallows'; in 'Dejection' 'tomorrow like a seagull hovers and cries: / *The windows will be open and the heart behind them*'; in 'Spring Sailor' the birds move 'with melody / Like kindly sirens', harbingers of a 'marvellous story without words, and still / Beyond your speech'; in 'Invaders' the 'Intelligences' are 'like black birds / come on their dire wings', but the heart must 'always ... indite / ... a good matter, while the black birds cry'; in 'Villanelle of Spring Bells' a bird 'in ten fine notes dispels twenty cares'; 'Poor Mary' gibbers with 'starling speech', trapped behind glass, and the children are 'twittering' behind the windows of 'L'Autobus'; in 'A God is Buried' a 'golden oriole fluting ... / colours the silence'; the rejected lover of 'I listen to the desert wind' is a bird whose 'sleepless eye / skims the cold sands'; the 'stooping man' in 'Words' has 'hollow birds' bones' which are a 'trap for words'; the doomed combatants of 'Landscape with Figures' are 'Perched on a great fall of air'. In all these cases birdsong and bird imagery are associated with the unsayable (whether painful or pleasurable), something like music's instantaneous power to articulate pure feeling, where words would be otiose or beside the point. Their song mediates between speech and silence, as their flight mediates between earth and heaven. Hence in 'Adams' the kingfisher is 'swallowing my thought'.

In trying to paraphrase 'The Sea Bird', then, one is reduced to performing an autopsy on the bird itself, since it has literally and metaphorically swallowed up in itself the mystery Douglas reaches towards. (Compare, once again, 'The Marvel', where the sailors turn their 'enquiring blade' on the body of the swordfish, whose 'burning eye', like the 'bright eye' of the bird, magnifies their own condition.) The 'demiarch', linked to the 'curtain of thought' through which the poet speaks, has some affinities perhaps with the arch in Tennyson's 'Ulysses':

> I am a part of all that I have met;
> Yet all experience is an arch wherethro'
> Gleams that untravelled world, whose margin fades
> For ever and for ever when I move.

Just as the world gleams and then fades for Ulysses, as it does also in many of Wordsworth's poems (e.g. the 'Immortality Ode'), so it flames into being – in the form of a bird – for Douglas, then escapes into its own ghost. It is a harbinger and symbol of the numinous, his own brief life and death, watched in fascinated detachment, which no logic save the Ovidian logic of 'marvels' can anatomize or comprehend. The bird itself links up with the grand Romantic tradition of cuckoos, larks, nightingales, kingfishers, et cetera, right down to Hardy's 'aged thrush' and Yeats's 'dying generations'. Andrew Young's meditation on some 'trembling feathers' he finds on the ground is very close to one aspect of Douglas's poem:

> Feathers without a bird!
>   As though the bird had flown away
> From its own feathers, fired
>   By strange desire for some immortal spray. ('Killed by a Hawk')

Later still come Ted Hughes's two hawk poems, 'The Hawk in the Rain' and 'Hawk Roosting', the second of which perhaps owes something to Douglas's example. But there are crucial differences in tone and emphasis between the three poets. Young's last line grabs too eagerly at the mystery, closing on a fistful of adjectives ('strange . . . immortal'); Hughes's certainties ('The sun is behind me'; 'There is no sophistry in my body') are as dictatorial as his tyrannical hawk, leaving hardly any room for mystery at all.

The collapse of the live bird into its own dead body is also related, I have suggested, to the fate of the combatants in 'Landscape with Figures', who are 'Perched on a great fall of air' only to descend into 'scattered wingcases and / . . . heads', in section I, or to 'dead men' wriggling in a 'motionless struggle' in section II. But this connection is tenuous and implicit; and the title of the latter poem makes it clear that the human figures are almost incidental to the inhuman ecology of the battleground. In 'Adams' Douglas rewrites and expands his epiphany to make its human implications clearer, and give them a new focal point. 'Along', in line 1, becomes 'alone'; the second triplet alters 'through a curtain of thought I see' to 'walking thinking slowly I see'; 'I turn from the dead bird' becomes 'leave the dead bird to lie' – otherwise the first four and a half stanzas are substantially the same. At this point he introduces his new material; the legendary flowers and their incendiary tints are

> a focal point
> like Adams in a room.
>
> Adams is like a bird
> alert (high on his pinnacle of air
> he does not hear you, someone said);
>
> in appearance he is bird-eyed,
> the bones of his face are
> like the hollow bones of a bird.
>
> And he stood by the elegant wall
> between two pictures hanging there
> certain of homage from us all
>
> as through the mind this minute
> he draws the universe
> and, like our admiration, dresses in it

[115]

towering like the cliffs of this coast
with his stiletto wing
and orange on his breast:

he sucked up, utterly drained
the colour of my sea,
the yellow of this tidal ground,

swallowing my thought
swallows all those dark fish there
that a rock hides from sunlight.

Till Rest, cries my mind to Adams' ghost;
only go elsewhere, let me alone
creep into the dead bird, cease to exist.

The closing stanza of 'The Sea Bird' has such an air of
finality about it that it seems to forestall further
questioning, even though the live and dead bird are as
irreconcilable as, say, the love and treachery of Ying-
cheng, or the child and man of 'How to Kill', or the lover
and killer of 'Vergissmeinnicht'. In 'Adams' this torment
is specifically located in the eponymous figure who takes
on the bird's attributes; he is elegant as the pictures in
the officers' mess, glossy as a bird in his polished cavalry
plumage. The deleted 'curtain of thought' is replaced by
the flatter 'walking thinking slowly . . .', but then taken
up again in a much more exciting metaphor: 'through
the mind this minute / he [Adams] draws the universe',
just as the kingfisher, in the other version, drew the
mind of the 'I' through its peregrinations. But now it is
'my' sea, the narrator's own colour and thought and
essential being, that is 'utterly drained'; and it is
'Adams' ghost' that is instructed and implored to 'let me
alone / creep into the dead bird, cease to exist'.

The plot thickens, and so does the ontology: two
corpses to explain, and a narrator threatened and
intrigued both by the marvel of life and death, as in
'The Sea Bird', and by an ego which seems to swallow

[116]

the universe of his own. Adams' ghost and the dead bird arrive as suddenly, and as inexplicably, in this alternative ending as the 'ghost . . . into . . . dead bird' in its previous incarnation. The phrase 'high on his pinnacle of air' links Adams, as I suggested earlier, to the opening of 'Landscape with Figures'. The impotence of the narrator of that poem – 'I am the figure writhing on the backcloth' – is related to the anguish apparent here; the dead men draw the drama of the universe through their minds, dressed in the 'colours death has the only list of', just as Adams, 'certain of homage from us all', drains and swallows the vitality of his comrades. The hardest word to interpret in both poems is 'ghost', since it seems to imply both the living spirit and the dead body, or some mysterious bridge between the two.

The word crops up quite frequently in Douglas's poems from 1940 onwards. In 'A Mime', about the twin villains Time and Death who are on his track, Time is 'limber as a ghost'; in 'An Exercise Against Impatience' ghosts are associated with an 'exchange . . . of foreboding' between 'youth and age'; in 'Negative Information' 'You and I are careless of these millions of wraiths' [the dead]:

> For as often as not we meet
> in dreams our own dishevelled ghosts;
> and opposite, the modest hosts
> of our ambition stare them out.

In 'The Marvel',

> I suppose the querulous soft voice
>
> of mariners who rotted into ghosts
> digested by the gluttonous tides
> could recount many [names and devices]. Let them
>   be your hosts
> and take you where their forgotten ships lie . . .

In both these last examples the *ghosts* of the dead turn into or meet the *hosts* of our ambition, which is to satisfy our hunger for experiences as fully as possible. The two

stand opposite each other like the dancers in 'Haydn –
Clock Symphony', moving 'in eternity'; each reflects the
other's face; both are metamorphosed, psychically and
physically, falling from some high pinnacle or perch to
crawl in desert sand ('Landscape with Figures') or be
digested by the 'gluttonous tides' ('The Marvel'). In
'Enfidaville' 'No one is left to greet /the ghosts tugging at
doorhandles / opening doors that are not there.' In 'How
to Kill' death turns flesh into dust: 'How easy it is to
make a ghost.' The active verbs – tugging, opening,
making – heighten the dizziness of the paradox. In the
war between 'substance' and 'nothing' ('Simplify Me
When I'm Dead') it is 'nothing' which becomes the
substantive victor. 'The centre of love is diffused / and
the waves of love travel into vacancy' ('How to Kill'). It is
some such diffusion which takes place in 'The Sea Bird'
and 'Adams'. A ghost is the agent who introduces a man
to his shadow ('man and shadow meet' – 'How to Kill'),
the vulnerable body to the soaring ego of the spirit,
which commandeers the entire universe for *Lebensraum*
('towering like the cliffs of this coast / with his stiletto
wing') then creeps abjectly into death, or recklessly
commits self-slaughter. Douglas returns to the image
again in his very last poem: 'There is an excitement / in
seeing our ghosts wandering' ('Actors Waiting in the
Wings of Europe').

Ghosts mediate, then, between the visible and the
invisible, between that which is both desired and feared;
they are guides to the underworld, like Virgil in Dante's
Inferno, or the sages in Yeats's Byzantium poems. Thus
they are mirrors in which to read our own fate: 'Now in
my dial of glass appears / the soldier who is going to die'
('How to Kill') – 'appears' suggesting that the ghost
itself takes physical shape in the glass. The pararhymes
rest/ghost/exist in the last stanza of 'Adams' –

> Till Rest, cries my mind to Adams' ghost;
> only go elsewhere, let me alone
> creep into the dead bird, cease to exist

– underline the nexus of elation and horror that is at the
heart of the two poems, a celebratory dramatization of
joy and foreboding. For the bird/Adams figure can also
be construed as an aspect of Douglas's own ego: 'the live
bird discovered *me* / stepping from a black rock into the
air' (my italics). Detached for a moment from his body and
surroundings, he watches the flight of his own spirit,
engrossed and appalled by the ferocity of his ambition to
consume the universe. There is a further connection,
noted by Geoffrey Hill, between Adams' 'hollow bones'
and the figure described in the later poem 'Words':

> this stooping man, the bones of whose face are
> like the hollow birds' bones, is a trap for words.
>   . . .
> There are those who capture them . . .
> But I keep words only a breath of time
> turning in the lightest of cages – uncover
> and let them go: sometimes they escape for ever.

The contrast between the stooping man who traps words
and the poet who lets them go parallels to some extent
the contrast between narrator and subject in 'Adams'.
Words trap or release their meanings as the ego traps
the self or releases it into immortality/oblivion. But
whether we construe Adams as a brother officer or as an
aspect of the self, the antinomies remain inescapable.
Explanation itself becomes a scatter of cerebral wingcases,
squashed dead by the opposing army of contradictions.

> Consume my heart away; sick with desire
> And fastened to a dying animal
> It knows not what it is; and gather me
> Into the artifice of eternity.
> (W. B. Yeats, 'Sailing to Byzantium')

Creep into the dead bird, cease to exist.

There seems to be some doubt, incidentally, as to the
order in which the two poems were composed. *CP(PL)*
and *CP* print 'The Sea Bird' first; the latter has a note

[119]

stating that 'Adams' is presumably the later version, though dates (often misleading) on the MSS suggest otherwise'. *TCP* reverses the order on the evidence of the Texas MS, an autograph airletter to Blunden. The matter is of some signficance, from a critical as well as an editorial standpoint. Geoffrey Hill has said, 'In my estimation, 'Adams' is by far the finer of the two poems ... It is conceivable that Douglas composed 'Adams' first, and, for reasons best known to himself, decided later to break this almost-perfect poem down ... If there is the slightest chance that 'Adams' is the more authentic text that chance should be seized. And, although a delicate point of ethics is involved, I would feel sympathy for any degree of casuistry that resulted in this poem becoming widely known.' Graham hints at an opposite valuation ('Adams' is a 'more hazardly ambitious poem'), and also admits that if 'Adams' *is* the later of the two poems it goes against Douglas's normal practice, which was a matter of 'paring away material from an extensive first draft' rather than one of addition. Clearly both poems should be printed in any good edition, whatever the scholars finally decide. I incline to the view that 'The Sea Bird' is the finer achievement, partly because it is all of a piece. However puzzling the riddle posed by the bird, it is cognate with the riddle Douglas feels at the centre of his own existence. The puzzle represented by the man Adams is slightly different. His superiority, unlike the bird's, is not spiritual or metaphysical but largely social, a matter of 'elegant' pictures and facades.* The 'homage' he exacts is that due to an aristocrat. True, he is a

* The model for 'Adams' may be Lt-Col. J. D. Player, the 'Guy' of *AZZ*, a notoriously sharp dresser, and the most colourfully aristocratic officer in the regiment. If this is so, it links the poem with 'Gallantry', 'Aristocrats' and 'I watch with interest . . .' (*CP* p. 142). Douglas may have unconsciously associated the self-confidence of such figures – 'certain of homage from us all' – with his father (see Edgell Rickword's wise comments on Douglas's psychology in chapter V).

'marvel' of sorts and hence to be studied with some care, but his marvellousness is of a slightly different order from that of the swordfish or kingfisher, who are lords of creation, not of the country house and the officers' mess. 'The Sea Bird' refines away this social element, and the slightly clumsy egotism ('my sea', 'my mind'), and hence one term in the multiple identities of bird–Adams–Universe–self–ghost, leaving only the potent isomorphic flight of bird into ghost and self into death.

'Time, time is all I lacked . . .' says Douglas's last poem. The theme runs through a good deal of his juvenilia, and (as noted earlier) is echoed by his contemporaries, most notably by Sidney Keyes in 'Time Will Not Grant':

> Time will not grant the unlined page
> Completion or the hand respite . . .
>
> . . .
>
> Take pen, take eye and etch
> Your vision on this unpropitious time . . .*
>
> . . .

* *Collected Poems*, Routledge and Kegan Paul, 1945, p. 44. There are some striking similarities between the lives of Douglas and Keyes (1922–42). Both had soldier fathers, whom they hardly knew, and were brought up largely by grandparents (Keyes's mother died six weeks after he was born); both were rather solitary, bright, imaginative children who liked books and nature; both won scholarships to public schools (where an intelligent master encouraged them) and then to Oxford; both wrote accomplished poetry as schoolboys, and grew up to be somewhat prickly. At Oxford Keyes too had a foreign girlfriend (a German girl called Milein Cosman, who later married Hans Keller) with whom he fell one-sidedly in love, as Douglas did with Yingcheng. Keyes then became close to Milein's room-mate Renee, who found him 'goblinish', much as Betty Jesse found Douglas erratic and cynical. Keyes joined the Royal West Kent Regiment and also fought in North Africa, where he died in mysterious circumstances (possibly, like Alun Lewis, by his own hand) in the battle for Tunis. He was known to his men as Puss in Boots, a name which catches something of the soft swagger of his poems. See John Guenther's *Sidney Keyes: a biographical enquiry*, London Magazine Editions, 1967.

Keyes is a more literary, plangent sort of a poet than Douglas, but there is no doubting his promise. Douglas makes his most lasting peace with the subject in 'Time Eating', which gathers up earlier preoccupations (e.g. in 'A Mime'), and also points forward to such later meditations as 'Snakeskin and Stone'. It is a fine witty poem which manages to be both angry and utterly objective, like Donne grappling with the great abstractions of love and death. I have used the text given in *CP(PL)* and *CP* in preference to *TCP*. The latter substitutes 'bigness' for 'smallness' in stanza 2, line 2; and the cacophonous 'it's his art' for 'his effort' in line 3.

Ravenous Time has flowers for his food
In Autumn, yet can cleverly make good
each petal: devours animals and men,
but for ten dead he can create ten.

If you enquire how secretly you've come
to mansize from the smallness of a stone
it will appear his effort made you rise
so gradually to your proper size.

But as he makes he eats; the very part
where he began, even the elusive heart,
Time's ruminative tongue will wash
and slow juice masticate all flesh.

That volatile huge intestine holds
material and abstract in its folds:
thought and ambition melt and even the world
will alter, in that catholic belly curled.

But Time, who ate my love, you cannot make
such another; you who can remake
the lizard's tail and the bright snakeskin
cannot, cannot. That you gobbled in
too quick, and though you brought me from a boy
you can make no more of me, only destroy.

Time is seen as yet another marvel, like the swordfish, or the bird in the two kingfisher poems. The heavy reversed stresses of the opening – 'Ravenous Time' – contrasts with the lightness of touch in the second stanza – 'If you' – which will take a stress on either syllable, and which introduces the human element under a hypothetical sentence-form. Moreover what you discover will only 'appear' to be the case, 'secretly' guessed at and 'gradually' taken in, whereas time devours, eats, makes, gobbles in declarative short-order. The strangeness of 'stone' as an image of smallness is noteworthy (and it is not a very good rhyme for 'come'). It seems to combine the idea of a seed, from which we 'rise' to become the flowers that time eats, with that of a foetus curled like a pebble. It functions as one element in a dialectic about being and becoming, permanence and change, juxtaposing the hard certainties of the childish ego with the vulnerability of the adult. By stanza 4 the world itself has become a stone-shaped foetus, curled in the huge belly of time, which unmakes animals and men in a parodic mirror-image of maternal solicitude.

The casual mastery of the poem, as it proceeds to digest the volatile facts and paradoxes of experience, is highly impressive. The forceful diction and syntactical parallelism ('he makes he eats'; 'you cannot make', 'you who can remake', 'you can make no more'); the relishing vowels and *al dente* perfection of 'Time's ruminative tongue'; the piled-up stresses and sibilants of 'slow juice masticate all flesh' all make sound an important part of the sense. The rhyming couplets are neither tentative nor polished to incorrigible epigram but work argumentatively through to the close with complete assurance. At the centre of the poem is the image of a huge snake coiling on itself, suggesting a world in thrall to cyclical events. But whereas 'The Marvel' accepts and rejoices in the 'burning eye' of the sun, which 'concentrates all the energies of creation as

the poet does . . . proclaim[ing] a unified . . . cosmos'
(Longley, p. 16), 'Time Eating' adopts the dissident
posture of the outraged lover. 'Cannot, cannot' under-
lines the cycle, by repetition, and vehemently protests
against it.

Time can remake everything but not 'my love'. This
may refer to Yingcheng ('Yingcheng seems to linger
behind it,' *KD*, p. 120; Graham also quotes an interest-
ing first draft, showing how far the poem has come
from its clumsy beginnings), who has abandoned him
as Cressida did Troilus ('even the world / will alter'); or
to his own capacity for love, which has been destroyed
by the mutability and infidelity of the world he grows
up in. The final rhyme on boy/destroy recalls the child
turning into a man in the opening stanza of 'How to
Kill', who becomes a 'man of dust' damned by the
absence of love.

What is perhaps most jolting in Douglas's poems is
his steadfast antinomianism. 'Time and Death', those
two 'unnatural uncles on my track' ('A Mime'), are to be
feared and avoided, and yet are in their own way as
creative as love and life, their dialectical opposites.
They may be 'villains' but their villainy has a heroic
logic which exactly mirrors the processes and values we
applaud; their ceaseless decreative manufacture of
'ghosts' and 'skulls' and 'dust' is no less natural and
marvellous than the procreative forces they mimic and
oppose. Like Keyes and Lewis, Douglas was an admirer
of Rilke (see *KD*, p. 222), whose ideas of *der eigene Tod*
(a death of one's own) and *Weltinnenraum* (a world of
inwardness) were congenial to all three. This is the real
burden ('the beast on my back') of all the minute
descriptions of dead or wounded men wriggling and
writhing on the sand in a parody of birth and of sexual
desire; or 'abased' before their equipment ('Vergiss-
meinnicht') in a parody of prayer. For Douglas the true
'drop fences' are not bad luck or bad management but
the irrevocable and insoluble paradoxes and parallel-

isms built into every impulse to act, a verb which stares into the mirror of its own ambiguous face. Thus love and war are not polar opposites, or not only that, but two aspects of a single world of behavioural energy which would be fatally distorted and impoverished by any attempt at their logical disjunction. Look! the poems keep saying, the price of conciliation is death, our devoutest wish. This entails a particular view of poetic truth, which is overtly taken up in 'Snakeskin and Stone'.

As so often in Douglas, beneath or alongside the polarities of the poem there seems to run an assertion of identity, collapsing or contradicting the initial dichotomy. Poetry is identified with the subtle crypto-grams of the snake, and the truth it expresses with the irreducible hardness and simplicity of stone; 'the pebble is truth alone'. Unlike the stone image in 'Time Eating', which denotes a foetus or young child, 'the stone is old / and smooth, utterly cruel and old'. Furthermore the pebble is 'truth *alone*' (my italics), in a world governed by interrelations and complications. Then, in an abrupt change of image, snakeskin and stone become 'two . . . pillars. Between / stand all the buildings truth can make.' The bald head and public speech are lying facsimiles of stone and poetry, 'deserts' of untruth, peopled only by flies and dead words, as opposed to the 'city' of stanza 2, which accommodates the unsung heroes ('lovers / murderers, workmen and artists') of daily life who do not hide behind masks. In the next three stanzas Douglas develops and intensifies these analogies, trying to establish causal and moral connec-tions between public platitudes and private tragedy. The words that 'lie in rows' are columns of type in the newspapers, 'awaiting burial' by the poet's truth, just as the dead soldiers await literal burial by the living. Their stopped mouths give the lie to 'The speaker's mouth / . . . that sucks and spews them out / with insult to their bodies'. Such untimely mouths are 'a cold sea',

like the 'jewelled cerulean seas' that turn cold and grey
in 'On a Return from Egypt'; and the 'mariners' bodies
in the grave of ships' recalls the 'mariners who rotted
into ghosts' of 'The Marvel'. But they at least turned
into the 'hosts' of the living, caught up in the marvel-
lous cycle of death and rebirth, whereas the dead men
in 'Snakeskin and Stone' are the victims both of lying
elegies and of an unrequited inner lust. Their fate is to
be the victims of a halfway state – 'from the skin the
life half out' – which connects with the 'desert' of the
'bald head' lying midway between 'country of life and
country of death'. (Edna Longley sees it as an attack on
'the "bullshit" of in-between states . . . all that belies a
glowing skin'.) The poem ends:

> Borrow hair for the bald crown
> borrow applause for the dead words
> for you who think the desert hidden
> or the words, like the dry bones, living
> are fit to profit from the world.
> God help the lover of snakeskin and stone.

There are traces of Eliot here (the 'desert' and 'dry
bones' of 'Ash Wednesday'). And the contempt for
public platitudes is a little like that of Sassoon and the
First World War poets. These allusive traces are
symptomatic of the poem's uncertain organization, as is
the accumulation of heterogeneous imagery (which
includes most of Douglas's favourites, such as stone,
mask, house, sea-death and sea-change) and the
attempt to impose order and relationship on their
variety. There are clumsinesses of diction and syntax
too, suggesting that the poem is 'obviously unrevised'
(CP, p. 152). This in turn, if true, is probably because he
went on to work out the material broached here in
better poems, such as 'Desert Flowers', 'Landscape
with Figures', and 'Vergissmeinnicht'.

After the metaphysical flight of 'Adams' and 'The Sea Bird' Douglas's 'amazed mind' turns, in the *Collected Poems*, to consider the countries he finds himself serving in, and his own uncomfortable role as enforced tourist and possible killer. 'These grasses, ancient enemies' explores in typically dualistic fashion the beauty of Syria, a 'two-faced country' in which 'you think you see a devil stand / fronting a creature of good intention'. The two faces are those of peace and war, 'fertile' and 'vicious' respectively, productive of 'a mantrap in a gay house / a murderer with a lover's face'. It is an uneven poem, one which begins very well but is weakened by Douglas's readiness to abandon particulars for a somewhat facile dialectic between good and evil in the middle stanzas. A similar schematic baldness is visible in 'Bête Noire', whose dealings with heaven and hell parallel this poem's description of the 'interdependent state' of angels and devils. One learns to beware such terminology in Douglas's poems since it can so easily impoverish and oversimplify the experience it seeks to record. The obsession with duality is such that one might amend Owen's famous statement to read: The poetry is in the paradox.

The paradox with which this poem opens is, however, rooted in fact. For the soldier, grass *is* an enemy, since it can conceal snipers and other dangers. The paradox is increased by 'a movement of live stones', which are lizards of 'hostile miraculous' age. Thus the natural connotations of nature and fertility are reversed, as are those of miracles (the ghostly cousins of 'marvels'). Furthermore nature is set in opposition to the town itself, grass and lizard ever-ready to reclaim the 'gentle ornaments' of civilized beauty, handed down from generation to generation. At the same time there is a suggestion, familiar to us already in 'Snakeskin and Stone' and improved into art in 'How to Kill', that the 'ancient enemies' are also a metaphor for the soldier-self: the initial dichotomy is collapsed into a perception

of underlying unity between predator and prey, rein-
forced by the pun on eye/I, by which 'hooded eyes'
might also imply the hooded I. The second stanza is as
minutely convincing as the first, registering the topo-
graphy with concise precision, developing the mystery
of appearance and reality, and deepening the air of
appreciative apprehension. 'Green spurs' is a perfect
fusion of the visual and moral taxonomy governing the
best parts of the poem; it enforces both a visual and a
tactile contrast with the snow and the dark 'velvet
beauty' of the girls, playing off the sharpness of 'spur'
against the gentleness of 'populous ... fruit' and
ornamental beauty. This synaesthetic delicacy is con-
veyed in an equally delicate verse (octosyllabics and an
unusual five-line stanza, with an unrhymed last line)
which just barely heightens the rhythms of prose, yet
can also encompass the resonant marriage of syntax,
sense, and rhythmic inevitability of the final stanza.
The less convincing cerebrations of stanzas 3, 4
and 5 are signalled by a marked decrease in rhythmic
vitality –

> You think you see a devil stand
>
> . . .
>
> But devil and angel do not fight
> they are the classic Gemini
> for whom it's vital to agree –

lines in which the iambic thump snaps on the binary
handcuffs, and a whole country is tidied away into the
conceptual lock-up Douglas carries about with him into
mental battle.

The companion poem, 'Syria', deletes the last four
stanzas of 'These grasses ...' and substitutes two new
ones. This deletion of weak material is typically acute,
but it is a pity he could not have found a way to
incorporate the fine ending of his first version. Unfor-
tunately he also replaces 'green spurs' with the

anodyne 'green space'. The new verses, however, are certainly an improvement on the old ones:

> Here I am a stranger clothed
> in the separative glass cloak
> of strangeness. The dark eyes, the bright-mouthed
> smiles, glance on the glass and break
> falling like fine strange insects.
>
> But from the grass, the inexorable lizard
> the dart of hatred for all strangers finds
> in this armour, proof only against friends,
> breach and breach, and like the gnat is busy
> wounding the skin, leaving poison there.

This circles back to the poem's beginning, bringing back the lizard and ending with an image of death which prefigures the memorable last stanza of 'How to Kill'. The 'separative glass cloak of strangeness' is an interesting metaphor, combining several of his favourite themes – glass, which both distances and reflects; the cloak, which is part theatre prop, part mask – but one whose metamorphosis into 'armour, proof only against friends' is not altogether convincing. The irony of the last phrase recalls some parts of 'Bête Noire' ('takes a dislike to my friends and sets me against them / ... makes enemies for me'). It is not entirely clear either why some insects break against the glass, and others 'breach and breach ... leaving poison there'. In the first poem the enemy lizard parallels the atavistic impulses of the self, whereas here it is merely the enemy *tout court*.

The narrator's foreignness is his fatal weakness, a carapace which cuts him off from the 'dark eyes' and 'bright-mouthed / smiles' of the inhabitants. His glass cloak is protective and yet vulnerable to the (reciprocal?) 'dart of hatred' of 'ancient enemies', which are internal as well as external, 'a mantrap in a gay house', as the first version puts it. This is a variant of 'the

house that devils made' in his earlier poem 'The House':
'I am a pillar of this house / of which it seems the whole
is glass'. In the earlier poem too this glassiness reflects
his dilemma, symbolizing a 'queer magnificence' full of
'substances' and 'shadows', the 'beautiful strangers'
who seem to thrive on death, 'eyes turned to fine
stones'. Some form of armour is necessary to survive
but is fatal to emotional intimacy, including intimacy
with the self. Given, however, that a part of the self is
destructive, such armour is also a shield against
'mortal hurt' inflicted from within. Hence 'I am a
stranger', in 'Syria', is also self-referring, a confession
that he is a stranger to himself (like the lover-and-
killer of the war poems) as well as to others. It is this
antinomy, I think, that he grapples with in such images
as 'live stones' and the many lenses and mirrors and
glasses that reflect his troubled identity. The inexor-
able marvel is that such incompatibles should coexist in
'one body and one heart' ('Vergissmeinnicht'). In this
metaphysical context the trite phrase 'forget-me-not'
takes on a whole new significance, and so do the
particulars of the two Syria poems. Do not forget that
'wounding the skin and leaving poison there' is as
natural an activity as picking fruit, that 'bright-
mouthed smiles' can 'breach and breach', that grass
itself can turn into the 'vicious scrub' that conceals
death.

The two Syria poems are dated November 1941
(though the exact date of the second one is uncertain).
The next thirteen months were the most hectic of
Douglas's life, during which he fought from Alamein to
Zem Zem in the final offensive against Rommel's
Afrika Corps and its Italian allies. During this period
he wrote only ten poems, two of them love poems about
Milena, five of them continuations of his off-duty pieces
about the Middle East, two of them about preparations
for battle ('The Offensive 1 and 2'), and one slight
meditation ('Devils') lying somewhere between 'The

House' and 'Bête Noire'. Not until his wounding and hospitalization at El Ballah in January 1943 did he get the necessary time to think and write about his experiences. The six weeks of his convalescence, and the following six months of relative calm, saw the production of most of his major poems and the beginning of *Alamein to Zem Zem*. The ten or eleven months of January–December 1943 were thus the most richly creative of his life. It may well be that we owe his best work to the respite granted him by treading on a mine and narrowly avoiding death, an irony of circumstance that Douglas himself would no doubt have relished.

The first of his poems about Egypt is 'Egyptian Sentry, Corniche, Alexandria', a character study which might be called painterly, but one which quickly abandons externals for empathetic biography. Very occasionally, in letters home, Douglas patronizes or dehumanizes Arabs, but in none of his poems – which is to say, his best and deepest self – is there any trace of racism or English superiority. The sentry is seen as an emblem of stoic endurance and fatalism, falling from his mother's shoulder to the gutter, a 'millionaire' only of smells, impervious to pleasure and pain; yet representative too of the 'real or artificial race / of life, a struggle of everyone to be / master or mistress of some hour'. The poem is organized around the familiar contraries, 'heaven or hell', 'birth and dying', 'real or artificial', but is also rich in detail of the sort of unflinching, clear-eyed honesty that generates its own compassion. For all that the sentry is a 'statue', bent on surviving his 'monotone' existence, he is surrounded by all sorts of marvels, the 'animal smell' of the sea, the moon shining on water or stone, the 'stinks and noises' of a world crammed with possibility. Even his gun is companionable: 'rests / a hot hand on the eared rifle muzzle' is not altogether unlike the feeling of Lewis's marvellous line 'The killing arm uncurls, strokes the soft moss' in 'The Jungle'. The 'seizing limbs' of stanza 3

[131]

may be seized by disease and death, but have also reached out to seize the day, or at least whatever the gutter had to offer. When it comes, death 'lifts him to the bearer's shoulder' like a trophy, out of the gutter at last, on a level with the 'mother's shoulder' from which he fell. He represents the stony truths of 'Snakeskin and Stone', as the 'supple / women of the town' and the 'rich gutter' represent the cryptograms of complexity. The moon shines down on 'rich couples / . . . loving . . . sleeping . . . eating', as it does in the opening of 'Dead Men', or is 'shut out with slats'.

The line-ending which punctuates the 'struggle of everyone to be / master or mistress of some hour' suggests two modes of being within the single sentence, stoic quietism and endless conflict. The sentry stands at the edge of many things, or rather at a place where many edges meet, land and sea, moonlight and town-light, gutter and cabaret, mother and lover; he holds a rifle and croons a song; wears a tarbush with a 'khaki cover', a civilian disguised as a soldier, or a soldier steeped in civility. The three verbs that govern his life – standing, leaning, sleeping – are hypostatized into psychic geography, and made into a noun-like declension. The 'struggle . . . to be' is summed up in the paradox of the first and last lines, picturing a statue that sweats.

'L'Autobus' is a slighter piece whose lively observations are hitched to a somewhat conventional historicism, linking the schoolgirls with 'Odysseus' bond-women' and the stereotypical wiles of Alexandrian beauties through the ages. This scheme of reference buries the poem's energy in the sands of public-school Hellenism, despite such good things as the vivid sketch of the bus 'making bulldog grunts in its nose' and the 'neutralizing beam of holiness' of the nuns, who will have to cope with the grunts and the girls' twittering as best they can. The last-quoted phrase recalls Blake – 'Damn braces, bless relaxes' – reminding one just how

the aspirates and plosives dragging the line along in marked contrast to the sprightly opening, fusing once more (in 'dolour') mental and physical suffering. Ghosts don't normally demand food; elbows are not normally jogged by voices or ghosts; 'you and I / and the table' are not normally seen as items of the same logical furniture; informal and formal registers ('blind of an eye', a tautology which is not tautological; 'heavy with habitual dolour') are not normally employed side by side – but the poem assimilates everything in its path with casual ease. As well as suffering from glaucoma, her very self is blinded by poverty and disease. Beggar or prostitute or both, she too struggles to be 'master or mistress of some hour', like the figures in 'Egyptian Sentry', but is defeated at every turn by forces beyond her control. The 'fine / clash' – synaesthesia, oxymoron, enjambement and spondee fused in two expressive syllables, if you will forgive the pedagogy – of events results in the moving summary of stanza 4, whose syntax and rhymes make plain the repetitive burdens of this ancient fifteen-year-old. As in 'Vergissmeinnicht', this penultimate verse is almost hymnlike. The poem tracks back from close-up to longshot, before ending in an angry yet compassionate diagnosis. Ugliness and beauty play the same dialectical parts here that love and death play in the war poems. The last stanza, like the first, employs four pararhymes. 'Cloud', in 'cloud / of disease' (whose repeated sibilants pick up the 'sinful taste' of the opening), suggests something like a cloud of flies or the biblical cloud of pestilence, contrasting with the 'God ... king ... country' triumvirate that looks complacently on at such horrors. Hughes's 'casual speech' is matched by the seemingly casual versification, which is in fact a series of variations played over an octosyllabic base. There is just one regular line in the whole poem, the last line of the first stanza. Though the girl herself 'knows no variety' (in ironic contrast to the 'infinite variety' of Shakespeare's Cleopatra?), the rhythms of this vignette are as supple as the voice in conversation. G. S. Fraser wrote a poem of the same title, which makes an instructive comparison:

> Who knows the lights at last, who knows the cities
> And the unloving hands upon the thighs
> Would yet return to seek his home-town pretties
> For the shy finger-tips and sidelong eyes.
>
> Who knows the world, the flesh, the compromises
> Would go back to the theory in the book:
> Who knows the place the poster advertises
> Back to the poster for another look.
>
> But nets the fellah spreads beside the river
> Where the green waters criss-cross in the sun
> End certain migratory hopes for ever:
> In that white light, all shadows are undone.
>
> The desert slays. But safe from Allah's justice
> Where the broad river of His Mercy lies,
> Where ground for labour, or where scope for lust is,
> The crooked and tall and cunning cities rise.
>
> The green Nile irrigates a barren region,
> All the coarse palms are ankle-deep in sand;
> No love roots deep, though easy loves are legion:
> The heart's as hot and hungry as the land.
>
> In airless evenings, at the café table,
> The soldier sips his thick sweet coffee up:
> The dry grounds, like the moral to my fable,
> Are bitter at the bottom of the cup.

This is decently competent verse, but compared with Douglas's economy and penetration its rhythms, perceptions and ironies – 'the heart's as hot and hungry as the land' – are monotonous and pedestrian. Similarly if one compares Terence Tiller's 'Egyptian Beggar' or

'Egyptian Dancer' with Douglas's swift evocations in
'Egypt' or 'Cairo Jag' or 'Behaviour of Fish . . .' one
realizes afresh just how powerfully original and incisive
his poetry is. Tiller's elaborate phrases are not much
more than a set of leaden western responses to the
words 'belly dancer'. Hardly a phrase conjures the
dancer's physical presence. When he reaches for com-
parisons and metaphors – 'the drift of the sandspout
the wavering / curve of the legs' – they are simply too
vague and imprecise to be convincing. There is more
eroticism in Douglas's single observation 'Slyly red lip
on the spoon/ / slips in a morsel of ice-cream' ('Behav-
iour of Fish . . .') than in the whole of Tiller's 'shrieking
desire of the flesh'. Douglas was fully alive to sexual
pleasure but never falls into heartlessness or inflation,
as he might easily have done if he were as unfeeling as
some of his critics have maintained. Cairo and Alexan-
dria have always been full of variegated delights, never
more so than in war-time, as Lawrence Durrell testifies
in his novels, and again in the memoir he contributes to
an anthology of Middle East writing (Victor Selwyn *et
al.*, eds., *Return to Oasis: War Poems and Recollections
from the Middle East 1940–1946*, Shepherd-Walwyn,
1980, p. xxiii.):

> The country basked in its fictitious neutrality, the shops
> were crammed, the cinemas packed; the Allied armies
> marooned here sharpened their claws in preparation for
> the desert battles to come, but in fact it seemed
> extraordinary to live in such oriental splendour with a
> battlefield which was only an hour's drive away. The
> cities had been declared 'open'. Cairo was one blaze of
> light all night long. The phrase 'fleshpots of Egypt' took
> on a new meaning when one saw such fortunes being
> made and spent by army contractors . . . People flown out
> from bombed and rationed England stared aghast at the
> bulging shops, the crowded nightclubs, the blazing
> lighted thoroughfares of Cairo – made all the more
> grotesque by the glaring poverty of the *fellaheen*, by the

beggars which flocked everywhere ... The sores, the leprosy, the smallpox, syphilis and bilharzia completed the throbbing panorama of the night life with its swirling *souks* and tinsel brothels.

It is against this phantasmagoric background, with its shifting whirlpools and cosmopolitan agglomeration of intellectuals and artists ('. . . Cairo became a brilliant intellectual centre. It seemed at times that every poet and painter from London was in our midst'), that Douglas's Middle East poems should be set. Cavafy and Seferis both contributed to *Personal Landscape*, the magazine run by Robin Fedden, as did Bernard Spencer, Olivia Manning, Robert Liddell, Durrell, Tiller, Fraser and Douglas himself. Other poets who served in the North African campaign included Hamish Henderson, Sorley Maclean, Ian Fletcher, John Waller, and F. T. Prince, whose famous poem 'Soldiers Bathing' is set on the Mediterranean coast. But although much was written about the war in the desert, very little of it is of lasting interest. Apart from Douglas himself and some portions of Hamish Henderson's elegies, which I shall return to, the only desert poetry of any distinction is Norman Cameron's 'Green, Green is El Aghir', a wry celebration of small mercies that has only tangentially to do with war, and the little-known Patrick Anderson's 'Desert', reprinted in Robin Skelton's *Poetry of the Forties*:

Hereabouts is desert, it's a bad country,
grows nothing, nothing to show for, sand has no
   whereabouts,
goes everywhere and nowhere like a sea:
yes, I said, and noticed the flash of sun on grit
and knew that all the hourglasses in the world had
   broken
and this was the sum of all the hours of the world.

Did you ever see a man bleed in sand? I
asked him, did you ever see a soldier, a khaki
hero with his life blood blotting entirely and quickly

into the khaki sand? Did you ever see a man drown in
   quicksand
or, let alone a man, a tree or a bedstead?

It's not just that there's so much of it, he said,
nor the bitter heat of it nor its blinding glare
but it's the shiftlessness, that there's no purpose here,
nothing but a blanket warming a blanket, or a sum
multiplying and dividing itself forever, a sum
adding and subtracting itself for ever and ever.

The middle stanza recalls the fate of Peter in Douglas's
'Aristocrats' and his original in *Alamein to Zem Zem*;
and the casual prose rhythms are also reminiscent of
'Cairo Jag' or 'Words'. It lacks Douglas's formal skills
and organizing intelligence, but the laconic, colloquial
tone ('grows nothing, nothing to show for') and vivid
imagery ('nothing but a blanket warming a blanket')
effectively catch the place and the time and the
arbitrariness of the soldier's existence. The sand will
bury a tree or a bedstead as readily as it will bury a
man; the sum of things is that there is no sum.

Douglas's next off-duty piece is 'Mersa', set in a small
town in Libya. He wrote it in a lull before the fighting
anticipated in 'The Offensive', and the final assault on
Tripoli. It is written in the same deceptively casual
style as 'Egypt' and 'L'Autobus', one which neither
salutes nor disregards the disciplines of metre and
rhyme but adapts them to his own purposes, rather as
the men themselves went into battle in a mixture of
official uniforms and raffish personal variation:

> This blue halfcircle of sea
> moving transparently
> on sand as pale as salt
> was Cleopatra's hotel:
>
> here is a guesthouse built
> and broken utterly, since.
> An amorous modern prince
> lived in this soured shell. . .

[139]

The 'amorous modern prince' is presumably Farouk, whose 'scoured shell' is in direct line of descent from Cleopatra's sumptuous palaces and Aphrodite's birthplace, in the famous painting by Botticelli. Now it is simply part of a bombed town; the image links death and sexuality again, suggesting that a single impulse lies beneath them both. The 'halfcircle of sea' recalls the 'demiarch' of the two Adams poems, through which the narrator puzzles over the mystery of the live and the dead bird. 'Cherryskinned', in the third stanza, picks up both the colour and the uncomfortable tautness of the soldiers' sunburnt skin, and gives them an air of seeming innocence as they 'idle on the . . . beach', though they are a part of the mechanism that has 'broken' the 'guesthouse' and made a 'skeletal town', exposing its secrets to 'wind' and 'dust'. This time the puzzle lies in the town itself, 'whose masks would still / deceive', and in the fate of its despoilers, who have exchanged peace for war, gossip for a dead tank.

Another frame of reference is the one mapped and discussed in the 'Soldiers Bathing' section of Paul Fussell's classic study *The Great War and Modern Memory* (Oxford University Press, 1975, pp. 299–309). Fussell traces the symbolic uses of this theme – soldiers momentarily released from war, stripping off to swim and relax – from Brooke's sonnet ('swimmers into cleanness leaping') to the blackly comic death of Kid Sampson in *Catch-22*, who is chopped in half by McWatt's plane as he stands up on the raft in the bay. Such scenes recur 'not because soldiers bathe but because there's hardly a better way of projecting poignantly the awful vulnerability of mere naked flesh. The quasi-erotic and the pathetic conjoin in these scenes to emphasize the stark contrast between beautiful frail flesh and the alien metal that waits to violate it. . . . These latter-day soldier boys of Douglas and Prince and Kirstein and Heller are objects of concern . . . because they are surely doomed.'

The contrast between hard metal and vulnerable flesh is one that Douglas never ceases to register. Poem after poem juxtaposes the two, tracing links between inner and outer 'doom', and providing a critique of the ethos which allows war an honourable role in human affairs. Death falls 'Into the ears of the doomed boy, the fool / whose perfectly mannered flesh fell / in opening the door for a shell / as he had learnt to do at school' ('Gallantry'). The Colonel praises such 'heroes' for their bravery, 'But the bullets cried with laughter, / the shells were overcome with mirth.' In 'Mersa' the houses threaten too, become frighteningly reductive avatars of the human face, like the faces in a Brueghel painting or the mask of Cheng's face in 'The Prisoner'; they have been stripped of their covering to reveal what lies beneath, and the soldier-lovers have come to poke fingers in wounds of their own making. Death is omnipresent, both in the 'immensely long road' that goes on to Tripoli (memorably described in *Alamein to Zem Zem*), and even in the innocent pastime of swimming. The 'I' of the poem only makes one appearance, in the last stanza, and is instantly seen by the 'logical little fish' as 'one of the dead'. The ubiquitous stone-image is used here to convey the appearance of his white feet underwater. The fishes' logic is akin to that of the wild dogs in 'Dead Men' finding 'meat in a hole'; they too 'converge' to 'nip the flesh', just as the lover and killer converge in one man to satisfy his material, emotional and spiritual needs. The word 'Now', common to this poem and 'How to Kill', is used as a mental fulcrum or resting point (as 'Tonight' is in 'Dead Men', and 'today' in 'Vergissmein-nicht') from which to view the past and predict an all to certain future. It occurs again in 'Behaviour of Fish . . .': 'But now the ice-cream is finished, is / paid for'. *Now* has paid whatever it costs to reckon up history, psychology, and biology to find the sum of things.

'Cairo Jag' is partly an evocation of the city and its fantastical inhabitants, partly a meditation on the marvels of this particular war, in which soldiers are metamorphosed into tourists and tourists into corpses. It might almost have been called 'Correspondences': 'it is all one' whether you get drunk or eat cake, indulge in casual sex or dedicate yourself to 'dull dead' love, like Marcelle, shriek or beg, dance or sleep. Tragedy and comedy are interchangeable, like the echoing phrases 'stamped *Décédé*' (deceased) and 'stink of jasmin'. Whichever 'conventions' you choose to read the evidence by, whatever drug you favour – drink or sex, 'fatalism' or 'hashish', love or death – whether you reach for a bundle of letters or of rags, whether you live sleeping ('somnambulist') or sleep dying 'scattered on the pavement like rags' it all amounts to the same bewildering fate, signed and decreed by 'Holbein's signature', the skull. Just an hour or two away from all this, however, is a 'new world' which parodies both the world of nature ('gun barrels split like celery', 'metal brambles', 'all sorts of manure') and the fleshpots of Cairo. Here the logic of desire has been taken to its ultimate conclusion. There is neither sense nor propriety in this brave new world, in which men trade their lives for 'a packet of chocolate and a souvenir of Tripoli'. Imagination here is of the essence: 'you can imagine the dead themselves' mirrors the logic of the little fish in 'Mersa', 'imagining I am one of the dead'. It suggests at least two possibilities, the imaginative rehearsal of one's own death, and the idea that in death men are most 'themselves', at one with the 'triumphant silence of the dead'.

'Jag' is used in the sense of 'spree' or 'drinking bout' (*SOED*), and also picks up associations of fragmentariness and sharpness from 'jagged'. The collocation of death and photography ('she has all the photographs . . .') is something I have already remarked on in *Alamein to Zem Zem* and 'Vergissmeinnicht'.

This distancing effect is used again later in the poem with the introduction of Holbein's signature, the skull, naming the unnameable (which is also what 'stains' the 'white town') by periphrasis. Death is not an experience we can know, only one we can imagine. Thus 'you can imagine / the dead . . . / clinging to the ground', as Marcelle clings to her letters and photographs, and the dead themselves cling to their chocolates and souvenirs. The 'mauve ink' of the official stamp, and the dead men's tinselly mementoes, are in one sense more real, because more comprehensible, than the subject of which they are the literal and metaphorical predicates. Beneath the heterogeneous images, the poem's anger and pathos, there runs a network of implications about the values we live and die for, the links between 'mundane conventions' and the 'new world' of fearful symmetries implicit in their adoption. (The symmetries are brought out more clearly in a longer draft of the poem sent to Olga Meiersons. See *TCP*, pp. 136–7.) The scene described at the close has some affinities with the no-man's-land of the First World War, insofar as both are unnatural, man-made desolations; and there is a corresponding trace of Sassoon or Graves, perhaps, in the writing. But the poem also underlines the enormous gulf between the two wars, and between the attitudes of the two generations that fought them. Thanks to modern technology it is possible to be a soldier and a tourist at the same time. Likewise it is possible to be a moral tourist, almost an anthropologist, noting the customs of the natives and of oneself, but committed to no more than a sardonic description of either. Not that Douglas is ever a complete relativist. If anything he is rather too wedded to the conceptual apparatus that he wields, finding comfort in explanation and symmetry, however comfortless the paradigms he is compelled to adopt.

The obvious comparisons to make are with his gentler contemporaries Alun Lewis and Philip Larkin, both far from being optimists, yet both abjuring Douglas's brand of intellectual impatience; or with the American poet Louis Simpson. What one might call the predatory side of Douglas's gift, hungry for confirmation of the worst yet powered by a soaring imagination, is the one inherited by Hughes. If it is true, as Hill suggests, that Douglas keeps changing holds to get a better grip on his experience, we must not think so much of a mountaineer patiently inching his way up a chimney or an overhang as of a geologist or mapmaker shuttling between the field and the laboratory, trying to get a proper match between sample and theory. In his best poems there is precisely that 'balance or reconciliation of opposite or discordant qualities . . . of . . . the idea, with the image . . . a more than usual state of emotion, with more than usual order' that Coleridge speaks of in his famous description of poetic imagination.

The two love poems of this period, both inspired by the loss of Milena to Norman Ilett, are 'The Knife' and 'I listen to the desert wind'; and these too wrestle with problems of explanation and reconciliation. (A tender drawing of Milena asleep is reproduced in *KD*, p. 160.) 'The Knife' – an oblique title for a love poem, related to the 'enquiring blade' of 'The Marvel', perhaps – celebrates his pleasure in familiar images, interiors, caves, a blessed sea, stones, islands, and sea marvels. All this is 'explicable as a waterfall', which is to say dazzlingly inexplicable: 'Your hair . . . / fell across my thought' and 'in a moment' becomes 'a garment I am naked without'. Physical pleasure is such that 'in your body each minute I died', though 'moving your thigh could disinter me / from a grave in a distant city'. So far, so orthodox: the little deaths of sex and the larger death-wish of the soldier are countered by the marvels of love. Inner and outer meet in fruitful union: the caves of the flesh are not threatening or demonic but loving exits and entrances which 'filled me with tears, sweet cups of flesh'. The tears *are* sweet cups of flesh, just as the 'blessed sea' and 'fine day' reflect the 'dream' of love, or 'hair' and 'thought' become members of the same logical family, 'swooning in elements without form or time'. The shock of betrayal comes in the final stanza:

> This I think happened to us together
> though now no shadow of it flickers in your hands
> your eyes look down on ordinary streets
> if I talk to you I might be a bird
> with a message, a dead man, a photograph.

The shock is made all the stronger by its casual introduction, and by the unexpectedness of the images of grief. The 'bird / with a message' is much like the live and dead bird of 'Adams' and 'The Sea Bird', and the silent omens discussed in connection with those poems. The message is linked to 'a dead man, a photograph', which is to say a spectral image bereft of 'interiors' and hence of danger and delight. The word 'now' comes again into the reckoning ('now no shadow of it flickers'), homophonically back-to-back with 'no'. Periphrasis works for utmost pain as well as pleasure: 'it' refers back to 'This', which in turn goes back to the marvels of the preceding four stanzas. 'Shadow' cleverly prefigures the bird image which is yet to come in the last two lines; she steps back into her ordinary self as the live bird crept back into the dead bird, 'ceased to exist', while he is still aloft, uttering his desolating cry of the knowledge of death. 'Man and shadow meet' ('How to Kill'), and this meeting is a 'photograph' of the psychic world.

'I listen to the desert wind' is closer in tone and organization to a conventional lyric and is possibly the finest of the lost-love poems, though 'cruel' in stanza 2 is a nudge-word, and the opening lines of 4 and 5 are adapted from Auden. ('All the elements agree' echoes Auden's 'O all the instruments agree' in his elegy 'In Memory of W. B. Yeats'.) Here the 'elements' of 'The Knife' have changed their magnetic field from positive to negative; stars, moon, wind, cloud are as indifferent to his fate as she is. Her face is now only a 'reflection', like a photograph, or thought unmodified by her bodily presence. The setting has changed from enchanted sea to pure desert, and the 'bird' of his 'sleepless eye' (cf. 'I') neither soars nor creeps but remains forever parallel to the hot and cold sands of its environment, as the lover's mind stays cruelly awake to his rejection. Like Cressida she 'denies her former way', and yet in doing so she merely complies with her own being as one of nature's marvels, 'wonderful and hard' as the stars and moon, which never stoop to poke their fingers in human wounds. The 'swarthy mistress' of the close recalls Shakespeare's dark love in the sonnets, and also the 'swart flies' of 'Vergissmeinnicht', feasting on the dead. Almost every line is a sentence; the language is simple and the rhythms repetitive; each quatrain hammers out one cluster of pararhymes (eight successive ones in stanzas 3 and 4; and the last returns to the same consonantal rhyme as the first, minus the terminal 'd'). The 'last / and most of love', as he puts it earlier in 'The Two Virtues', is to turn the 'drowned heart' itself into yet another marvel, 'that stone, that jewel tranquillity'. Such consummations are easier to arrive at in an intellectual exercise such as this early poem than in the aftermath of Yingcheng's or Milena's real-life behaviour; yet Douglas really does aspire to what he says. Since the elemental is by definition unalterable, ruling over a world of marvels made in its own image; and since, in Yeats's words, 'all is from antithesis', each wondrous particular being a union of 'substance and shadow', marvel and anti-marvel, given to metamorphic reversal without notice, it would be morally and intellectually futile not to bite on the consequences. Childish not to love, for fear of getting hurt, and equally childish not to recognize that pleasure entails pain. The toughness is a product of his honesty. The affront to liberal sensibilities occasionally posed by

Douglas's attitudes springs from his recognition that energy is eternal delight, and that in the personal life selfishness is the last sincerity – not social selfishness but the sort that Lawrence urged against Russell and Moore and the abstract sterilities of Cambridge, or that Yeats invokes in his 'Prayer for Old Age': 'God guard me from those thoughts men think / In the mind alone; / He that sings a lasting song / Thinks in a marrow-bone.' No doubt a preturnatural eye for 'bullshit', such as Douglas's, carries its own built-in dangers, but he stops well short of pharisaism or self-mutilation. One way and another all his poems, including the love poems, echo the old proverb that seeing is believing. Hence his alertness to every last nuance of poeticism and falsification, which, in the words of his letter to Hall, 'is dangerous to oneself and to others'.

The feeling of being an outsider, explored in the two Syria poems, is taken up again in a group of three poems set in Jerusalem and Tel Aviv. The first of them, 'Saturday Evening in Jerusalem', records the sight of happy families and friends on a summer evening, 'a collaboration between things / and people' from which the poet feels entirely excluded. I have used the last line of the *CP(PL)/CP* text, which is slightly different from *TCP*.

> But among these Jews I am the Jew
> outcast, wandering down the steep road
> into the hostile dark square:
> and standing in the unlit corner here
> know I am alone and cursed by God
> as if lost on my first morning at school.

The rhyme scheme breaks down (Jew/school), and 'cursed by God' is rather baldly hyperbolical. No doubt personal disappointment played a part; he had learnt recently that Kristin, his youthful love, was now married, and that Milena had become officially engaged to Norman Ilett. While on leave in Tel Aviv with Olga he also read in the newspaper of the death of Colonel Kellett (Piccadilly Jim). So the poem pits the fragility of love ('we whose drug is a meeting of the eyes') against human indifference and 'the many heads of war'. The history of his relationship with Olga is somewhat complicated; Graham says that she soon settled into the role of friend and confidante, rather than that of lover, especially while his infatuation with Milena ran its course (*KD*, p. 149). The latter was 'one of these women in the world who send me mad', from whom he rebounds back to Olga: 'ours is an understanding, and I think we love each other ... I don't like, almost I hate and fear many Jews [Olga was of Latvian-Jewish descent] – yet I feel more and more that in the end it will be a Jewess I marry. Probably from constantly suffering real or imagined injustice, I have acquired something of a Jewish mentality myself.' The holiday with Olga, then, coming after his double wounding by Milena and the mine which put him into hospital, was something in the nature of a return from the dead. The image with which the next poem 'Tel Aviv' opens, therefore, has an extra touch of appropriateness: 'Like Ophelia in a pool of shadows lies / your face, a whiteness that draws down my lips'. (In *CP(PL)* and *CP* her face is 'a flower that draws down my lips'. This version also contains an extra stanza.) The simile is partly literal, and partly the conjuration of a submerged parallel between Hamlet's rejection of Ophelia and Douglas's complex feelings towards Olga, whose white face recalls the 'white stone ... on the seafloor of the afternoon' of 'Behaviour of Fish . . .' The tensions between Ophelian innocence and carmined experience, together with those we have already seen associated with glass and submarine life, of houses and walls (stanzas 3 and 4), reflect the poet's uncertainty vis-à-vis Olga and his treatment of her. They are not exactly lovers, who can refer backwards and forwards to past and future intimacies (the old and new buildings

[148]

of stanza 3), nor are they not lovers, but in some strange area between the two; 'not unaware' of their disparate minds and worries, yet finding 'this evening . . . heavier / than war' because of their problematical youthful entanglement. The final stanza tries to wring coherence from this confusion; he does not want to use her, nor to destroy their friendly independence, yet is immensely hungry for something more:

> Do not laugh because I made a poem
> it is to use what then we couldn't handle –
> words of which we know the explosive
> or poisonous tendency when we are too close. If
> I had said this to you then, BANG will
> have gone our walls of indifference in flame.

Lines 3 and 4 may refer back, as Graham suggests, to something Douglas had written Olga earlier in a letter: 'As you see, I am as bitter and sickened as you are . . . When we meet it'll be good for us both if we do more kissing than talking' (*KD*, p. 190). The rhyme joins 'poem' and 'flame' together in action, which will verbally and sexually destroy the stasis of 'indifference' and mutual independence. The capitalized BANG underlines the extent to which Douglas constantly draws parallels between lover and killer, the battle-fields of war and human relations. (Cf. the capital-ized NOW in 'How to Kill'.) To act is always to penetrate or be penetrated, motivated either by love or hate or some irreducible mixture of the two. Such action will result in the destruction of 'our walls of indifference', which shelter the ego as the walls and proscenium arch of the theatre shelter the spectator from the events onstage. Douglas's honesty compels him to recognize that he inhabits both worlds simul-taneously, and in both his roles as soldier and lover. He is 'the figure writhing on the backcloth' ('Landscape with Figures'), impossibly trying to unite action and inaction in a single metaphor of catharsis, writhing like a snake that has itself been penetrated by the stony truth of death, or the bird and mosquito that fuse with their own shadows.

The themes of the two poems are tackled again in 'Jerusalem', 'This is the Dream' and the version called 'I Experiment' in *CP(PL)* and *CP*. 'Jerusalem' draws explicitly on the theatrical metaphor I have just mentioned ('Now the dark theatre of the sky / encloses . . . the whole city'), and also sets the lovers between the poles of 'movement' and 'wonder'. The opening stanza of 'Tel Aviv' becomes stanza 2, followed by a new and more explicit version of stanza 3: 'But now, and here / is night's short forgiveness / that all lovers use' – as they use each other too for emotional and physical gratification. This is certainly an improvement on the oblique imagery of angels and pinpoints in 'Tel Aviv'. And the word 'Now', which introduces the last stanza, is once more the price that will have to be paid for leaving their seats and becoming actors in their own drama.

'This is the Dream' is virtually a blueprint of the typical Douglas obsessions; its links with the other love poems and war poems are clear both in its organization and characteristic imagery. The 'tinkle . . . buzz . . . BANG' crescendo acts out an etiolated abstract version of the dialectical sorcery that is so richly particular in 'Vergissmeinnicht', 'Dead Men' and 'How to Kill'. The Audenesque 'Adventures' are those of love ('Discoveries of sea creatures / and voices') and war, the everlasting 'cycle' of action and inaction, played out against a 'lurid / decor' of faces and spirits. The 'finale' to all his role-playing is 'the moment my love and I meet' – a formula which mirrors the meetings of mosquito and shadow, man and ghost, live bird and dead bird, elsewhere. Since the poem tells us nothing about who or what 'my love' is, and the final image of 'the rose of love' is similarly bereft of context (apart from the earlier 'pot pourri' of the mind), the ending is not particularly illuminating. The poem's detachment, reflected in its alternative title 'I Experiment', means that everything is seen as from a great height, and in considerable weariness of spirit. The self-protectiveness becomes self-regarding, reducing 'happiness and pain' to stage counters.

Back in England in early 1944 he wrote his last short meditation on the women he had loved, 'To Kristin Yingcheng Olga Milena':

> Women of four countries
> the four phials full of essences
> of green England, legendary China,
> cold Europe, Arabic Spain, a finer
> four poisons for the subtle senses
> than any in medieval inventories.
>
> Here I give back perforce
> the sweet wine to the grape
> give the dark plant its juices
> what every creature uses
> by natural law will seep
> back to the natural source.

The swift reduction to 'essences' displays his impatience to classify, the 'finer ... / poisons' his love of paradox. In the second stanza he finds new images for the 'natural law' of loss, pivoting now on the word 'Here'. Every creature uses and is used. The 'dark plant' of line 3 suggests various possibilities, including nightshade, grape vine, and metaphorically the 'dark secret love' of Blake's 'The Sick Rose'. Whichever, the 'dark plant' yields 'sweet wine'. Much as 'the body can fill / the hungry flowers' in 'Desert Flowers', so the lover-scientist 'perforces' gives back his distillations to the natural cycle to which all living things are subject. 'Creature' nicely bridges the animal, vegetable and human world; the used ('One who owes his position to another' – *SOED*) and the creative user, the alchemist who looks for the philosopher's stone of love. By now Douglas can look back with some equanimity to the 'natural source' of all pleasure and pain. This quiet coda took six successive drafts to achieve (*KD*, p. 240). It represents a sort of tidying-up of his emotional affairs before the final carnage of the Normandy landings.

I want to go back now to the two poems called 'The Offensive', which act as prologue to the eight or ten major poems of 1943 on which Douglas's reputation stands. Alternative titles were 'Midnight, Wadi Natrun' and 'Reflections of the New Moon in Sand', the latter of which carries a strong premonitory charge. The moon occurs so frequently in his poetry that it is tempting to look for some consistent symbolism in its use, but I think he simply draws on its traditionally rich associations with the wonders of existence. 'I look back as to a period spent on the moon, almost to a short life in a new dimension,' he wrote of his Middle East experience. There are obvious connections between the aridity of the moon and that of the desert, and between it and the 'new dimension' entered by someone who falls in love or takes part in a battle. Moreover a desert moon has its own distracting splendour, from which the eye is not solicited by cloud or wood or sea. The landscape thus lends itself to hard-edged allegory and the dream world of psychic prophecy and fable.

The title Douglas settled on is close to that of one of Owen's finest poems, 'Spring Offensive', but where that deals with all three phases of a battle, anticipation, offensive, and aftermath, Douglas's much slighter piece deals only with the first. It is constructed around some of his favourite polarities, and broods 'in a passion / of foreboding' on what the coming battle of El Alamein will hold for him. As Graham says, it is 'an outsider's poem' (*KD*, p. 162), written before he had taken part in any fighting, but it contains one excellent stanza:

> So in conjecture stands
> my starlit body. The mind
> mobile as a fox goes round
> the sleepers waiting for their wounds.

The starlight is literal and a natural metaphor for mystery and fate, too far off to 'descry' with the certainty of interpretation. The image of the mind as a fox (anticipating Hughes's later thought-fox) brilliantly fuses the idea of the restless imagination wondering which soldiers and friends will be wounded or killed with the suggestion that it is the mind itself which ultimately inflicts such wounds, a worried circularity of thought emphasized in the pararhymes mind/round, stands/wounds. The repetition of stanza 5, with its pun on 'piece' and peace, underlines the theatrical metaphor and the poet's unavailing attempt to write his mental review in advance of the spectacle. It is clear, however, especially in part II, that he is already armed with dialectical apparatuses and preconceptions, all ready to grapple with the ultimate 'test' of war. If this sounds limiting, the point must be to some extent conceded; Douglas's weaker poems are victims of their own explanatory mechanisms ('all our successes and failures are similar'), which can work to exclude the vivid particularity on which all poetry depends. But this shifting relationship between form and content is one that is common to all writers. 'You can refute Hegel but not the Saint or the Song of Sixpence', Yeats memorably remarks in a late letter, contrasting abstraction with incarnation. Apart from one or two local and transitory borrowings in youth Douglas is not at all a Yeatsian poet, but like the great Irishman he packed more and more lived experience into the forms and cadences he had slaved to perfect as a young man.

TCP prints a significantly different version of 'The Offensive' from that of the two previous editions, breaking it into two poems and adding an extra stanza to the second. None of the drafts, however, is particularly satisfying or coherent. (Part II rehearses ideas which find a superior expression in 'Time Eating' and 'Snakeskin and Stone'.) By the time he came to write 'Dead Men', though, he had undoubtedly come of age. The poem gathers together all his shards of innocence and experience and locks them into a cyclical structure which combines great delicacy and strength, pity and pitiless self-knowledge. It is also the completest statement he had yet achieved of his antinomian view of the forces of creation and destruction:

> Tonight the moon inveigles them
> to love: they infer from her gaze
> her tacit encouragement.
> Tonight the white dresses and the jasmin scent
> in the streets. I in another place
> see the white dresses glimmer like moths. Come
>
> to the west, out of that trance, my heart —
> here the same hours have illumined
> sleepers who are condemned or reprieved
> and those whom their ambitions have deceived;
> the dead men, whom the wind
> powders till they are like dolls: they tonight
>
> rest in the sanitary earth perhaps
> or where they died, no one has found them
> or in their shallow graves the wild dog
> discovered and exhumed a face or a leg
> for food: the human virtue round them
> is a vapour tasteless to a dog's chops.
>
> All that is good of them, the dog consumes.
> You would not know, now that the mind's flame is gone,
> more than the dog knows: you would forget
> but that you see your own mind burning yet
> and till you stifle in the ground will go on
> burning the economical coal of your dreams.

Then leave the dead in the earth, an organism
not capable of resurrection, like mines,
less durable than the metal of a gun,
a casual meal for a dog, nothing but the bone
so soon. But tonight no lovers see the lines
of the moon's face as the lines of cynicism.

And the wise man is the lover
who in his planetary love revolves
without the traction of reason or time's control
and the wild dog finding meat in a hole
is a philosopher. The prudent mind resolves
on the lover's or the dog's attitude for ever.

This comes to the very edge of cynicism and despair,
yet Douglas keeps a miraculously sure balance as he
picks his way between the awful facts. 'Hours ...
illumine', in stanza 2, suggests appropriately enough a
book of hours, in which canonical texts are accompanied
and illustrated by brilliant symbolic icons. So here we
have a graphic moral primer on death and love with
corpses centre stage and a supporting cast of white
dresses, wild dogs, guns and mines, reason and time and
love, set against a velvet background of moonlit night.
The same hours illumine (literally by the light of the
moon, figuratively by the light of human need and
aspiration) the most diverse experiences, whether the
white dresses and exotic scents of the city, the pow-
dered dead rotting in the desert, or the dog following its
appetites as naturally and inevitably as the lover who
follows his. The two extremes of 'planetary love' and
'meat in a hole' (suggesting (i) buried corpses; (ii) flesh
in a fix; (iii) sexual consummation) characteristically
meet and merge into a single category, exemplifying a
wisdom beyond 'reason or time's control'.
Is the speaker of the opening, who sees the moon as a
pandar, standing literally in Cairo among the finery of
women or 'here' in the desert where another kind of
'doll' is available for contemplation – or shuttling in

imagination between the two? 'I in another place' suggests, but doesn't specify, some metaphysical standpoint above and between the various possibilities, looking down objectively at the tangible and intangible facts which make up the self, including its simultaneous impulses towards detachment and involvement. The city-experience may be a 'trance', as opposed to the 'sanitary earth', but the blandishments of the 'west' lead also to a variety of sleep in which condemnation and reprieve look very much alike. The wild dogs, seeing off the vapour of human virtue, are a grimly literal instantiation of Time Eating. 'Virtue/vapour' is exactly right, reductive in the manner of some of Hamlet's speeches yet paradoxically affirming the value of that which they deny.

The white dresses glimmering 'like moths' are subtly recalled in the 'mind's flame' of stanza 4, which 'till you stifle in the ground will go on / burning the economical coal of your dreams'. The metaphor is both lyrical and sardonic: dream as you may, you will eventually stifle – an active, transitive verb for the stasis of death. Similarly the move from 'I' to 'you', first to second person, remains self-referential. The grammar of the poem performs the same balancing act as its concepts and logic, all in the present continuous tense, jostling difference against unity, visible against invisible, the particular against the universal. Even the coal is from Douglas's antinomian stockpile, 'economical' in two senses because (i) you will always dream, until you die, and (ii) you will tailor your dreams to suit the brutal reality in which you live. Similarly the love who 'revolves' like one of the planets is both majestic, at one with the cosmos, and merely going round in circles, a gratuitous collection of mental and physical states subject to the twin logics of 'food' and 'good'. The teasing paradoxes and cycles are even reflected too in the rhymes, lover/revolves/resolves/ever, which play phonological and anagrammatical games with each other.

The word 'doll' is cognate with all those other images taken from ballet and theatre and concert hall that are found throughout Douglas's poems. From the mummers and marionettes of early pieces to the 'effigy' of 'Poor Mary' and 'Song: Dotards . . .' to the 'demon' of 'Vergissmeinnicht' and the 'fallen . . . dancers' of 'Enfidaville', actors, wraiths, spirits, phantoms, mimes, waxworks and the like offer their impersonations of humanity, dramatizing the pathos and theatricality of action, which lives in dialectical harness with its opposite, inaction and death. 'Doll' is an interesting – and almost unique – variation on this image, all the more convincing for its casual accuracy, and for not owing any obvious debt to Douglas's schematic system of contraries. Much as a doll aids and abets a child's imagination, so the dead call up a similar exercising of the poet's power to look before and after. Here it is powdered with a maquillage of dust, put on by the wind that bloweth where it listeth, pointing backwards to childhood and forwards to death. There is no question now, as there was in 'A Ballet', of saying 'I don't like this dance'. Since it is the only dance there is, the question is rather what attitude the 'prudent mind' will adopt towards it, that of the lover or the dog; and whether prudence is any more to be trusted than white dresses, or bones, or dreams.

> All in different degrees
> embody the celestial thing
> and the wise man will learn of these
> analysis in worshipping.

Thus the early 'Extension to Francis Thompson', 'these' being the 'natural laws' of life. What analysis discovers in 'Dead Men' is 'nothing but the bone / so soon'. Should death itself, then, be the object of our worship? No, 'leave the dead in the earth' for they are not 'capable of resurrection'. The grimly humorous contrast with the resurrection of mines (one of which had nearly killed

[157]

the poet) is echoed by the tone of the final sentence, which undermines certainty even in the act of announcing it. The 'I' cannot be tethered to a single point of view, dog's or lover's, any more than it can be tied to a single place or time. Like 'The Sea Bird' it soars and it creeps, as the scenes in this poem are correspondingly seen in close-up and longshot: 'you see your own mind burning yet' ('yet' too is momentarily ambiguous, out on the end of the line – adverb or conjunction?) and so cannot help identifying with the virtue of life, which is to burn and be burnt, even as you identify also with the fate of the dead.

Guns can become fetishes too, no less than dolls or the planets in which we invest our 'fate'. 'Dead Men' takes a cool and passionate look at all the options and settles for a traditional wisdom-in-sadness, finding the ultimate prudence in surrender to the polymorphous needs of the self. There are just eight regular iambic pentameters in the poem's thirty-six lines, most of them uttering orthodoxies ('and those whom their ambitions have deceived', 'who in his planetary love revolves') which are questioned and jostled by the surrounding irregularities – e.g. 'the dead men, whom the wind', which refuses to be metrically varnished, and whose brevity may owe something to Eliot's practice of using longer and shorter lines over a pentameter base. By such means Douglas finely renews the lyric voice in verse which is 'fighting fit', as Edna Longley says, yet alive to every emotional nuance which comes its way.

'The Trumpet' and 'Gallantry' are transitional poems, pointing forward to 'Aristocrats' and 'How to Kill'. The first was published in the *Times Literary Supplement* of June 1943 under the title 'The Regimental Trumpeter Sounding in the Desert', and perhaps answered to conventional expectations of what the new generation of war poets should sound like. Arcturus is the brightest star in the Great Bear, and in

Greek means literally 'the Bear-guardian'. As I re-marked earlier, the poem's anti-war theme is essentially a minor variation on Owen's 'Dulce et Decorum'. In finding a voice in which to speak credibly of war, Douglas had to combat purplish tendencies ('men dressed to kill in purple') on two fronts, substantive and formal. 'Gallantry' is an interesting dry run for the finely achieved compassion of 'Aristocrats', those fools and heroes who constituted a sub-class of marvels that never ceased to amaze their subordinate officer-poet.

Once into their vehicles the only communication between tank commanders is by radio, and the opening of 'Gallantry' parallels scenes that are described in detail in *Alamein to Zem Zem* (see chapter 17, pp. 110–15). Douglas does not tell us what the Colonel's joke is, but implies that it leads to the ultimate joke of death. 'Doomed' is repeated in successive lines; the well-mannered child is father of the well-mannered subaltern, both doomed to the battlefield's peculiar brand of *noblesse oblige*, and hence to obsolescence. This anticipates the 'child turning into a man' of 'How to Kill', who similarly finds that the ball has turned into bullet or a bomb. The description of Conrad's death in stanza 3 – 'only his silken / intentions severed with a single splinter' – exactly prefigures the manner of Douglas's own death in Normandy just over a year later. 'Silken' refers to his impeccable manners, perhaps, and to their inutility in the face of modern warfare. The next stanza is even better, though weakened by a stiffly regular last line and the slightly pompous formality of 'surmise'. By the close Douglas has exchanged his own inimitable voice for a satirical one derived from Rickword or Sassoon. Where 'Aristocrats' holds exacerbation and applause together in admirable poise, 'Gallantry' dissipates the tension in surreal irony. (But see the opposing view of Lt-Col. John Stubbs, who particularly liked this poem and its last stanza. 'That really did, that caught the feeling of what it was like, the noise, the chattering and screeching noise of that shell and ammunition whirring through the air. He really portrayed the thing.' *PN Review*, 47, vol. 12, no. 3, p. 28.)

One notable feature of the desert war, commented on by many of the soldiers of both sides, was lack of hatred for the enemy. Rommel and his Afrika Corps were respected, even liked and admired, by the Allied troops. There were few or no atrocities. Prisoners of war were well treated and often exchanged. 'The troops confronting each other . . . were relatively small in numbers. In the early stages . . . they were to a large extent forced to live off each other. Motor transport, equipment of all kinds and even armoured fighting vehicles changed hands frequently. The result was a curious 'doppelganger' effect . . . enhanced by the deceptive distances and uncertain directions of the North African wasteland . . . After the . . . campaign had ended, the memory of this odd effect of mirage and looking-glass illusion persisted, and gradually became for me a symbol of our human civil war, in which the roles seem constantly to change and the objectives to shift and vary. It suggested, too, a complete reversal of the alignments and alliances which we had come to accept as inevitable. The conflict seemed rather to be between "the dead, the innocent" – that eternally wronged proletariat of levelling death in which all the fallen are comrades – and ourselves, the living . . .' Thus Hamish Henderson, in the Foreword to his *Elegies for the Dead in Cyrenaica* (John Lehmann, 1948, reprinted *EUSPB*, 1977, p. 59). Another poet-combatant, Sorley Maclean, speaks of the desert's 'cold on winter nights, its sandstorms and occasional Khamsins . . . It prolonged little cuts in desert sores, and though the glitter and mirages of mid-day sometimes stopped the firing, they could also lead astray, as the sandstorms could too, and being led astray could sometimes mean death or captivity. It was a good battleground in that there was little of human achievement in it that could be destroyed except soldiers themselves and human means of destruction. The combatants were as if abstracted from a real world to fight on a remote moon-like terrain, and in general the only bitterness against the "enemy" was when a soldier got news of deaths of his near and dear by civilian bombing at home' (*ibid.*, Introduction to 1977 reprint, p. 10). The general picture is confirmed – though he calls the struggle 'brutal' – by a German witness. 'The war in Africa is quite different from the war in Europe. It is absolutely individual. Here there are not masses of men and material. Nobody and nothing can be concealed. Whether in battle between opposing land forces or between those of the air or between both it is the same sort of fight, face to face; each side thrusts and counter-thrusts. If the struggle were not so brutal, so entirely without rules, one would be inclined to think of the romantic idea of a knight's tourney' (from the war diary of Lieutenant Schorm, Afrika Corps, 1941; Desmond Flower and James Reeves, eds., *The War 1939–1945*, Cassell, 1959, pp. 232–3).

Douglas never entertained such romantic ideas, though he does once liken the pursuit of retreating tanks across the desert to a fox-hunt, in *Alamein to Zem Zem*. Henderson and Maclean both confirm the accuracy of his prose and poetry. They even use similar images, such as the 'moon-like terrain', the 'looking-glass' effects of desert war, and what Henderson calls 'our human civil war', in which the conflict is between the dead and the living, and in the very mixed feelings of the individual soldier, rather than between abstract ideas of good and evil. Even the 'enemy' is put in inverted commas, as though the notion was archaic and faintly embarrassing. It is in this context, then, that Douglas is able to identify so unhesitatingly with the 'lover and killer' on either side of the lens of war, the

[161]

'burning eye' that looks inwards as naturally as it looks out towards its supposed enemy and prey. Henderson's 'Second Elegy' attempts to evoke just this fusion at its close:

> The Sleepers toss
> and turn before waking: they feel through their blankets
> the cold of the malevolent bomb-thumped desert,
> impartial
> hostile to both.
>
> The laager is one.
> Friends and enemies, haters and lovers
> both sleep and dream.

The elegies contain some interesting and vivid detail, and a moving compassion for the dead, but are seriously weakened by inflation and Eliotesque ambition, as the symptomatic reference to the 'North African wasteland' implies. MacDiarmid too is a discernible influence, but unfortunately it is the posturing Marxist 'intellectual' side of that fine poet that Henderson chooses to imitate, abandoning particulars for portentous historical juxtaposition.

Despite the fellow-feeling that undoubtedly existed between the opposing forces, it would be sentimental to endow them with contemporary pacifist attitudes, or to underestimate the actual carnage that took place. John Pudney's account of the aftermath of the battle of Alamein makes this very clear:

> Below them stretched death and destruction to the very horizon. Shattered trucks, burnt and contorted tanks, blackened and tangled heaps of wreckage not to be recognized; they scattered the landscape as thickly as stars in the sky. Like dead stalks in the sand, rifles were thrust upright – a denuded forest. And each one meant a man who had been maimed or killed . . . (*ibid*., p. 474.)

Perhaps it is a tribute to the sanity of Douglas and his contemporaries that they were able to remain free of nationalism and hatred in the face of such experiences as this. Pudney concludes his description with a poem whose lack of distinction does not disguise its essential continuity with Douglas's 'Vergissmeinnicht':

Graves: El Alamein

> Live and let live.
> No matter how it ended,
> These lose and, under the sky,
> Lie befriended.
>
> For foes forgive,
> No matter how they hated,
> By life so sold and by
> Death mated.

Passing over 'Desert Flowers' for the moment, which is in some ways Douglas's profoundest epitaph on the war, the next important poem is 'Enfidaville', where he rejoined his regiment after his hospitalization and convalescence. The town had been devastated by shelling. Douglas learnt of the 'new scale of fighting' that had developed while he had been out of action (*KD*, p. 197). His regiment was waiting to go into battle again, in the attempt to join up with the encircling Allied armies in the last push towards Tripoli.

> In the church fallen like dancers
> lie the Virgin and St. Thérèse
> on little pillows of dust.
> The detonations of the last few days
> tore down the ornamental plasters
> shivered the hands of Christ.
>
> The men and women who moved like candles
> in and out of the houses and the streets
> are all gone. The white houses are bare
> black cages. No one is left to greet

the ghosts tugging at doorhandles
opening doors that are not there.

Now the daylight coming in from the fields
like a labourer, tired and sad,
is peering about among the wreckage, goes
past some corners as though with averted head
not looking at the pain this town holds,
seeing no one move behind the windows.

But already they are coming back; to search
like ants, poking in the debris, finding in it
a bed or a piano and carrying it out.
Who would not love them at this minute?
I seem again to meet
the blue eyes of the images in the church.

It is the most directly tender of all his poems,
completely free of irony or self-accusation. The rhyme
scheme is an unusual one for Douglas, ABCBAC until
the last stanza, which alters slightly to ABCBCA. As in
'Dead Men' the prosody too is variable, playing varia-
tions on octosyllabic, pentameter and trimeter lines.
Once again the poem pivots on the word 'Now' half way
through, dividing past from present, shattered houses
and ghosts from daily labour, gratuitous violence from
the benign art of Christian iconography. These 'fallen
. . . dancers' do not bleed emblematically like those in
'A Ballet', for they have fallen 'on little pillows of dust',
an image at once visually exact and morally compas-
sionate. 'Shivered the hands of Christ' reminds one
subtly of the crucifixion, as well as of the literal effect of
'detonations'. Hands, and the sense of touch, often play
an important part in Douglas's poems: 'which of us will
catch tears in our simple hand?' ('Point of View'); 'our
hands move out . . . / certain they hold the rose of love'
('This is the Dream'); 'Today . . . I touched your face /. . .
as a gesture love' ('The Prisoner'). So the twice-
splintered 'hands of Christ' are guarantors of mercy

and love, even though the saints have fallen and the Lord's name is set to rhyme with 'dust'.

The simile which opens the next stanza is not so much visual (though perhaps the men's white burnouses are being likened to tall white candles) as emotional, linking the moving figures with the devotional practices in church, and with silence and fragility. 'Perched on a great fall of air', like the 'pilot or angel' of 'Landscape with Figures', both the saints and the human beings are subject to the twin forces of creation and destruction, physically embodied in the 'white houses' of hope and the 'bare / black cages' of despair. Are the 'ghosts tugging at doorhandles' inside or outside the houses, and where have they come from? In my discussion of 'Adams' I suggested that a ghost is the agent who introduces a man to his shadow, mediating between life and death; they are what is left when 'the centre of love is diffused / and the waves of love travel into vacancy' ('How to Kill'). 'Enfidaville' enacts a declension from saints and Christ to men and women, from men and women to ghosts, from ghosts to 'daylight . . . with averted head'. Presence and absence change places: the saints are passively sleeping, the men and women 'all gone', whereas their ghosts are actively tugging and opening 'doors that are not there'. The house of the self has become a black cage from which the spirit has escaped, vainly seeking reentrance. Stanza 3, employing the same so-called pathetic fallacy as Eliot's *Preludes* ('Morning comes to consciousness . . .'), movingly describes the wreckage as seen by the labourer of daylight 'coming in from the fields' –

> not looking at the pain this town holds
> seeing no one move behind the windows.

The second line fuses absence and presence in an image reminiscent of the ghost of 'Poor Mary' trapped behind glass in the house of her withered self. It is all the more

[165]

effective for unhitching 'no one' from its usual hyphen. In the final stanza the people return to their homes to claim what is salvageable, and the poem similarly circles back to 'the images in the church'. They too have been dispossessed, turned out of the house of God to earn their keep in a world of 'wreckage' and 'pain'. Their symbolic potency is not lessened but increased by this fate, since it exactly mirrors that of the human world they preside over. The last two lines enact another meeting, of the sort we are familiar with in 'Vergissmeinnicht', 'Dead Men' and 'How to Kill'; this time, however, Douglas meets not another version of himself but 'the blue eyes ... in the church'. The meeting is qualified by 'seem', and by the double refraction of 'eyes of ... images', but is none the less as affirmative as the close of Larkin's 'An Arundel Tomb'.

'Aristocrats' is published in *TCP* under the title 'Sportsmen', for reasons Graham gives in his Notes (*TCP*, pp. 139–40), notably the inference that the British Library MS 'is later than the version in an autograph letter to Tambimuttu 11 July 1943'. He also defends his text, which differs significantly from *CP(PL)* and *CP*, on the grounds of its 'metrically more regular third stanza, more precise title, and misdating of Player's death'. None of these points is entirely convincing, or cogent enough to justify printing a decidedly inferior version of one of Douglas's best-known poems. The new title is narrower but no more precise. Graham's third stanza is indeed more 'regular' than Tambimuttu's, but he has substituted an inferior last line ('The fool and hero will be immortals' for 'Each, fool and hero, will be an immortal'). I accept the substitution of 'fading' for 'falling' in line 3 of the stanza (see *KD*, p. 279), and the new lineation, but otherwise find the accepted text much more satisfying than that printed in *TCP*, and accordingly retain it here.

The unfinished poem printed as 'Fragment' in *TCP*, and 'I Watch With Interest, For They Are Ghosts' in *CP(PL)* and *CP*, is an obvious forerunner of 'Aristo-crats'. It sketches out Douglas's mixed feelings towards his superior officers both in images – 'ghosts', 'skeletons', 'gypsies', 'gentlemen' whom 'Time ... behind their backs turned ... to smoke' – and in discursive analysis: 'I feel the hand of pity on my heart / shaken by their fealty to the past.' He adds 'Look, / their gestures...' in the manner of 'Vergiss-meinnicht's' 'Look. Here in the gunpit spoil...'; impartiality as between friend and enemy, each sum-med up in their possessions and postures, could hardly go further. But he abandoned this first attempt at a portrait of 'the noble lunatics', and then made his definitive version a month or so later. 'Never was such antiqueness of romance' wrote Graves in 'Recalling War', and it is this theme which Douglas takes up and explores:

Aristocrats

'I think I am becoming a God'

The noble horse with courage in his eye
clean in the bone, looks up at a shellburst:
away fly the images of the shires
but he puts the pipe back in his mouth.

Peter was unfortunately killed by an 88:
it took his leg away, he died in the ambulance.
I saw him crawling in the sand; he said
It's most unfair, they've shot my foot off.

How can I live among this gentle
obsolescent breed of heroes, and not weep?
Unicorns, almost, for they are fading into two legends
in which their stupidity and chivalry are celebrated.
Each, fool and hero, will be an immortal.

The plains were their cricket pitch

and in the mountains the tremendous drop fences
brought down some of the runners. Here then
under the stones and earth they dispose themselves,
I think with their famous unconcern.
It is not gunfire I hear but a hunting horn.

The ghosts and gypsies of the first attempt are replaced
with the much more powerful image of the 'noble horse
. . . / clean in the bone'. For those familiar with
Douglas's poetry, and perhaps even for those who are
not, the word 'bone' implicitly introduces intimations of
death. Horses (which, incidentally, he loved) have
time-honoured associations with war in all the arts,
from Homer and Renaissance painting and sculpture
through to Picasso's *Guernica*. The Sherwood Rangers
was itself a cavalry regiment whose senior officers were
more at home on the back of a horse, hunting or
fighting, then they were in the turret of a tank.
Piccadilly Jim, it will be recalled, was killed while
standing up in his tank – as it were in the stirrups –
shaving. 'Shellburst' and 'shires' alliteratively yokes
together the incongruities, and so does the surreal
notion of a horse with a pipe in its mouth, like a parody
of a gun. Stanza 2 is probably based on *Alamein to Zem
Zem*'s account of Robin in chapter 8:

> Presently I saw two men crawling on the ground,
> wriggling forward very slowly in a kind of embrace.
> As I came up to them I recognized one of them as Robin,
> the RHA Observation Officer whose aid I had been
> asking earlier in the day: I recognized first his fleece-
> lined suede waistcoat and polished brass shoulder titles
> and then his face, strained and tired with pain. His left
> foot was smashed to pulp, mingled with the remainder of
> a boot . . . I spoke to Robin saying, 'Have you got a
> tourniquet, Robin?' and he answered apologetically: 'I'm
> afraid I haven't, Keith.'

The tone of this is exactly preserved in the poem by the
adverb 'unfortunately', and by the plethora of under-

stated pronomic constructions: 'Peter was . . . it took . . . he died . . . I saw . . . he said . . . they've shot'. Peter's reported speech comes *after* the dryly factual noting of his death, so that the speech is as though delivered by a dead man, or a ghost. 'Crawling' relates him to the dead men of 'Landscape with Figures' who 'wriggle' on the sand, and the narrator 'writhing' in futile anguish; yet in another sense of the word he doesn't crawl at all, but heroically understates his plight. The third and fourth stanzas, with their echoes of Owen ('Weep, you may weep, for you may touch them not' – 'Greater Love') and Sassoon, bring the poem close to the ironic-elegiac modes of his Great War predecessors. The last line, too, for all its gruff scansion, is instinct with Owenesque nostalgia ('And bugles calling for them from sad shires' – 'Anthem for Doomed Youth'). It may well be this aspect of its appeal which has made it, together with 'Vergissmeinnicht', Douglas's best-known poem.

The 'fool and hero', seen inevitably in tandem, is the obsolescent equivalent of 'Vergissmeinnicht's' up-to-the-minute 'lover and killer'; yet the poem resists, until its last line, the luxury of single vision and simple sadness. Cricket pitches and runners and drop fences were the staple language of radio code, as boyishly native to English officer-unicorns as they were easily decipherable, one would imagine, by German intelligence. In using this public-school lingo for his peroration, Douglas achieves a delicate fusion of tones of voice, mimicking the officers' stiff upper lips and yet uttering a wholly sincere tribute to their 'famous unconcern' – a phrase as sharply accurate as it is paradoxical:

> Here then
> under the stones and earth they dispose themselves,
> I think with their famous unconcern.

The two-way suggestiveness of 'dispose' ('the verb blending graceful disposition and the disposal of their bodies'; *KD*, pp. 201–2) and the pun on dis-pose; the languid qualifier 'I think' and the decreative form of the noun *un*concern', leaving 'famous' spotlit in the middle of the line; and the blending of colloquial and formal rhythms, with slight caesuras after 'earth' and 'think', provide a countermovement to the elegiac swoon of the close. This ending reminds one of Geoffrey Hill's charge against Owen's 'Anthem for Doomed Youth', that 'irony in this poem cannot alter the fact that he takes thirteen lines to retreat from the position maintained by one' ('I in Another Place: Homage to Keith Douglas', *Stand*, vol. 6, no. 4, p. 7). The justice of this may be partly granted, and yet counted somewhat rough. Is civilian mourning to be forbidden, or counted as 'mockery', because men died 'as cattle'? Is Douglas's poem likewise vitiated by inadmissible or inappropriate pity? I suspect it is the tenor of resigned acceptance in Owen which Hill jibs at (compare the 'Wiped jaws of stone' of his own 'Funeral Music'), yet what in this realm would count as adequate, and who is to legislate? Since there is nothing new to be discovered, we make what tautological noises about death we can.

The poem's epigraph, 'I think I am becoming a God', is attributed to the Roman emperor Vespasian by Suetonius: 'Nothing could stop [his] flow of humour, even the fear of imminent death . . . His death-bed joke was: "Dear me! I must be turning into a god"' (Graves's translation). Vespasian was brought up by his grandmother and fought both in Britain and in Cyrenaica, the scene of Douglas's own desert war. Presumably the application here is to the 'immortals' of the title, who die in the service of their own sublimely self-sufficient values. Their reticence, especially in the face of death, parallels Roman stoicism; and the 'hunting horn' of the fox meet is their appropriate Last Post. It has also been suggested by the editors of *CP* that the horn is a deliberate echo of the scene of Roland's death at Roncesvalles in the *Chanson de Roland*. Perhaps no single poem of Douglas's has been so often misinterpreted as this one, or used more often as evidence of his supposed attachment to outmoded values. G. S. Fraser, for example, says 'the aristocratic morality, evoked in this poem, was the morality to which in the depths of his nature Keith Douglas was most profoundly drawn' (*Essays on Twentieth-Century Poets*, Leicester University Press, 1977, p. 219). This is almost as unperceptive as his pronouncement on 'Behaviour of Fish . . .': 'One doubts that *that* is a good poem.' In fact Douglas is absolutely clear-eyed and unsentimental about his fellow officers; he weeps *at* their stupidity as well as *for* their doomed bravery. To confuse this honest appraisal of their vices and virtues – and it is absolutely typical that he insists on both – with an identification with their code is to flatten and distort the subtlety of his art. (Fraser's judgement is echoed by Alvarez, Crossley-Holland, Hamilton, Fuller, Carey and others – see chapter V.)

I have referred often to 'Landscape with Figures' in discussions of other poems but not so far considered it in its own right. Each of the three poems is a sonnet (the third having an extra line), in which the sestet rhymes EFG, EFG after the manner of French sonnets. I think the poems should be printed as such, with spaces between the quatrains and tercets, as in Douglas's translations of Rimbaud. Parts I and II are a companion poem to 'Desert Flowers', attempting to summarize the feel of the war and Douglas's place in it. As the title suggests, human beings are almost incidental to this landscape, no more important than the squashed and stunned beetles their hardware soon resembles. It is the 'plain' which 'discerns' the lunatic ecology of warfare after 'the haze settles'. The godlike viewpoint of the opening swiftly changes to baffled close-up; and the ironic rhymes of the sestet – come/ tomb, wounds/fronds, posies/explosive – underline the replacement of the natural world by one dedicated to artificiality and death. The Doubting Thomas who comes to 'poke fingers in the wounds' is perhaps the poet himself as much as it is the reader, fascinated to know what death looks and feels like. Part II focuses unremittingly on the familiar, obsessive paradoxes: the dead 'wriggle', their 'aims' no more than 'mimes' of silence and futility. They are actors who find themselves 'at a queer angle to the scenery' – queer physically and morally, since they are less heroes than failed actors whose fate is emblematic of the larger struggle between engagement and detachment, itself a product of the unsigned antinomian script. All the images insist on the unreality of the supreme reality, personified as the anonymous prompter 'who opens his mouth and calls / silently'. This could be either the dead calling out to the dead, or the poet-witness, who is 'the figure writhing on the backcloth' impotent to affect or penetrate the mystery being acted out in front of him:

> The eye and mouth of each figure
> bear the cosmetic blood and hectic
> colours death has the only list of.

The sentence is at once self-important and offhand, offering to tell us something crucial and then trailing off to end in a preposition (a type of construction that has almost become a cliché in contemporary poetry, forty years later). There is no doubting its mimetic power to engage and repulse; 'hectic' beckons us compulsively on, only for us to find ourselves fobbed off with the abstraction we had hoped to circumvent and get inside. 'A yard more' repeats the process; once there the most we can do is to trace the make-up on a stone, held at arm's length as ineluctable spectators. The mirror-images multiply in reciprocal parody – vehicles like insects, metal like vegetation, air like iron, steel like gauze, ritual ('posies') like 'lunatic' madness, men like insects ('wriggle') or actors whose incompetence is their highest skill, death like an over-enthusiastic make-up artist, volition altogether motionless – but not one catches a trustworthy likeness of the 'I', whose suffering is both real and yet purely vicarious.

The grotesquerie culminates in the collision of 'maquillage' and 'stony', flesh and blood as mere make-up disguising the stony reality of the skull; and in a complex image of the poet writhing in a horrible parody of the living and the dead, not quite of either party, 'at a queer angle to the scenery' like an angel or a devil, perhaps, or the twin masks of comedy and tragedy on the theatre curtain, or a ghost hovering about the collapsed walls of the self, trying to tug open doors that are not there. Everything is frozen as in a *tableau vivant*; yet the very strength of the exertion of impersonality bears witness to a passionate involvement. The 'figures' of the title might almost be art-school illustrations, after the manner of 'The Hand', 'the imaginary true focal / to which infinities of motion and shape are yoked', and the narrator's helplessness a 'drilling of the mind' in useless rehearsal of death.

Part III assembles a large cast of 'angels and devils . . . / the arguments of hell with heaven' and analyses the self in the same dialectical terms used later in 'Bête Noire'. In both cases the fable is too schematic for comfort and the pressure of feeling drops, not because of any conscious dishonesty but because the triteness of the terms excludes any real play between experience and analysis. '. . . Not passing from life to life / but all these angels and devils are driven / into my mind like beasts': I take this to mean that his will is paralysed by disbelief, a stasis induced by multiple antitheses. For the moment the contraries lead to no progression.

For all their differences as men and poets, there are interesting similarities between Douglas's predicament and that of his fine contemporary Alun Lewis. 'Accept-ance seems so spiritless, protest so vain,' he wrote. 'In between the two I live' (letter to his wife Gweno, *In the Green Tree*, George Allen and Unwin, 1948, p. 36). This is close to the spirit of Douglas's letter to Hall: 'I suppose I reflect the cynicism and the careful absence of expectation (it is not quite the same as apathy) with which I view the world . . . To . . . admit any hope of a better world is criminally foolish, as foolish as it is to stop working for it.' Both disliked many aspects of army life, especially the officers' mess. 'I get tired so quickly of the conventional life of the Mess, the officer-mind and its artificial assumptions, the rigid distinctions of rank which so rarely go with quality and character, the back-biting and watching each other that is a seething obbligato to our daily bread' (*ibid.*, p. 31). Yet both saw service as inevitable. Douglas's view of 'the experience of battle' as 'something I must have' is echoed in Lewis's 'I want to run the gamut . . . They [the men in his battalion] seem to have some secret knowledge that I want and will never find out until I go into action with them and war really happens to them. I dread missing such a thing' (Ian Hamilton, ed., *Alun Lewis: Selected Poetry and Prose*, George Allen and Unwin, 1966, p. 56). This was prompted by his refusal of the offer of a safe Staff job, which parallels Douglas's desertion of his Staff post to rejoin his regiment. Lewis, essentially a socialist and a pacifist, is content to let war 'happen' to him rather than go belligerently in search of it, but his motives for fighting, his enjoyment of 'the boyish pleasure of it all – and the unreality of it also' (*In the Green Tree*, p. 55), his search for 'a robustness in the core of sadness. What else is there by which we can live now?' (*ibid.*, p. 22), and his self-analysis – 'I've got the enemy of life inside me' (Hamilton, p. 35) – are all close to Douglas's own experience. He grapples with the same problems of moral and poetic integrity, and with the same dead-weight of paradox, dramatized in his short story 'The Orange Grove': '. . . it became a struggle between himself and the corpse, who was trying to slide off his back and stay lying in the road.' Lewis shoulders the corpse, whereas Douglas would

like to get the beast off his back. None the less both
identify the enemy as something interior which will not
let them rest. Both too shared premonitions of early
death. 'He often thought he'd die; it was a familiar idea;
why shouldn't he, if there's a war on and you're young
and you try to be in it, somewhere? He'd got into the
army easy enough, but the war seemed to elude him all
the time . . . he'd think of the Eighth Army glowing in
the desert, attracting him like a moth to its fiery circle'
(*In the Green Tree*, pp. 85–6). And, in another letter to
Gweno: 'Death is the great mystery, who can ignore
him? But I don't *seek* him. Oh no – only I would like to
"place" him. I think he is another instance of the
contrary twist we always meet sooner or later in our
fascinations . . .' (*ibid.*, p. 39). That 'contrary twist' is
precisely the burden of many of Douglas's best poems,
and is there, too, in many of Lewis's poems and stories.
There is a superb description in the latter's journal, for
example, of the killing of a snake:

> We killed a wonderful Russell's viper, *so* beautiful, too
> cold in the early morning to writhe away quickly enough:
> and the dew glistened on its lovely diamonded skin. We
> also started a ten-foot snake from the long grass and G.
> had three shots at it as it flickered across the clearing. He
> got it: and it curled up slowly and raised its fine little
> head above its shattered body and stared at us inscrut-
> ably until the Colonel slashed it with his stick and it was
> dead. (*Ibid.*, p. 54)

The incident is not analysed at all, and yet is so charged
with feeling ('A highly civilized soul would *feel* the
connexion'; Hamilton, p. 20) as to make of it a fable, the
lover and killer staring his own handiwork in the face.
The snake recurs in section II of Lewis's fine poem, 'The
Jungle':

> But we who dream beside this jungle pool
> Prefer the instinctive rightness of the poised
> Pied kingfisher deep darting for a fish

To all the banal rectitude of states,
The dew-bright diamonds on a viper's back
To the slow poison of a meaning lost
And the vituperations of the just.

This is close, and not merely in imagery, to the burden
of 'Snakeskin and Stone', just as the kingfisher starts
up echoes of the sea bird described in Douglas's letter
home to his mother and used in the two sea-bird poems.
'Cargoes of anguish in the holds of joy, / The smooth
deceitful stranger in the heart', the poem goes on; 'And
though the state has enemies we know / The greater
enmity within ourselves':

Grey monkeys gibber, ignorant and wise.
We are the ghosts, and they the denizens . . .

A trackless wilderness divides
Joy from its cause, the motive from the act;
The killing arm uncurls, strokes the soft moss . . .

The bamboos creak like an uneasy house;
The night is shrill with crickets, cold with space.
And if the mute pads on the sand should lift
Annihilating paws and strike us down
Then would some unimportant death resound
With the imprisoned music of the soul?

Or does the will's long struggle end
With the last kindness of a foe or friend?

Lewis is a great man for interrogatives, Douglas for
declarations of identity. Lewis is sensuous, descending
from Keats, Hopkins, Yeats, Edward Thomas, where
Douglas looks to Donne, Eliot, and Auden. Yet beneath
the differences run deep similarities. Both see them-
selves as 'ghosts'. Both see a 'wilderness' between
'motive' and 'act' (symbolized in the jungle and the
desert respectively). Both employ complex mirror-
images of the self as enemy:

[176]

Now in my dial of glass appears
the soldier who is going to die.

The face distorted in a jungle pool
That drowns its image in a mort of leaves.

Much of 'The Jungle' is close in spirit to 'Desert
Flowers' and 'How to Kill', and so are 'The Patrol' and
'The Run-In'. 'The Sentry' is perhaps his version of
'Simplify Me When I'm Dead'. Douglas notes with
appalled honesty how the lover turns into a killer, is
the one by virtue of being the other. Lewis reverses the
action, seeing the killer uncurl into the lover, but it is
the same conjunction of the same two forces. In 'How to
Kill' the 'closed fist' is urged to 'open' and behold an
ambiguous gift; in Lewis's poem 'The killing arm
uncurls, strokes the soft moss' – a gentle unfolding of
the paradox that haunts them both. Lewis's 'alone-
ness', Douglas's 'waves of love' travelling 'into vacancy'
are one and the same, 'the imprisoned music of the soul'
powerless to alter human nature.

How to Kill

Under the parabola of a ball,
a child turning into a man,
I looked into the air too long.
The ball fell in my hand, it sang
in the closed fist: *Open Open*
Behold a gift designed to kill.

Now in my dial of glass appears
the soldier who is going to die.
He smiles, and moves about in ways
his mother knows, habits of his.
The wires touch his face: I cry
NOW. Death, like a familiar, hears

and look, has made a man of dust
of a man of flesh. This sorcery
I do. Being damned, I am amused

[177]

to see the centre of love diffused
and the waves of love travel into vacancy.
How easy it is to make a ghost.

The weightless mosquito touches
her tiny shadow on the stone,
and with how like, how infinite
a lightness, man and shadow meet.
They fuse. A shadow is a man
when the mosquito death approaches.

The ball in the opening line, describing a 'parabola' (cf.
'parable'), is in part a plaything, in part a figure for the
earth and planets, and in part a precursor of the bullets
and bombs that will be used in the adult game of war.
Thus the birthday 'gift' metamorphoses into something
'designed to kill', as the open hand finds itself clenched
into a fist. 'I looked into the air too long' suggests a child
enamoured of dreams and long perspectives, ignorant
of those things implicit in its own flesh, the skull
beneath the skin. 'I looked . . . I cry . . . I do . . .'

The 'dial of glass' is literally the telescopic sight on a
rifle. (One draft of the poem is called 'The Sniper' – see
TCP, p. 141. The later phrase 'I cry / NOW' makes one
wonder whether Douglas does not also have in mind
the tank commander, who gives orders to his gunner
when and how to fire.) It also picks up all the
associations of 'glass' I have discussed earlier: the
'house . . . of glass' ('The House'), the 'lens' of 'time's
wrong-way telescope' ('Simplify Me When I'm Dead'),
the 'separative glass cloak of strangeness' ('Syria'), the
'powerful enlarging glass' of the fish's eye ('The Mar-
vel'), and the predictive 'with a crash I'll split the glass'
('On a Return from Egypt'). All these are figures for
what Isabella, in *Measure for Measure*, calls 'man's
glassy essence' (II, ii, 120), at once remote and yet
closer than breath. The glass reflects one's own face,
and at an unquantifiable distance – the 'trackless

wilderness' of Lewis's jungle, making of it an image that is far-off and unreal. Thus 'the soldier who is going to die' is the 'I in another', and the first 'now' rehearses the fusion of predator and prey that will follow in this alchemical drama.

Tenderness flickers momentarily at the mention of the soldier's mother, who knows his every move and look. The second 'now' mimes perhaps the doubleness of the glassy reflections, and the exertion of will required to summon death into the present tense. Even the sense of touch is nullified, since it is only 'wires' that 'touch his face'. (The word recurs in the last stanza, but again at one remove from direct sensation: 'touches / her tiny shadow . . .' The fact that the mosquito is given a gender is interesting, implying that the meeting of man and shadow is also a meeting of the sexes.) Instantly the first person gives way to the third, and the tense changes to past; though the 'I' admits to sorcery and damnation, it is the 'familiar' death who actually does the killing, relegating killer and killed to the passive status of onlookers, like Faustus bound hand and foot to the master he has summoned up from his own psyche. 'Sorcery', like 'demon' in 'Vergissmein-nicht', is not a 'shoddy' evasion of the facts, as Ian Hamilton asserts, but an acknowledgement of guilt, and an attempt to explain the theatricality of engaging in war. The detachment is psychologically truthful and, I imagine, tactically essential to survival – though what survives is not much more than a 'ghost'.

The brilliant last stanza, as precise as it is riddlingly suggestive, is one of Douglas's finest achievements. Like the 'weightless shadows' of 'The House', death is 'unreal' yet instantiated in the fusion of mosquito, man, shadow, stone. 'Mosquito' and 'shadow' meet (cf. the 'overshadowing' gun of 'Vergissmeinnicht'), phoneti-cally as well as semantically, in 'stone'; and with how isomorphic a lightness the poem's alliterations, asso-nances, half-rhymes and metrical dexterity effect that

introduction. 'How like, how infinite . . .' deploys syn-
tactical identity and phonetic variation, the short vowel
of 'like' followed by the virtuoso expansion and
diminuendo of the vowel in 'infinite' and 'lightness'.
'They fuse' in an action, or cessation of action, at once
explosive and yet so delicate as to be almost impalp-
able. The mosquito is the whining bullet, the poison
sting of death (cf. Rosenberg's 'swift iron burning bee'
in 'Dead Man's Dump' and Douglas's own 'gnat . . . /
wounding the skin, leaving poison there' in 'Syria'), its
landing the tiniest conceivable alteration in the ecology
of a landscape which is utterly indifferent. Indeed the
landscape is present only in the barest particulars, air,
shadow, stone: in which an appearance briefly occurs,
then turns to dust. Masculine endings accompany the
first two stanzas, feminine ones ('touches/approaches')
the delicacies of the last, the *t* sounds playing off
against the long vowels in a further mimesis of the
sting of death.

In nearly all the major poems 'stone' leads an
ambiguous life as Douglas's favourite polyvalent image
of that which is both feared and desired. It seems to
relate to a whole series of overlapping associations:
with houses, which imprison or release the self; with
the planets and stars and a 'petrified' God ('The
Creator'), as relatedly with the cruelty of Yingcheng ('a
mask stretched on the stone- / hard face of death') and
Milena ('as wonderful and hard as she'); with the dead
(the obsolescent heroes of 'Aristocrats' disposed 'under
the stones and earth', the 'stony actors' of 'Landscape
with Figures') and with war ('War can be the famous
stone / for turning rubbish into gold' – 'Christodoulos');
with inscrutability (lizards as 'live stones' in the two
Syria poems, the sweat-lined 'statue of a face' of
'Egyptian Sentry', the poet's own feet 'like stones /
underwater' in 'Mersa'); with potentiality and its
opposite ('you've come / to mansize from the smallness
of a stone' – 'Time Eating'); and especially, in an erotic

context, with women, where 'stone' and 'jewel' are juxtaposed in a variety of ways. Thus the 'drowned heart' is 'that stone, that jewel tranquillity' ('The Two Virtues'); the 'women old and young at once' are 'pretty stones' ('Negative Information'); the visitors to 'The House' might have 'that creative stone / to . . . turn all alive', unless death turns the eyes to 'fine stones'; the beautiful but hard and cruel woman in the Egyptian tea garden is 'a white stone' in the first and again in the last stanza, 'useless except to a collector, a rich man'. A related use, as Graham points out (*PM*, p. 34), occurs in a schoolboy paragraph on the power of words: 'Words are . . . like diamonds, stones to the beast, and useless, but to the connoisseur most valuable in the world.' Used badly, they become the 'dry bones' of 'Snakeskin and Stone'.

It is hardly surprising, then, that 'How to Kill' begins with a ball in a fist and ends with a pararhyme on 'stone' and 'man'. The image focuses steadily on the unbearable paradox of death-in-life, a fusion ('fuse' too embraces both union and separation) which locks safety and danger together in eternal tension, exemplified in the stone house of the self which shields and entombs, and in the jewelled beauty of women, irresistible as the 'hot coast . . . of love' ('Song: Do I Venture'), and its anti-type, the desert landscape of war. Stone is also cognate with the durable metal of guns and tanks, as opposed to the decaying flesh of the lover. Always hot for certainty, there is a side of Douglas that yearns for the clarity of stone, not because of a death-wish but because he wants to be 'all alive' or all dead. There is a stony quality in his rhythms and diction, springing partly from the ruthless interrogations of a painter's eye – all his poetry is intensely visual – and partly from a disposition to wring meaning from appearances at all costs, like a logician let loose on an unknown planet. This cerebral belligerence, chivvying the world into satisfactorily humbling antitheses, is leavened by a scrupulous honesty which generates its own passion and wit, continually referring the part to the whole and the whole to the verifiable part. Death is stonelike because it 'singles' ('Vergissmeinnicht'), thus resolving the logical and the psychological problems of identity, the 'I in another place' that haunts all the desert poems. Love shares the same ambition to annihilate contingency in favour of necessity; it is yet another 'marvel' which metamorphoses from one thing to another. The commonest imperative is *Look*, often accompanied by the axes *here* and *now*.

Though he can be impatient there is nothing bullying or sentimental in Douglas's view of the world, as there is in writers with whom he is sometimes compared such as Hemingway. If it is true that he seldom entertains mysteries and doubts in the manner of Keats and Lewis, it is equally true that he never descends into bathos or rhetorical mysticisms of the sort Lewis tends to puff up into capitalized abstract nouns. 'How to Kill' ends as tenderly and mysteriously as one could wish, and so does that other serene meditation, 'Desert Flowers', which might be construed as a reply to the youthful certainties of 'Simplify Me When I'm Dead'. The poem begins with an acknowledgement of the point he had made in his essay 'Poets in This War': the 'hardships, pain and boredom; the behaviour of the living and the appearance of the dead, were so accurately described by the poets of the Great War that every day on the battlefields of the western desert . . . their poems are illustrated. Almost all that a modern poet on active service is inspired to write, would be tautological.' But his exploration of his own poetic mission is wonderfully original and fresh:

> Living in a wide landscape are the flowers –
> Rosenberg I only repeat what you were saying –
> The shell and the hawk every hour
> are slaying men and jerboas, slaying

[182]

the mind: but the body can fill
the hungry flowers and the dogs who cry words
at nights, the most hostile things of all.
But that is not new. Each time the night discards

draperies on the eyes and leaves the mind awake
I look each side of the door of sleep
for the little coin it will take
to buy the secret I shall not keep.

I see men as trees suffering
or confound the detail and the horizon.
Lay the coin on my tongue and I will sing
of what the others never set eyes on.

Douglas's social and intellectual background, and his
role in the army as a junior officer, were far closer to
Owen's experience than to that of the Jewish private
from the East End of London who was so small he was
enlisted in a bantam regiment. Yet the identification
with Rosenberg, that other poet and artist, is tempera-
mental as well as thematic. Douglas even identifies, at
times, with Jewish alienation from gentility, notably in
'Saturday Evening in Jerusalem' and in the already-
quoted letter to Milena. Both possessed a 'sinewy and
muscular aliveness' and penetrating 'imagination'
(Siegfried Sassoon, Foreword to *The Collected Poems of
Isaac Rosenberg*, ed. Gordon Bottomley and Denys
Harding, Chatto and Windus 1962, p. vii), and both
came close to treating war as a modern morality.

The poem Douglas alludes to specifically is 'Break of
Day in the Trenches', a title which may owe something
to Jeremiah 51,20: 'with thee will I break in pieces the
nations, and with thee will I destroy kingdoms' (used
also by Hardy in his juxtaposition of war with quotidian
life in his fine lyric 'In time of "The Breaking of
Nations"'):

> The darkness crumbles away –
> It is the same old druid Time as ever.

> Only a live thing leaps my hand –
> A queer sardonic rat –
> As I pull the parapet's poppy
> To stick behind my ear,
>
> Poppies whose roots are in man's veins
> Drop, and are ever dropping . . .

The concern with Time and antinomianism are both calculated to appeal to Douglas, as is the enjambement and reversed stress of the last two lines, which he uses so often himself. Douglas assembles and juxtaposes a similar list of marvels. The 'shell and the hawk . . . / and jerboas' (desert rats) and 'dogs' are all seen as predators of the same order of reality, all caught up in the same cyclical economy of life and death anatomized in 'Vergissmeinnicht' and 'Dead Men'. Parallel with these are the 'wide landscape' with its miraculous flowers that spring up in the desert overnight, and the 'mind' with its 'slaying of words / . . . the most hostile things of all'. The latter phrase characteristically undermines his own dialectic, for even as the contraries are assembled they are collapsed back into uneasy logical identity, like the electrons whirling about an atom. The flowers are just as 'hungry' as the dogs and rats; the rhyme on 'saying' and 'slaying' hints that words too are hostile, like the hawkish minds that produce them. Literally the dog's word is a howl for comfort and food; metaphorically it is the *reductio* acted out in 'Dead Men', mirroring the plight of man's animal nature. Minds are slain too, from within and without, by shells and by paradox, yet remain 'awake' to the options they face.

The paradoxes are emphasized by the strange logic of the long opening sentence, and especially by the repeated 'but' of stanza 2, whose function is both connective and disjunctive, miming this landscape's macroeconomy; and by the double enjambement of 'discards//draperies', where the verb enacts and refutes its own meaning. That is to say we initially read 'night' *as* a 'drapery', even as the poem forces us to discard that meaning, for the mind will have none of it, remaining nakedly awake to its riven identity, midway between waking and sleeping.

Throughout the poem details line up both in opposition and in resemblance: the 'wide landscape' and 'every hour'; shell and hawk; body and mind; night and day; repetition and newness; poetry and a dog's howl; the intelligible and the secret; beauty and hostility; 'buy' and 'sing'; detail and horizon. The 'little coin' is a bullet, the currency of death, and the fee placed on a dead man's eyes or tongue to pay Charon the ferryman to row him across the Styx. 'Buy' also puns on the slang phrase 'He's bought it', which links modern warfare and ancient mythology. Perhaps, too, the coin is an offering to Janus, god of doorways, who looks both ways; and hence to those 'antinomies . . . which are the inexhaustible source of all mental effort and provide the problems of thought in all times and in all civilizations' (C. G. Jung, 'Archaic Man', *Modern Man in Search of a Soul*, Routledge and Kegan Paul, 1981, p. 172).

The 'secret' of stanza 3 is of course death. Why will the poet 'not keep' it? 'I look . . . I see . . . I will sing . . .': like the birds at the end of Yeats's 'Sailing to Byzantium', the poet's function is to 'sing of what is past, or passing, or to come'. But this visionary possibility belongs only, in Yeats's words, to those who are 'out of nature'. A dead man is just such a being, forfeiting knowledge of death in the very act of acquiring it. The tenderness of the final stanza recalls the emotional tenor of 'Enfidaville', which similarly ends with a meeting of narrator and the 'eyes' of certain images of love. 'Men as trees' alludes to Christ's healing of a blind man in St Mark, 8, 23–6: 'And he took the blind man by the hand, and led him out of the town; and when he had

[185]

spit on his eyes, and put his hands upon him, he asked him if he saw ought. And he looked up, and said, I see men as trees, walking. After that he put his hands again upon his eyes, and made him look up: and he was restored, and saw every man clearly. And he sent him away to his house, saying, Neither go into the town, nor tell it to any man in the town.' The narrator thus identifies with the blind man at the point where he is partially sighted. The metaphor of men as trees makes perfectly good lay sense too, since there is a natural affinity between the two species.

'Desert Flowers' preserves the mystery, but not the outrage, that clings to Douglas's other poems about death. For once there are no 'stony actors' and theatrical metaphors, save the 'draperies' of night. Nothing here sprawls or wriggles, indeed there are no other people at all, just an 'I' set amid 'detail and . . . horizon'. Trees do not stand or lie 'at a queer angle to the scenery'. It is a poem of horizontals and uprights, correlatives of clear-sighted life and death, in which the resolved self, cured of its doubleness, will sing like a bird.

Douglas's ability to map psychic energies and connections without falling into archaism or self-consciousness is one of his most attractive qualities. It is demonstrated in the brilliance of his last major poem, 'The Behaviour of Fish in an Egyptian Tea Garden', which employs a single extended metaphor of submarine life to conjure up a woman's effect on a variety of men in a Cairene institution. The title itself is a little surreal, like the horse and pipe in 'Aristocrats' or the nightmarish pantomime in 'Vergissmeinnicht', but the poem owes nothing to French surrealism or its English counterpart, though it was precisely at this time that the New Apocalypse, and the poems of David Gascoyne, were making themselves felt. (The Surrealist Exhibition took place in London in 1936, during Douglas's formative years. Gascoyne's *Poems*

1937–1942 was published by Tambimuttu's Editions Poetry London in 1943. *The New Apocalypse* and *The White Horseman* were published in 1939 and 1941 respectively.) Douglas's imaginative flights, however, are never self-serving or didactic or covert manifestos about how poetry should be written. As in the war poems, he takes in detail and *Gestalt* at a single glance, and never lets go of the electric current magnetizing part to whole:

> As a white stone draws down the fish
> she on the seafloor of the afternoon
> draws down men's glances and their cruel wish
> for love. Slyly red lip on the spoon
>
> slips in a morsel of ice-cream. Her hands
> white as a milky stone, white submarine
> fronds, sink with spread fingers, lean
> along the table, carmined at the ends.*

The drawing Douglas made of the scene (reproduced in *CP*, p. 112) is a good deal less accomplished than its verbal counterpart, but gives some idea of a picture-hatted woman sitting beneath a parasol at a café table, surrounded by men, and watched also by a sardonic-looking bird in the lower right foreground who might be a figure for the poet himself.

The woman is dressed in white, with red lips and 'carmined' nails, 'a beautiful red or crimson pigment obtained from cochineal', says *SOED*, which is made from the dried bodies of an insect that lives on cactus. Thus she unites the clarity and hardness of stone, or a jewelled insect, with the soft undulations of 'fronds' that 'sink' into the deceptive element of water. (Her

---

* *TCP* hyphenates 'slips-in' and substitutes 'Her' for *CP*'s 'Slyly'. It also moves the adverb 'coldly' in line 14, and prints 'But now' rather than 'Now' in line 25.

surprisingness is mirrored in the surprising syntax of stanza 2, which introduces its main verbs after an adjectival clause and an identity clause; the frond-like sentence moves about in unexpected ways.) The ice-cream, too, is both liquid and solid, like the 'milky stone' of line 6, as potently erotic as her 'red lip on the spoon' moistened by the succeeding play of sibilants. 'Slyly' enforces a pause after its double stress, miming her self-conscious action; 'Slyly . . . lip' is effortlessly elided into 'slips'; the plosive labial 'li*p*' is taken up in 's*p*oon' and 'sli*p*s' and swallowed as softly as the cold ice in her warm mouth. This single short sentence about the ice-cream is a microcosm of Douglas's virtuoso handling of sound and sense throughout the poem. At every level the language is as vivid and economical as only good poetry can be:

> A cotton magnate, an important fish
> with great eyepouches and a golden mouth
> through the frail reefs of furniture swims out
> and idling, suspended, stays to watch.
>
> A crustacean old man clamped to his chair
> sits coldly near her and might see
> her charms through fissures where the eyes should be,
> or else his teeth are parted in a stare.
>
> Captain on leave, a lean dark mackerel
> lies in the offing; turns himself and looks
> through currents of sound. The flat-eyed flatfish sucks
> on a straw, staring from its repose, laxly.
>
> And gallants in shoals swim up and lag,
> circling and passing near the white attraction:
> sometimes pausing, opening a conversation;
> fish pause so to nibble or tug.

What could be more evocative of commercial power and the Midas touch than 'great eyepouches and a golden mouth'? 'Gold' might have done nearly as well, but 'golden' picks up 'Magnate' and gives him the rounded-ness of a complete man of the world. The inversion in the next line ('through . . . frail reefs . . . swims out') subtly mimes his negotiation of the tables and chairs; 'frail reefs', with its hint of paradox, is a marvellous image for the wrought-iron delicacy of the furniture; and the sentence fizzles out in its delayed verbs – what he is is more interesting than what he does. The stanza virtually abandons rhyme, or stretches it to near-invisibility ('fish / out', 'mouth / watch'), yet it is difficult to see how it could be improved.

An equally brilliant image closes the next stanza, evoking a predatory old man whose 'teeth are parted in a stare'. Instead of eyes he has 'fissures', like the 'recesses' and 'cavernous slots' of 'Poor Mary' and 'The Deceased'. Like these avatars he is dying or dead, all but his teeth and claws, extremities which relate him to the woman he stares at, who is also characterized by hands and mouth, although they are at an earlier stage in the cycle of appetite. Each character is picked out in this way, just one or two details magnified by the lens of the sea, and by the poet's imagination. The captain on leave 'lies in the offing' to see what might be on offer, and 'looks / through currents of sound': sight, sound and touch brought deftly together in acknowledgement of the lightening synaesthetic skills that operate under water, and above it too. In the simple act that 'turns himself' he tells us as much about his character as the woman does in slipping in a morsel of ice-cream. And the 'flat-eyed flatfish' is as near-comatose as the syntax in which he lives, governed by repetition and by the superbly lifeless adverb 'laxly', which makes a supine sort of rhyme with the previous three lines.

> Now the ice-cream is finished, is
> paid for. The fish swim off on business
> and she sits alone at the table, a white stone
> useless except to a collector, a rich man.

The ice-cream has been paid for in more senses than one. She has bought her treat with the weapons she has to hand, as, in a very different context, the narrator of 'Desert Flowers' buys his experience of death, or the German soldier of 'Vergissmeinnicht' has 'paid' for his. The little drama has played itself to a conclusion and now she 'sits alone' like the protagonists of the war poems, a 'stone' that's as ambiguously 'hard and good' as the powers she potentiates and symbolizes. The ending is typically double-edged: 'useless' to whom, and what kind of a 'rich man'? Rich with, say, Antony's riches? Or only nastily rich, like Christodoulos? A 'collector' of marvels, like a poet or a sailor, or the curator of naked impulse and desire? If the desert is a theatre, Cairo is a fishbowl. In both, 'the presences of love and mortality harden into sexuality and death' (Vernon Scannell, *Not Without Glory*, p. 46).

Early and late, Douglas's poems assemble a vivid cast of animals, birds, reptiles, fish and insects, personifying physical and psychic powers which are both delightful and terrifying, and which seem to rule a world that is at once alien and wonderfully unalterable. These powers extend upwards into the air and downwards into the sea and inwards into the skull. The mind gropes for its place in a body which is part skeleton, part divinity. Thus the terms of the dialectic lie ready to hand, like a theologian's categories or a painter's festal tubes of colour. Unlike Hughes, however, who sometimes seems to believe that reason is largely a form of rationalization, Douglas is also gripped by the drama of the brain's desire to grasp its own divided inheritance. At bottom he is a passionate holist, like Donne, but one who perhaps looked into the Manichaean air too long and so stumbled off the *via media* of tender hope.

Back in England in the early spring of 1944 Douglas attempted to write a poem which wouldn't come out right, 'Bête Noire', and the two versions of his inter-regnum piece, 'Actors Waiting in the Wings of Europe' and 'On a Return from Egypt'. 'Bête Noire' was partly prompted by Betty Jesse's use of the phrase, jokingly, to refer to his moodiness (*KD*, p. 233). It combines elements of the disappointed-love poems, the house-poems, the bestiary-poems, the metaphysical-analytical poems, but remains an obstinate failure. He made a drawing of the beast for the cover of his first full collection of poems, which was to be published by Tambimuttu; it is reproduced on the covers of *KD* and *TCP*. (Another is reproduced in *CP(PL)*, p. 129.) In a note written to accompany the drawings he acknow-ledges his inability to write the poem, and acutely confesses to a suspicion that he has in fact already written it:

> Bête Noire is the name of the poem I can't write; a protracted failure, which is also a protracted success I suppose. Because it is the poem I begin to write in a lot of other poems: this is what justifies my use of that title for the book. The beast, which I have drawn as black care sitting behind the horseman, is indefinable: sitting down to try and describe it, I have sensations of physical combat, and after five hours of writing last night, which resulted in failure, all my muscles were tired. But if he is not caught, at least I can see his tracks (anyone may see them), in some of the other poems. My failure is that I know so little about him, beyond his existence and the infinite patience and extent of his malignity . . . he is so amorphous and powerful that he could be a deity. Only he is implacable; no use sacrificing to him, he takes what he wants. (*TCP*, p. 120)

Douglas seems to have held the beast responsible for his failures in friendship and love, his own emotional paralysis; it was the 'enemy . . . inside' that also plagued Alun Lewis and Edward Thomas. The word 'infinite' recalls the meeting of man and shadow in

'How to Kill'. 'Don't kiss me. Don't put your arm round/ and touch the beast on my back' says one of the draft fragments; for the beast had banished all tenderness. He returns to the image of kissing in his very last poem, 'On a Return from Egypt':

> The next month, then, is a window
> and with a crash I'll split the glass.
> Behind it stands one I must kiss,
> person of love or death
> a person or a wraith,
> I fear what I shall find.

Just three years separate this 'depleted fury' from the youthful imperatives of 'Simplify Me When I'm Dead'. What the murderers of the opening stanza kill deadest of all is themselves and their own gentleness, 'sloe-eyed' as the feminine presences in 'These grasses, ancient enemies'. The 'jewelled . . . seas' fade into hard 'grey rocks', and the heart too, with all its emotional and creative ambitions unfulfilled, is a Shelleyan coal fading into death. The final image of the 'window' and 'glass' circles back to the looking-glass image of *Alamein to Zem Zem*, to the effigy of 'Poor Mary' trapped in a lifeless house, and to the innumerable lenses and mirrors that reflect the soldier-lover's own ghostly features, the 'one I' gazing at himself who must be kissed into a 'person' or a 'wraith'. The pun on 'wreath' indicates what sort of 'I' he expects this last meeting to bring.

V

Critical Reception

Though he received useful encouragement at home, at school and at Oxford Douglas remained a loner who went his own way, and this fact continued to be true of his posthumous reputation. Sidney Keyes was elected 'the spokesman of a generation' (Michael Meyer, Memoir in *The Collected Poems of Sidney Keyes*, Routledge and Kegan Paul, 1945), like Rupert Brooke before him, and his poems were collected in 1945. Alun Lewis's *Raiders' Dawn* (1942) went through six impressions in four years. Douglas's poems were not collected until 1951, when new sorts of poetry were in the air – notably Dylan Thomas and the first stirrings of the Movement – and the war was a fast-receding memory. 'The poems, by that time, had no longer the impact of news; they had not yet acquired the impact of history' (G. S. Fraser, 'Keith Douglas: A Poet of the Second World War', 1956). Friends and acquaintances, mostly other poets such as Bernard Spencer, Lawrence Durrell, John Hall, John Waller, G. S. Fraser and Alan Ross discerned his quality, and these were later joined by some of the best poets of our time; but for twenty years or more after his death Douglas was largely neglected. Kenneth Allott's influential *Penguin Book of Contemporary Verse* (1950) omitted him altogether, even in the revised edition of 1962; so did A. Alvarez's *The New Poetry* (Penguin, 1962), though it included work by American modernists of the same generation such as Berryman and Lowell. Lucie-Smith's *British*

Poetry Since 1945 (Penguin, 1970) also left him, and
Lewis, out of account. Not until Charles Tomlinson's
essay on 'Poetry Today' in 1961 (Pelican Guide to
English Literature, vol. 7, *The Modern Age*, ed. Boris
Ford), Ted Hughes's brilliant Introduction to his
Selected Poems of Douglas in 1964, and Geoffrey Hill's
Stand review of the same year, did Douglas begin to get
something like his due. In the past twenty years
reviews and essays have multiplied, partly in response
to the indefatigable efforts of Douglas's editor and
biographer Desmond Graham, partly because the
poetry itself has outlived irrelevant strictures and
appreciations and created its own audience.

The early notices of *Augury* (1940), *Eight Oxford
Poets* (1941) and *Selected Poems* (1943) are uniformly
uninteresting, though reviewers included Edwin Muir
(*New Statesman*, 31 January 1942) and Stephen
Spender (*New Statesman*, 17 April 1943). T. S. Eliot's
response to the poems sent him by Blunden was polite
– 'They seem to me extremely promising' – but
uncomprehending, especially of the second batch sent
by Douglas himself in spring 1941, 'The House', 'Song:
Dotards do not think', 'The Marvel' and 'Time Eating'.
Eliot responded in June with a letter and marginal
comments on the typescripts. '. . . I think that the one
called 'Song' is very nearly written. The others seem to
me to need a good bit of work with special attention to
ineffectual adjectives . . .' (*PM*, pp. 71–81). Eliot's
failure to see or feel the accomplishment of 'The
Marvel' and 'Time Eating' is disappointing. In his
defence we may note that this was a difficult and
unhappy time in his life, when he had no proper home
and was constantly ill (*T. S. Eliot* by Peter Ackroyd,
Hamish Hamilton, 1984, pp. 260–61). It was thus left
to Tambimuttu to become Douglas's publisher and
champion. His 'Tenth Letter: In Memory of Keith
Douglas' (*Poetry London*, vol. 2, no. 10, 1945) is a warm
valediction upon his death. 'Auden was the barometer

of the weather during the thirties, Keith Douglas was the crystallization of poetic experience in the war generation ... He believed in discipline and order although he was a rebel all his life ... One is impressed by the chasteness and precision of the writing as if it had been engraved with the burin. His lines, stripped to the bare essentials of thought itself, carried his meaning through directly and without fuss ... He seems to have been born with an eye for the exact shape and topography of things ... His conclusions about life in action are the most mature any poet has arrived at in this war ...' It is not altogether easy to separate sense from nonsense in Tambimuttu's career, and it was his hopeless inefficiency that led to the long delay in the publication of Douglas's *Collected Poems*. None the less he was a tireless publicist of Douglas's work once he had read it. Perhaps his championship was itself an element in Douglas's tardy recognition, since the literary world viewed his endorsements with understandable suspicion. But whatever his shortcomings he must be counted amongst those who had some real insight into the quality of Douglas's achievement. Olivia Manning also spotted his talent early on: 'Among the younger men whom the army has brought out here [Cairo] Keith Douglas stands alone. He has been in contact with the enemy much of the time and he is the only poet who has written poems comparable with the works of the better poets of the last war and likely to be read as war poems when the war is over' ('Poets in Exile', *Horizon*, October 1944). Bernard Spencer wrote a brief obituary note for the Cairo magazine *Personal Landscape* (vol. 11, no. 4, 1945). Douglas's friend Norman Ilett, to whom he lost Milena, contributed a perceptive assessment of his character to *The Christ's Hospital Book* (1953): 'I think many people knew a part of him, as much as he cared to show them or thought would occupy or amuse them. He was interested in a number of things which do not usually go together. This brought him a wide acquaintance who formed not only large but a number of smaller circles, in each of which he could feel at home without permanently residing in any . . .' Another service friend at El Ballah hospital later recalled that Douglas's favourite record and virtual signature-tune was 'It Ain't Necessarily So' (Lt-Col. John Stubbs; see Bibliography).

John Waller, who had reviewed *Eight Oxford Poets* (*Poetry Review*, May–June 1940), wrote an early appreciation for the American magazine *Accent* (Urbana, Illinois, 1948), but it is a fey and woefully inadequate piece which insists on picturing Douglas as an Oxford 'dreamer', one who stumbled bravely through the war recording 'wistfully bright moments'. Alan Ross's British Council booklet *Poetry 1945–1950* (Longmans, 1951) numbered Douglas among the 'four outstanding' poets of the war, together with Keyes, Lewis and Fuller. He thought many of the poems (in the poetical supplement to the first edition of *Alamein to Zem Zem*, an arrangement Douglas perhaps copied from Blunden's *Undertones of War*) 'only rough drafts, unrevised and incomplete', a view echoed by R. N. Currey's *Poets of the 1939–1945 War* (British Council, Longman, 1960): 'Many are drafts, not fully polished . . .' Currey holds that 'The spirit underlying the best writings about both wars was fundamentally the same. It is impossible to understand the good poetry of the Second War except in relation to Owen . . .' Douglas's is a 'poetry of true compassion . . . like Keyes and Lewis he was a poet in direct succession to Owen . . . He was a conscious artist and his poems of battle are the best of the war, but he seems to me to lack their [Keyes's and Lewis's] creative range'. Alan Ross wrote a fuller appreciation of Douglas for *The Times Literary Supplement* (6 August 1954), hailing both *Alamein to Zem Zem* and the *Collected Poems* as enduring literature:

Douglas is often an elliptical poet, therefore of no interest to the slovenly reader who only wants to read what he (or she) expects. . . . He wrote very close to life, very idiomatically and naturally, so that there is no sense of strain in his poems, nothing absurd or intense which a man of sensibility would find himself unable to say to another man in ordinary conversation . . . In the last resort, over and above techniques and themes, one judges poets – or, rather, likes them, because 'judge' is a depressing verb to apply to poetry – by whether or not one finds them sympathetic. To me, Keith Douglas is the most sympathetic poet of his (which is my own) generation: he wrote the kind of poetry I should like to have written, which is the most any writer can say about another.

Alamein to Zem Zem was published by Tambimuttu's Editions Poetry London in 1946, together with many of Douglas's drawings and a supplement of sixteen poems, ranging from 'Time Eating' (but not 'The Marvel', presumably because it did not fit the war theme) to 'On a Return from Egypt', and containing six of his best Middle East poems. There are two illustrations in colour, the first a striking watercolour frontispiece of a man trapped in a tank and burning to death. It is semi-expressionist in style, done in lurid orange and ochre, Indian red, and cobalt darkening to black. Like 'Vergissmeinnicht' and 'How to Kill' it is not based on a single incident but on an amalgam of various experiences, and seems to me essentially a self-portrait, the figure 'burning in hell' of 'Landscape with Figures 3'. (The watercolour portrait of Yingcheng reproduced in *KD*, p. 77, also bears a marked resemblance to Douglas's own features). This volume is in many ways the quintessential Douglas book; I agree with Geoffrey Hill that an enlarged scholarly edition, containing all the best of the Middle East poems, is eminently desirable (Desmond Graham is hoping to publish such an edition). *Alamein to Zem Zem* was enthusiastically greeted from the outset, and the three subsequent editions (see Bibliography) have continued to spread its reputation. I shall include critical comments on it in some of the extracts that follow.

Proper appraisal of Douglas's poetry begins in the early sixties with the essays by Tomlinson, Hughes and Hill that I have already mentioned. It took Hughes to turn the 'want of finish' charge on its head (originated perhaps by G. S. Fraser in his 1951 Chatterton Lecture – 'there are . . . certain technical roughnesses' in e.g. 'Cairo Jag', 'a vivid piece of documentation . . . But is it . . . a *poem*, is its painfulness resolved?' – and repeated by almost every critic since) and demonstrate, with ample evidence and authority, that Douglas was in fact a 'renovator of language' and poetic form. Predictably, his reference to Shakespeare (used to make a point about poetic style, not about Douglas's status in the canon) raised hackles, and several critics have read into the piece a covert self-portrait. Hughes's Introduction to the *Selected Poems* was arrived at by way of two preliminary pieces on Douglas written for a BBC radio broadcast, and for *Critical Quarterly*, in which he refines his sense of Douglas's originality:

By the time he was killed in Normandy, in 1944, he had produced what is to my mind a more inexhaustibly interesting body of poetry than any one of his generation has produced since, in England or America . . . It is a voice unique in modern English poetry for the endless variety of its intonations while still working at high artistic pressure and with the presence of a whole human being – not just a lyrical or metaphysical or formal fragment of one. Most important of all is this last: his special brand of honesty, which is also courage and also an obsession to get the facts down clear and straight, with no concessions to so-called poetry . . .

. . . Douglas comes to the subject of Time like a man coming to fight a bear. It is typical of him that he tackles it in its most practically effective aspect and that he first of all makes sure he himself is quite naked, and without ready-made approved weapons or bull-roarers or any mechanical advantage of any sort; then attacks openly. The result is crude, but in the powerful way that good proverbs are crude . . .

Keith Douglas has been dead eighteen years and since I began to read occasionally about modern poetry, ten or so years ago, I have seen his name mentioned not more than a dozen times. Yet if English poetry has lacked anything during that time, it has lacked his character: his hatred of self-regarding complacency and his effort against it; his hatred of cant and his effort against it, of that indulgent self-deprecation that passes in this country for charming good manners, while it excuses idleness; his hatred of all posturing and superciliousness, this passion radiates from his poems, even from his thorough misfires. Little about his work is dated, though the mass of it is exercise and unsuccessful attempt. And in this poetry there is the beginning of a style, a tempered wholeness of mind, that could deal in poetry with whatever it came up against, a versatile, ruthless, direct style not limited to certain subjects in certain moods . . . (*The Listener*, 21 June 1962)

It is not enough to say that the language [of 'Encounter with a God'] is utterly simple, the musical inflexion of it peculiarly honest and charming, the technique flawless. The language is also extremely forceful; or rather, it reposes at a point it could only have reached, this very moment, by a feat of great strength. And the inflexion of the voice has a bluntness that might be challenging if it were not so frank, and so clearly the advance of an unusually aware mind. As for the technique, insofar as it can be considered separately, there is nothing dead or asleep in it, nothing tactless, and such subtlety of movement, such economy of means, such composition of cadences, would do credit to any living poet. And behind that, ordering its directions, the essentially practical cast of his energy, his impatient, razor energy . . .

We begin to see [in 'Forgotten the red leaves', titled

[199]

'Pleasures' in *TCP*] what one of Douglas's genuine gifts, to us, is going to be: a poetic speech that is life-size without being extroverted, the language of a man speaking his mind with a flexibility and nonchalance that contrast hypnotically with the ritual intensity, the emblematic density, of what he is saying ... (*Critical Quarterly*, Spring 1963)

At about the same time that the three poet-critics Tomlinson, Hughes and Hill were laying the foundations for a proper understanding of Douglas, Ian Hamilton wrote a substantial series of essays on the poetry of the forties for the *London Magazine* (the first appeared in April 1964; all are collected in *A Poetry Chronicle*, Faber and Faber, 1973). Hamilton takes Lewis to be the best poet of the period, and attacks Douglas for his narcissism (his 'eye for the statuesque is an aspect ... of Douglas's view of himself as the isolated artist, especially burdened by his sensitivity'), his lack of documentary realism ('very little ... of the sheer documentary impact of reluctant recruits like Fuller and Lewis'), and his highly suspicious militaristic attitudes: 'Just as at Oxford he had idealized the remote aristocrats of learning, so in wartime he tends to mythologize the chivalric hero, the "scarlet and tall / Leisurely fellows" who "stroll with royal slow motion", a "gentle / obsolescent band of heroes". This attitude somewhat uncomfortably co-exists with an intermittent, and much less convincing, recognition of the physical facts [quotes second stanza of 'Aristocrats']. Allowing for their attempt at a Sassoonish ironical terseness, these lines do instance a danger which Douglas did not always escape, that of reticence stiffening into the tight-lipped insensitivity of the officers' mess. A poem like "Vergissmeinnicht", which has a powerful plot and is probably Douglas's most famous "active service" poem, seems finally rather prim and frozen in its formality. It is shoddy in a number of key places – the "paper eye", "burst stomach like a cave", "the swart flies", "the entry of a demon" – and there is a constant, debilitating pressure to make fable: the facts seem wrenched and cerebrally reconsidered; rhyme words clot uncomfortably and there are irritating inversions and compressions. One feels that Douglas might have been happier had the plot been rather less powerful, less limiting to his taste for the spectral. . . . Douglas is at his best . . . when his verse can enact the unreality of its circumstances and be released by them . . . what one misses in Douglas, finally, is the sense of a firm, discovered personality . . .'

The indictment is compounded of moral smugness, falsification of the record, and critical ineptitude, as various critics have pointed out, including Vernon Scannell in *Not Without Glory* and Roger Garfitt in his fine review of Graham's biography (see below). The 'unreality of . . . circumstances' charge, for example, recalls Hamilton's later judgements, handed down with all the authority of a Fleet Street veteran, that Douglas's life was 'uneventful'. Likewise the notion that Douglas paraded his 'sensitivity' is totally false; in both his life and his poetry he conspicuously avoided aestheticism of any kind. To cite the lines on grenadiers from the early poem 'Haydn – Clock Symphony' as though they were from one of Douglas's mature war poems; and then to misconstrue the light tone of this playful piece (which nevertheless finds its imaginary heroes 'men of air . . . unreal . . . madmen') is culpably to distort the poetry to fit a preconceived thesis based on a selective and misleading account of Douglas's life. The supposed shoddiness of 'Vergissmeinnicht' is asserted but not demonstrated. The observation that 'there is a constant . . . pressure to make fable' is perfectly true, as it is of Rosenberg, but again Hamilton fails to show how or why this should be seen as 'debilitating'. Fable debilitates when the moral or conceptual scheme dictates to and impoverishes local detail – as in, say, some of the weaker poems of Edwin Muir and Andrew Young, or in the novels of Rex Warner. 'Vergissmeinnicht', however, is as convincing at every level as Rosenberg's 'Louse-Hunting' or 'Break of Day in the Trenches'. The notion that Douglas lacked a 'firm, discovered personality' is aired again in the anonymous *TLS* review of Graham's biography ('What seems lacking is any centre, to the work or to the personality' – 7 June 1974). But perhaps any critic who thinks that 'Bête Noire' and 'Cairo Jag' are of a comparable order of achievement – they 'mark his limitations just as they predict his likely development', says Hamilton – is not to be taken too seriously. Unfortunately for Douglas, however, Hamilton's misreadings and personal animus set the tone for much that was to follow.

Ted Hughes's edition of Douglas's *Selected Poems* was published by Faber in 1964 and provoked much discussion:

> ... what is striking about each of his best poems is its intensely distinctive personality, its 'once-only' character ...
>
> The key poems are two written in 1941, 'Time Eating' and 'The Marvel', the former about time the destroyer and remaker, the melter-down of all individual existences, and the latter about poetry, or the act of imaginative awareness. The more one thinks about the curious symbol 'The Marvel' is based on – a sailor, gouging out the eye of a dead swordfish, uses it as a lens with which to burn the name of a harlot into the ship's deck – the more it expands in the mind and seems to sum up everything that Keith Douglas wanted to say at that moment. The body of the fish is unceremoniously chucked aside; only the 'burning eye' (a beautiful ambiguity between 'burning with awareness' and actively burning a meaningful pattern into things) has any survival value. The fish is like the dead German soldier in 'Vergissmeinnicht', 'mocked at by his own equipment / that's hard and good when he's decayed'.

In versification Douglas's main master was Eliot, and he managed a wavering, loosened iambic measure or *vers libre* with great subtlety. He has a fine ear: listen to the perfectly contrived progression of vocables in 'as legendary flowers bloom / incendiary in tint'. Indeed, he was learning, like Eliot, to turn everything to expressiveness: syntax, transitions, and the mere placing of a highly-charged line, like that climactic one in 'The Marvel' – 'all this emerges from the burning eye'. (P. N. Furbank, *The Listener*, 5 March 1964)

... he ... leans heavily on the overworked Yeatsian trick of buttressing the noun at the end of a line with the double literary adjective: 'a simplified medieval view', 'the querulous soft voice', 'the ambitious cruel bone', 'hostile miraculous age', 'a lean dark mackerel', 'an amorous modern prince', etc. This is even employed in the good late poem 'On a Return from Egypt', where we find 'gentle sloe-eyed murderers' and 'jewelled cerulean seas', but here it has quick point: literariness breaking down under the pressure of experience, so that 'colour and sheen' are lost, and 'cold' itself is recognised as 'an opiate of the soldier'. The poem, on a technical level, becomes almost an argument between the two halves of Douglas's skill – the controlled impulse towards the beautiful, and the involuntary surrender to the stricter beauty of the true – and it is poetry, with its plainness and lack of comfort, which 'wins' through in the last stanza . . .' (Robert Nye, *The Scotsman*, 18 April 1964)

Douglas's completest gift [is] a radical inventiveness and distinctiveness of imagination, which sends some of his poems into strange, unpredictable and continually exciting orbits. And here, had he lived, he would have supplied something that poets like Larkin and Enright tend to lack, as the price no doubt of their coolness and discretion ... This journey of the total poem cannot transpire from brief quotations; but 'A Marvel' [*sic*] is a good example. So is 'The Sea Bird'; and it becomes a much better one if we go back to 'Adams' in the *Collected*

Poems of which it is a telescoped version. In this longer poem the writer's progress through the strangeness of his complex double image is one of truly marvellous intricacy, variety and assurance ... (John Holloway, *Granta*, 15 February 1964)

The introduction struck me as claiming too much, good though Douglas is. 'A utility general-purpose style, as, for instance, Shakespeare's was' – Douglas's poems are mocked by such an instance. Mr Hughes's earlier broadcast talk offered a vigorous praise which conceded more openly ... there is something crude about all but the best of Douglas's work. The war poems can stand some crudity, and are almost unflawed. Not just those on battle, daunting though they appropriately are – the whole Egyptian scene, with its brothels and beggars, opened Douglas's mind and heart into great generosity. The rest is speculation, but it is impossible to forget that Douglas was only two years older than Philip Larkin. (Christopher Ricks, *New Statesman*, 13 March 1964)

Every once in a long, long while a book appears that restores perspectives and makes nonsense of current judgements and values, a work that cuts right through the controversies and petty wranglings of those who would contain art within the confines of their own small homes: a work that hangs in the air and *exists* by dint of nothing but its own majesty and power ... Douglas may have written under the influence of war, but he cannot be restricted because of it. He also wrote under the influence of youth, of people he knew and loved, of books he read and of countries (notably Palestine and Egypt) he visited. But in whatever, from wherever, he breathes new life into the language and infuses it with a great dignity. And that is why he is a 'major' poet. (Jeremy Robson, *Tribune*, 13 March 1964)

I trust that the poems of Keith Douglas will finally be known for what they are: the finest poems written in our language by a soldier of the Second World War. ... The

best new English poet between Auden and Larkin.
(Donald Hall, 'World of Books', BBC Home Service, 21
March 1964)

The Faber editions of *AZZ* and *Collected Poems* of
1966 (published in America by Chilmark Press) pro-
voked widespread discussion and reassessment:

> The inescapable word for him is 'brilliant'. If war implies
> battle, he was probably our only ranking war poet of
> 1939–45. He was immensely gifted . . . tough, generous,
> and unsentimentally compassionate. (John Rowe Town-
> send, *Guardian*, 25 November 1966)

> As a decription of the vagueness, ignorance and off-hand
> courage of war, *Alamein to Zem Zem* is as good as Robert
> Graves's *Goodbye to All That*; it is also wittier and less
> obsessed. But it is Douglas's poems which most com-
> pletely express both the stupid, wasteful outrage of
> killing, and the tensions of guilt. They work by a kind of
> physical concentration of language, stripping away
> every inessential flourish of image or emotion, until they
> emerge as sharp, clean and 'simplified' as a knife, and as
> utterly lacking in self-pity. The feeling is all in state-
> ments without gestures, the bare facts of war. In their
> taut and restrained way they are a perfect elegy on that
> 'gentle obsolescent breed of heroes' with whom Douglas,
> in his self-deprecatory way, himself belonged. (A.
> Alvarez, *Observer*, 13 November 1966)

> He responded eagerly to action, to the vivid colours and
> smells of Syria and Egypt, and found a distinctive voice –
> utterly unsentimental, ironic, thrusting. Now, too, his
> poetry became more muscular, less facile. But some
> people may feel, as I do, that even his best work is flawed
> by inhibition. Douglas deliberately distances himself
> from all that he sees in such a way that it is difficult to
> feel close to him. He is a man to admire, not to love.
> (Kevin Crossley-Holland, *Poetry Review*, Spring 1967).

The idea that good war poets are anti-war is surely

wrong . . . Our culture implies war, and what it would be like to live in one that didn't, nobody knows. War is imaginatively liberating because it speaks to realities which 'peace' cannot directly cope with. War poets are priests, ritual sacrifices more often than not, in a half-hidden cult of Mars, and we respect them as profound truth-tellers. I'm not even sure that good war poetry is anti-death. Rosenberg's ability to make death sharpen his relish for life is peculiar to him, perhaps because he expected less of life than the more privileged Owen or Thomas, whom death fascinates and saddens. Alun Lewis felt affinity with Edward Thomas, and Keith Douglas aspired towards Rosenberg's negative capability, but both usually see death as reality, always present, making other experience temporary, shallow, and without actually being pleased about this, they convey little sense of outrage or protest. (Graham Martin, *The Listener*, 1 December 1966)

Death, especially in wartime and in action, is a great exaggerator . . . As a poet, Douglas had that dangerous youthful facility which prompts writers to put pen to paper without really having anything to say. (Anonymous, *The Times Literary Supplement*, 11 December 1966)

To paraphrase a famous remark of Eliot's, he knew more than Owen and Owen was one of the things he knew. The sense of outrage and sheer pain that marks the older poet is missing from Douglas, or, at least, trasmuted into something wonderful, thoughtful and contemplative. (Thomas Lask, *New York Times*, 29 March 1967)

Douglas, even at school, was a creative technician, and he became the best of his generation (which includes Philip Larkin and Donald Davie). While the influence of Owen, Auden, Donne, can be spotted in this poetry if one tries, there is no need to bother. Douglas was a nonpareil, entire unto himself. Perhaps we can compare him with an experimental scientist . . . He uses negatives a great deal, like a physicist discarding hypotheses. In his war poetry he describes horror, and his own reaction to it, as accurately as he can, and the result needs no sermons to reinforce its point. How much, oh how much, English poetry since the war has needed his superb intelligence, his refusal to fool himself or anybody else.

The prose of *Alamein to Zem Zem* is masterly. The problem in documentary writing is to satisfy two demands at once. We want to know what happened. But we are bound to be inquisitive about the narrator, and we want to know what sort of man he is, before we will trust him. Douglas's stance is exactly right. Because he treats his own feelings in the same level way as the landscapes and the corpses, we believe every word he says. Not 'I am a camera' so much as 'I am a lump of fallible humanity like these men'. (Angus Calder, *Tribune*, 18 November 1966)

The complex irony and pathos of that poem ['Aristocrats'], and of all Douglas's work that came out of the war, make him the one British poet of the Second World War who can bear comparison with those of the First . . . Not the least of Douglas's virtues as a poet and prose writer was a moral one which he owed to his upbringing – a passionate truthfulness. This truthfulness was nourished by an awareness of what was going on outside Britain. (Michael Hamburger, *The Nation*, 29 April 1968)

Douglas . . . preconditioned by his education, slipped without much effort into the assumptions of the Old Etonian cavalry officers, admired his beautiful, pomaded colonel, smiled loftily upon cringing prisoners ('poor little toad'). The Italians he despised: 'little beasts', and cowardly to boot, no respect for corpses, good for nothing except singing for their captors . . . he coveted the immunity of the less sensitive, and formulated a *sang froid* of his own . . . in his war poems the meticulously stiffened upper lip can cramp response . . . Even so good a poem as 'Vergissmeinnicht', which becomes concerned about observing the German's burst stomach and the 'dust upon the paper eye', and imagining his girl's grief, admits satisfaction at his abasement, and switches off so coolly as to edge on disdain. The strictly rationed compunction makes the poem more distinctive, but less humane. (John Carey, *New Statesman*, 18 November 1966)

The *Collected Poems* of Keith Douglas . . . is a classic . . . I'm sure of it. Douglas wrote poems about World War II; many poets today are writing poems against the war in Vietnam. What are the qualities that, in Douglas, strike deep, while much of what we write sounds like a newspaper? I think it was because Douglas was there in flesh as well as spirit:

> I am the man, I suffered, I was there . . .

Having experienced suffering gives a poet assurance. He knows what to leave out. He is not hysterical with continuous fantasies. Having suffered, he is rid of guilt; he may even be happy. Douglas recorded what he saw, and had pity for it [quotes second stanza of 'Aristocrats'] But, at the same time, he kept a sense of joy, the reality of his own life. He wrote:

> Remember me when I am dead
> and simplify me when I'm dead.

As time passes, real men and real books are simplified. Intelligence, feeling, rhythm, the poet's mystery, become clear. While poems that are only words soon fade. (Louis Simpson, *Harpers*, August 1967)

Desmond Graham's biography was published in 1974, and his editions of *The Complete Poems* and *Alamein to Zem Zem* in 1978 and 1979:

Keith Douglas was a poet of quite staggering resources. As a boy of fifteen he was writing with the skill and originality of someone twice his age: see 'Famous Men' and 'Images'. And the best of the mature poems written in the Middle East – 'Vergissmeinnicht', 'Behaviour of Fish in an Egyptian Tea Garden', 'How to Kill', 'Mersa', and 'Cairo Jag' – showed already, in his very early twenties, that he commanded an individual tone, a mastery of rhythm and an ability to handle poetic argument without loss of poetic intensity such as few poets ever attain. His death robbed English poetry of one of the most exciting talents to appear since Auden. (Vernon Scannell, *New Statesman*, 14 June 1974)

The *Selected Poems* of 1964, edited by Ted Hughes and with a preface by him ... not surprisingly picked up all that was most Hughesian (which was not a great deal) ... what emerges most strongly is how ambiguous, protean, contradictory and unknowable the man was ... What seems lacking is any centre, to the work or to the personality. (Anonymous, *The Times Literary Supplement*, 7 June 1974)

A critic has suggested that this story is uneventful. One can only be disgustedly aghast. The sadness of the death of this young, healthy and gifted man is intolerable. (Martin Seymour-Smith, *Birmingham Post*, 22 June 1974)

It's plain he cared acutely about ... impoverishment, and it may well account for his notorious snobbishness ... 'Simplify Me When I'm Dead' is a plea that suggests Douglas's unease about the yearnings and resentments that rankle beneath his well-polished buttons. But it also amounts to a request to have his complications put on record. It's not the simple that want simplifying, nor the simple, for that matter, that turn preparations for OTC parade into half a week's work ... Much of his best poetry grows out of this urge, on the one hand, to reduce himself and other people to objects (e.g. 'Behaviour of Fish ...' ... 'Mersa' ... 'The Prisoner' ...) and the claims, on the other hand, of emotional involvement that he could not withstand. (John Carey, *New Review*, September 1974)

He was a snob, with none of the thirties intellectual's

sympathy for or sentimentality about the proletariat. He
was a resourceful trouble-maker, with a cruel tongue and
(to give him his due) a lack of fear about consequences
... Yet such things (and a good few more of a similar
kind), allied with his brain-power and command of
language, operated to bring him to early maturity and so
to leave behind a remarkable body of work ... the
persisting influence (and it is there, though mastered by
Douglas's own voice, until the end) is the short-lined,
non-Latinate Auden of *Poems* ... What marks Douglas
off ideologically from practically all the poetically-
respectable poets of the Second World War is the large
absence in his work of what may be called the civilian
element ... On one level Douglas may be labelled an
incipient fascist (the logical fulfilment of his origins!) or
certainly as an Army 'pig' (if the Army used the term, as
the Navy did) ... His courage, interest in clothes ...
notion of himself as a horseman ... and convictions of
upper-class superiority drove him along ... (Roy Fuller,
Encounter, September 1974)

Perhaps the rigour of Douglas's attitude is one reason
why he has never been properly appreciated ... He did
not seriously imagine that he would survive the war. But
this anticipation of death must not be confused with the
flirtation that we find in his contemporary, Sidney
Keyes. Whilst Keyes was never properly possessed by
the death wish he was undoubtedly fascinated by it, for it
formed the basis of the romantic exploration of his
enemy's psychology which was so often the stimulus of
his verse. For Douglas, however, death was simply a fact,
an incisive and bounding line that could be used to
sharpen the definition of the living, seeing and writing
... The other quality that Douglas's poems have is
gesture, not in a rhetorical sense, but in the sense of
movement present within the poems, observed, recorded,
yet deliberately incomplete. The final statement is
notable for its absence, and its absence is precisely a part
of what Douglas is sying ... (Richard Luckett, *Specta-tor*, 8 June 1974)

He was intensely lonely and obsessed by death at an early age. He was generous, snobbish, spiky . . . Douglas tried to stabilize the demonic element in his personality in a number of uneasy relationships with young women, entering into engagements that could never have succeeded and threatening suicide if he could not have his way . . . One of Douglas's recurring images is the lens – the lens to focus, clarifying and concentrating what would otherwise dissipate or elude . . . The ethic of sight – the effort towards clear-sightedness and the moral entailment that it brings – demanded much of Douglas from early on . . . It is one measure of his fineness that so many poets have written so well about him – from Ronald Bottrall, Alan Ross and Edmund Blunden to Ted Hughes and Geoffrey Hill. Hill's essay in *Stand* is the classic appreciation, memorable for its use of Douglas's phrase 'I in another place' ('Dead Men') to suggest the alienness of the reality he was compelled to face in war . . . (Charles Tomlinson, *The Listener*, 9 January 1975)

Too much can be made of his spit-and-polish and boot-boning punctiliousness in the OTC. This was no doubt an off-shoot of the father-son relationship, which had been close in early childhood; they had even, up to a point, seemed playmates. With the father's character and army background this naturally led to Keith's adoption of masculine and military attitudes. But the father left home when the boy was about seven and made no attempt to keep in touch. This deprivation, inexplicable to the immature boy, must have been very wounding, and perhaps at boarding school he kept up the 'smart soldier' stance as support for a vulnerable ego . . . (Douglas uses 'dead' of tanks as naturally as of men.) . . . But enemy applied to the man has no meaning either; it was the tank that was the enemy. If this poem ['Vergiss-meinnicht'] reads harsh and thin after Rosenberg's 'Dead Man's Dump', it argues not less humanity in Douglas but a further dehumanization of war. This is more fully expressed in 'Dead Men'. This is a subtle poem, balancing between love and death, which indeed is the fulcrum on

[211]

which all his later poems balance. The awareness of death gives the edge to his eroticism, which has in any case a cool sensuality which he can turn against himself as, when deprived of his girl, he imagines her turning in bed towards her new lover ('I Listen to the Desert Wind') . . . (Edgell Rickword, *Stand*, vol. 16, no. 3, 1974–5)

Critics have mistaken his masterly verse control for a cerebral detachment. They have pointed to his succession of aristocratic heroes, from 'Famous Men' and 'Haydn – Military Symphony' to 'Aristocrats' themselves, as further evidence of an emotional detachment, without, apparently, noticing that defeat is implicit for all Douglas's hero figures, that they are votive symbols of survival much more than emblems of invulnerability. Douglas's emotional history confirms what I have always felt to be the animus of his poetry, that the detachment is not cerebral but is rather a strategy deployed against the strength of feeling, a means of controlling it and making it positive . . .

A clue to Douglas's strategy perhaps lies in his own phrase 'analysis is worshipping'; in other words, in the belief that the imagination's degree of response lies in its degree of control. Thus his conviction that one must enquire accurately even into those experiences that seem inhuman, and destitute of meaning: 'I will sing / of what the others never set eyes on.' This is not to deny feeling: it is to give to feeling a foundation in fact, and at the same time to make of those facts something that can exist in spite of them; to create something to stand against what is 'slaying the mind' . . .

. . . if one compares Lewis's 'Infantry' with Douglas's 'Christodoulos' or 'Dead Men', his 'Jason and Medea' . . . with Douglas's 'Cairo Jag', or his 'Indian Day' [quotes first stanza] with Douglas's 'Egypt', one finds at every point that Douglas is at once more incisive on human corruption and markedly more humane . . .

Douglas's poetry is almost an imitation of action in the vigour and compactness of its language, yet fully human in its response. It is poetry, not of a studied detachment, but of an achieved intensity. Accepting death as levelly as he accepted all experience, Douglas created a poetry that would be hard and good when he's decayed. (Roger Garfitt, *Poetry Nation*, no. 4, 1975)

The question, I am afraid, about Keith Douglas . . . is whether he had any talent; whether he is much more or anything more than a name in the gallery of the shadow-poets of the Second World War – poets who had only the smallest poetic existence . . . I must express my own disappointed conviction that Keith Douglas's poems are almost uniformly bad. Desmond Graham – and it is not his fault – does not find a convincing stanza, a convincing line to quote, let alone a convincing poem . . . (Geoffrey Grigson, *Country Life*, 18 May 1978)

And so one finds contradiction unreconciled but understood. (Cullen Murphy, *Queensboro Record*, N.C., 27 October 1974)

Douglas is no 'war poet' but rather a brilliant visionary who saw war as a metaphor for the agony implicit in all human life. (Fleur Adcock, *Encounter*, vol. 51, August 1978)

Individual poems share the elusive quality of his work as a whole. He wrote that he wanted his poetry to be read as significant speech, not music, but the speech is unemphatic. There is no Keith Douglas voice – the poems mould themselves to the reader's tones instead. The choice of words, the metaphors, seem unexceptional, intent even on making themselves inconspicuous . . .

It is a very young poetry, alert to every sensation, eager to discern the large meanings in a life that could be, and was, short, but tempering that eagerness with what the poet had already learned about death in the western desert . . . (Martin Dodsworth, *Guardian*, 30 March 1978)

Like the mosquito, Douglas's imagination hovers over the invisible point or frontier where extremes meet;

where life becomes death, flesh dust or bone, love indifference, Cairo the desert, man's creativity destruction (the 'excellent smooth instrument of war'). In 'Desert Flowers' he 'looks each side of the door of sleep'. In 'On a Return from Egypt' he lays his whole life and poetry on the line. [Quotes last stanza.] Does the incomplete rhyming of 'find' with 'window' stop just this side of the glass? The thinly dividing walls, doors, glass in Douglas's house of the imagination reflect a scrutiny as finely balanced as a coin on its edge; or the situation between wartime lovers who 'can never lean / on an old building in the past / or a new building in the future', but must

> balance tiptoe on a pin,
> could teach an angel how to stand. ('Tel Aviv')

Yet the amount of touching, meeting, sudden synchronisations at the end of poems – for good or ill – again suggests an ultimate integrity of vision . . . Give or take a few immaturities, a few incompletions ('time is all I lacked'), Douglas achieved a stylistic 'balance' since unmatched in English poetry. His economical prescription of economy – 'every word must work for its keep' – is not nearly as well known as it should be, in comparison with many inflated twentieth-century poetic manifestos . . . His lean periodicity, like MacNeice's ampler rhetoric, may have benefited from classical studies. Not skeletal poetry, but poetry with no superfluous flesh on it, fighting fit. (Edna Longley, 'Shit or Bust: The Importance of Keith Douglas', *Honest Ulsterman*, no. 76, Autumn 1984)

A number of interesting essays on Douglas have appeared in recent years, by Smith, Ormerod, Gibbons and others, details of which are given in the Bibliography. Desmond Graham's edition of *A Prose Miscellany* was published by Carcanet Press in 1985 and reviewed by Neil Corcoran (*TLS*, 4 October 1985), Bill Greenwell (*New Statesman*, 14 June 1985), Peter Levi (*Spectator*, 6 September 1985), and Valentine Cunningham:

. . . most important of all is an early draft of Douglas's strongest poem 'Vergissmeinnicht', found on the end-papers of Douglas's copy of his own *Selected Poems*, now in the Brotherton Library. Its variants are arresting ones – its Germans are treated with a contempt rinsed from the later versions . . . what's also expanded is one's sense of an occasionally very unlovable post-Audenic youthful brutality, an instinct for violence akin to the young John Cornford's . . . the zest in bloody cataloguings pervades the *Miscellany*'s stories as it does *Alamein to Zem Zem* and the poems . . . The attempt at dispassion is clear. But crunching over dead men's bones was also, it seems, what Douglas thought good war poets should do . . . Douglas is always compassionate towards the dead, but that compassion keeps jostling against his admiration of fighting machines . . .

. . . one of the busiest sites of accumulating hesitation and mixtures of feeling that the *Miscellany* confirms has to do with Douglas's obsessive poking, groping, prying into, or just looking at, the holes dug in the desert, the slit-trenches and gunpits, or the caves opened in the bodies of shot soldiery. These caverns, provokingly suggestive of female sexual orifices, receptacles for probing male eyes or recumbent male flesh, promise joy, plunder, the loot that Douglas describes in the letter to Jocelyn Baber printed here . . . But they're also the zones of horrific concealment and threat, of the rot of bodies, sneaky German snipers, death in some of its many forms. The text of 'Vergissmeinnicht' worries at what confronts the observer in its awful moment of frozen-frame vision – is 'the stomach like a cave' that is to be thought neutrally 'open', less neutrally 'burst', or deterringly 'stinking'? Such common confrontations in the desert fighting and in Douglas's writing turn even this most unflinchingly penetrative of poets . . . into a reluctant, Doubting Thomas. (Valentine Cunningham, *Poetry Review*, vol. 75, no. 2, August 1985)

Later that day, I think, when Mrs Douglas was again thanking me for all the pains I had taken [in organizing an exhibition of Douglas's graphics, manuscripts and memorabilia at the Bodleian Library, Oxford, June – July 1974, to coincide with the publication of his biography] and all the people I had found . . . she turned to Ted Hughes's broadcast of 1962. 'Did you hear Hughes's talk?' I had not. 'He understood Keith so well I was convinced he had known him. I wrote to him after the broadcast and was astonished when Hughes replied that he had not, and was ten years younger' . . . At the exhibition John Waller, who had known Douglas a little both at Oxford and in the Middle East had come up and confided to me: 'You know Ted Hughes looks like Keith, some fifteen to twenty years on!' I am sure there was truth in it: that powerful and distinctly physical presence; the impact on a room, which many reported of Douglas, before he had said a word; an animal energy; 'feline' a fellow officer had called him; though this was not the species Hughes referred to when he wrote a poem for the biography flyleaf – 'Poets and pigs are only valued when they're dead.' (Desmond Graham, 'An Unwilling Biographer', *PN Review* 47, vol. 12, no. 3, 1985)

'He complains now that my stuff gives him no asylum for his affections,' Pound wrote to a friend in 1916 about Yeats's reactions to his recent work, and the same complaint echoes through criticism of Douglas, from J. C. Hall and G. S. Fraser to such academics as John Carey and Valentine Cunningham. Much debate revolves around such biographical matters as whether or not Douglas was a snob, a killer, and a psychic amputee; whether the poems are passionate and sincere or coldly artificial, lacking in common humanity; and whether they renovate language and form, as Hughes suggests, or are simply trenchant jottings which fail to live up to the standard set by the poets of the First World War.

The condescension, misprision and occasional vindictiveness shown towards Douglas by Hamilton, Carey,

Fuller, Levi and Cunningham seems to have its origin in a heavily biographical reading (and misreading) of the poems, as though 'How to Kill' and 'Vergissmein-nicht' were reports Douglas had compiled on his previous day's duties rather than compound imaginative recreations of the experience of desert war, and its relationship to the abiding morphology of human nature. This is analogous to the supposition that Eliot had simian arms, or that Larkin's doctor and priest wore long overcoats.

Douglas's hatred of 'bullshit', moral and poetic, makes him a difficult and somewhat un-English figure for some critics; hence the many attempts to explain and defuse his disturbingness by assigning it to personal and technical inadequacies, or by concluding, as Martin Dodsworth does, that he has no voice of his own. The best recent criticism, however, following Hughes's insights, is beginning to grapple with Douglas's actual achievement. His poetry does not yet seem to have attracted the attention of any deconstructionists, though his lifelong obsession with binary and tertiary oppositions would seem to invite their critical attention.

Select Bibliography

Works by Keith Douglas

Augury: An Oxford Miscellany of Verse and Prose, ed. K. C. Douglas and A. M. Hardie, Basil Blackwood, 1940.

Eight Oxford Poets, ed. Michael Meyer and Sidney Keyes, Routledge and Kegan Paul, 1941.

Selected Poems: Keith Douglas, J. C. Hall, Norman Nicholson, John Bale & Staples Ltd, Modern Reading Library Number Three, 1943.

Alamein to Zem Zem, Editions Poetry London, Nicholson and Watson, 1946. New edition, ed. John Waller, G. S. Fraser and J. C. Hall, with an Introduction by Lawrence Durrell, Faber and Faber, 1966. Reprinted with corrections as a Penguin Modern Classic, 1969. New edition, ed. with an Introduction by Desmond Graham, Oxford University Press, 1979.

The Collected Poems of Keith Douglas, ed. John Waller and G. S. Fraser, Editions Poetry London, Nicholson and Watson, 1951.

Selected Poems Keith Douglas, ed. with an Introduction by Ted Hughes, Faber and Faber, 1964.

Keith Douglas Collected Poems, ed. John Waller, G. S. Fraser and J. C. Hall, with an Introduction by Edmund Blunden, Faber and Faber, 1966.

Faber editions of *Collected Poems* and *Alamein to Zem Zem* published in New York by the Chilmark Press, 1966.

The Complete Poems of Keith Douglas, ed. Desmond Graham, Oxford University Press, 1978.

Keith Douglas: A Prose Miscellany, Compiled and Introduced by Desmond Graham, Carcanet Press, 1985.

Biography

Keith Douglas 1920–1944, a biography by Desmond Graham, Oxford University Press, 1974.

'An Unwilling Biographer' by Desmond Graham, *PN Review* 47, vol. 12, no. 3, 1985.

'Keith Douglas' by N. L. Ilett, *The Christ's Hospital Book*, published for the Committee of Old Blues, 1953.

'A Soldier's Story: Keith Douglas at El Ballah' by Lt-Col. John Stubbs, recorded by Desmond Graham, *PN Review* 47, vol. 12, no. 3, 1985.

Anthologies

Personal Landscape: an anthology of exile, ed. Robin Fedden et al., Editions Poetry London, Nicholson and Watson, 1945.

The Poetry of War 1939–1945, ed. Ian Hamilton, Alan Ross Ltd., 1965; New English Library, 1972.

Components of the Scene: an anthology of the prose and poetry of the Second World War, ed. Ronald Blythe, Penguin Books, 1966.

The Terrible Rain: the war poets 1939–1945, ed. Brian Gardner, Methuen & Co., 1966; Magnum Books 1977.

I Burn for England: an anthology of the poetry of World War II, ed. Charles Hamblett, Leslie Frewin, 1966.

Poetry of the Forties, ed. Robin Skelton, Penguin Books, 1968.

Poetry of the 1940s, ed. Howard Sergeant, Longman, 1970.

Return to Oasis: war poems and recollections of the Middle East 1940–1946, ed. Victor Selwyn et al. with an Introduction by Lawrence Durrell, Shepheard-Walwyn in association with Poetry London, 1980.

Literary Criticism and Memoirs

Not Without Glory: Poets of the Second World War by Vernon Scannell, The Woburn Press, 1976.

Under Siege: Literary life in London 1939–1945 by Robert Hewison, Weidenfeld and Nicolson, 1977; Quartet, 1979.

The Truth of Poetry by Michael Hamburger, Penguin Books, 1972; Carcanet Press, 1975.

The War 1939–1945, ed. Desmond Flower and James Reeves, Cassell, 1959.

The Great War and Modern Memory by Paul Fussell, Oxford University Press, 1975.

British Poetry of the Second World War by Linda M. Shires, Macmillan, 1985.

The Poetry of the Forties by A. T. Tolley, Manchester University Press, 1985.

Second World War in Literature: Eight Essays, ed. L. Higgins, Scottish Academic Press, 1986.

'Poetry Today' by Charles Tomlinson, Penguin Guide to English Literature, vol. 7, *The Modern Age*, ed. Boris Ford, Penguin Books, 1961.

'Poetry Since 1939' by Stephen Spender, British Council, 1948.

'Poetry 1945–50' by Alan Ross, British Council, 1958.

'Keith Douglas' by Alan Ross, 'Personal Preference' column *TLS*, 6 August 1954.

'Poets of the 1939–1945 War' by R. N. Currey, British Council, 1960.

'Keith Douglas' by G. S. Fraser, British Academy Chatterton Lecture, 1956, reprinted in *Essays on Twentieth Century Poetry*, Leicester University Press, 1977.

'Oxford Poetry and Disillusion II' by John Waller, *Poetry Review*, May–June 1940.

'The Poetry of Keith Douglas' by John Waller, *Accent* 8 (Urbana, Illinois), 1948.

'War and the Writer' by Douglas Grant, *Penguin Parade*, second series, no. 3, 1948.

'The Poetry of Keith Douglas' by Ted Hughes, *The Listener*, 21 June 1962.

'The Poetry of Keith Douglas' by Ted Hughes, *Critical Quarterly*, Spring 1963.

Introduction to *Selected Poems Keith Douglas* by Ted Hughes, Faber and Faber, 1964.

'I in Another Place: Homage to Keith Douglas' by Geoffrey Hill, *Stand*, vol. 6, no. 4, 1964–5.

'The Forties' by Ian Hamilton, *London Magazine*, April 1964, reprinted in *A Poetry Chronicle*, Faber and Faber, 1973.

'Keith Douglas' by Roger Garfitt (review of Graham's
   biography), *Poetry Nation* 4, 1975.
'Shit or Bust: The Importance of Keith Douglas' by Edna
   Longley, *Honest Ulsterman* 76, Autumn 1984, reprinted in
   Poetry in the Wars, Bloodaxe Books, 1986.
'Keith Douglas and the Western Desert' by Philip Gardner, *A
   Festschrift for Edgar Ronald Seary*, University of Toronto
   Press for Memorial University of Newfoundland, 1975.
'Keith Douglas and the Name of the Poem I Can't Write' by
   David Ormerod, *Ariel* (University of Calgary), vol. 9, no. 2,
   April 1978.
'A Sharp Enquiring Blade' by Reginald Gibbons, *Parnassus*,
   vol. 9, no. 1, Spring/Summer 1981.
'Keith Douglas and the Dead Soldier: An Artistic
   Confrontation' by A. Bannergee, *Literary Half-Yearly*
   (Calcutta), January 1984.
'The New Keith Douglas Collection' (essay-review of *TCP*) by
   Rowland Smith, *The Dalhousie Review*, vol. 58, no. 4,
   Winter 1978–9.
'Last Lunch with Keith Douglas' by Tambimuttu, *Return to
   Oasis*, ed. Victor Selwyn et al., Shepheard-Walwyn in
   association with Poetry London, 1980.
'Keith Douglas' by Desmond Graham, *Dictionary of Literary
   Biography*, vol. 27: 'Poets of Great Britain and Ireland
   1945–60', ed. Vincent B. Sherry Jnr.

Sources for other reviews and appreciations are given in
   chapter V.

Radio and TV

'Breed of Heroes: The Poetry of Keith Douglas' by Vernon
   Scannell, BBC radio broadcast recorded 28 November
   1973, with contributions from Douglas's mother and
   friends from university and the army. Transcript in the
   possession of Desmond Graham.
'Keith Douglas', *Bookmark*, BBC2 TV programme 1985,
   presented by Ian Hamilton, with contributions from army
   and other friends, including Milena Pegnas and Betty
   Jesse. Video cassette in the possession of Desmond
   Graham.

[221]

Index